THE VALANCOURT BOOK OF VICTORIAN CHRISTMAS GHOST STORIES

VOLUME FIVE

THE VALANCOURT BOOK OF

VICTORIAN CHRISTMAS
GHOST STORIES

VOLUME FIVE

Edited with an introduction by
CHRISTOPHER PHILIPPO

VALANCOURT BOOKS
Richmond, Virginia
2021

CONTENTS

Introduction

> Myrrh is mine, its bitter perfume
> Breathes a life of gathering gloom;
> Sorrowing, sighing, bleeding, dying,
> Sealed in the stone cold tomb.
> "We Three Kings of Orient Are" (1857)

EVEN KNOWING THAT CHRISTMAS GHOST STORIES have roots in fireside winter's night tales and pre-Christian solstice festivals, one still wonders at the transition. Preceding Charles Dickens, two books are typically mentioned for having associated ghost stories with Christmas: *Round About Our Coal-fire: or, Christmas Entertainments: Containing, Christmas Gambols, Tropes, Figures, Etc. with Abundance of Fiddle-Faddle-Stuff; Such as Stories of Fairies, Ghosts, Hobgoblins, Witches, Bull-Beggars, Rawheads and Bloody-Bones, Merry Plays, &c.* (1732) and Washington Irving's *The Sketchbook of Geoffrey Crayon, Gent.* (1819).

Prior to the Victorian era, it's more common to find references just to the oral tradition, like a 1775 article, "On the Antiquity of Christmas Games," in which the author wrote "the conversation of the hearth-side was the tales of superstition: the Fairies, Robin Goodfellow, and Hobgoblins, never failed to make the trembling audience mutter an Ave Maria, and cross their chins"[1] or a lexicographer writing in 1787 that "ghosts, fairies and witches, with bloody murders, committed by tinkers, formed a principal part of rural conversation, in all large assemblies, and particularly those in the Christmas holy-days, during the burning of the yule-block."[2]

---

1 Thomas Chatterton, "On the Antiquity of Christmas Games," *Westminster Magazine* (Dec. 1775): 650.
2 Francis Grose, *A Provincial Glossary, with a Collection of Local Proverbs, and Popular Superstitions* (London: S. Hooper, 1787), vii-viii.

For these kinds of stories, "ghost story" or "goblin story" were terms used somewhat interchangeably or, paired, "invok[ing] a mood or point[ing] toward a domain: the eerie, the other, the night, the unknown."[1] There are specifically ghosts to be sure, but also demons, vampires, werewolves, mummies, sirens, sociopathic murderers, and more.

Would such observations have seemed current to readers, or mainly historical, particularly when it came to families that didn't have avid storytellers in them? There are reasons to think that many would have seen them as old traditions that did still have life in them.

One possibility is suggested by the dirgelike quatrain above: religious poetry and carols of the Christmas season. Many of the classic ones were rife with ghostly and morbid imagery.

> The flocking shadows pale
> Troop to the infernal jail,
> Each fettered ghost slips to his several grave:
> And the yellow-skirted fays
> Fly after the night-steeds, leaving their moon-loved maze.
> "On the Morning of Christ's Nativity," John Milton (1629)

> Vain with the pride of filthy flesh,
> Which is but dust and loathsomeness,
> 'Tis but a coffin turn'd with breath,
> By sickness broached, drawn out by death.
> "The Fountain of Christ's Blood" (bef. 1823)

Some of the most graphic are those that address the "Massacre of the Innocents," Herod's slaying of the children in Bethlehem, an event memorialized by several denominations with its own day during Christmastide.

---

1 Michael Ostling and Richard Forest, "'Goblins, Owles and Sprites': Discerning Early-Modern English Preternatural Beings through Collocational Analysis," *Religion* 44, no. 4: 547-572. For other bogey terms, see Henk Dragstra, "'Bull-Begger': An Early Modern Scare-Word," in *Airy Nothings: Imagining the Otherworld of Faerie from the Middle Ages to the Age of Reason*, ed. Karin E. Olsen and Jan R. Veenstra (Leiden: Brill, 2014).

> Then Bethlehem grew red with blood,
> And white with infants' bones,
> That nought was heard in Jury land
> But Children's mothers' groans
>   "Augustus Cæsar Having Brought" (bef. 1823)

A second possible bridge through time is the theatre. "Monk" Lewis's *The Castle Spectre*, first staged during Advent in 1797, was by 1809 presented as something of a holiday tradition, evoking some of the same bugbears from 1732.

> did the MONK ever suppose that his ghosts, his caverns, chains, lamps, and rusty daggers, would be laid on the dramatic shelf, merely to be brought forward to decorate a bug-a-boo, or a raw head and bloody bones in the Christmas Holidays?[1]

Another play, *The Mistletoe Bough; or, Young Lovel's Bride* (1834), in adapting the story from the song included herein, added a ghost, goblin, and murder.[2] The prefatory remarks by "D.—G." to its printing referenced a variety of old Christmas traditions, including "stories of hobgoblins, raw-heads, and bloody-bones—Buggy-Bows—Tom-Pokers—Bull-Beggars —witches, wizards, conjurors, Doctor Faustus, Friar Bacon, Doctor Partridge, and such like horrible bodies, that terrify and delight round about a coal-fire at Christmas,"[3] all taken from that 1732 book.

One last bridge is the media's coverage of ghost panics. In late November through late December 1839, for example, two of the most widely-reported were the Limekiln-street ghost in Dover, and a supposed haunting of Christ Church-yard in

1 *National Register* [London, England] (Dec. 31, 1809): 838, col. 1.
2 C. A. Somerset, *The Mistletoe Bough; or, Young Lovel's Bride: A Legendary Drama, in Two Acts* (London: G. H. Davidson, [1834?]).
3 "D.—G." was probably George Daniel, author of *Merrie England in the Olden Time*, Vol. 1 (London: Richard Bentley, 1842). An abbreviated version of the comment about "stories of hobgoblins" appears in *Merrie England* at p. 5, n. 1.

Southwark. There was a conscious association of such things with the oral story tradition.

> The inhabitants have been for many days past amusing themselves with a ghost story. Some gentle family has been greatly annoyed by hearing knocks on the walls of the rooms, and the latches of the doors jingle, and have charged the servant girl with the "spiritous" propensity. The girl has denied the charge in a lengthened affidavit, and the wonder-loving neighbours are making a portentous Christmas tale of the event.[1]

Such stories had been so typical for so long that in 1840 a writer could refer to "the usual ghost story, which country newspapers are expected to provide for Christmas tide."[2]

Examples of Christmas ghost story fiction in print do seem to be rare, however, until some years after the end of the Regency and the publication of the first literary annual *The Forget-Me-Not* in 1822. The regularly printed Christmas ghost story really does seem to be a thing of the Victorian age, not earlier.

Even with the advent of the annuals, while such Christmas gifts would often include Gothic tales (as did monthly magazines throughout the year),[3] early on they weren't necessarily tales of ghosts. When they were, the stories were frequently of the variety that proves to have a rational explanation.[4] Those stories may have been in part an attempt to instruct readers, to

---

1 "Dover," *Kentish Gazette* (Dec. 24, 1839): 3, col. 1.
2 *Western Times* [Exeter] (Dec. 1840): 4, col. 3.
3 See, e.g., Katherine D. Harris, *The Forgotten Gothic: Short Stories from British Literary Annuals, 1823-1831* (Zittaw Press, 2012); Jennie MacDonald, *Schabraco and other Gothic Tales from the* Ladies' Monthly Museum*, 1798-1828* (Richmond, Va.: Valancourt, 2020).
4 See Harris (2012), xxxi. *E.g.*, Barbara Hofland, "The Regretted Ghost," *Forget-Me-Not; A Christmas and New Year's Present for 1826* (London: R. Ackermann, 1826): 79-101; John Roby, "The Haunted Manor-House," *Forget-Me-Not; A Christmas and New Year's Present for 1827* (London: Ackermann, 1827): 133-159.

educate them to avoid ghost panics. The problem with panics
wasn't merely the embarrassing naïveté of the observers, but
the consequence of the crowds. The aforementioned 1839
Christchurch "ghost" had attracted 200 people, and pickpock-
eting resulted—as had also happened in earlier cases.[1]

Texts might still explicitly conjure the image of the fireside
ghost story in passing, though.

> When cluster'd round the fire at night,
> Old William talks of ghost and sprite,
> And as a distant out-house gate
> Slams by the wind, they fearful wait,
> While some each shadowy nook explore,
> Then CHRISTMAS pauses at the door.[2]

When did printed Christmas ghost stories start to become
common? Tentatively one might point to the publication of
T. H. Bayly's "The Mistletoe Bough" and J. G. Lockhart's
"Little Willie Bell" (1827) in this volume, and Sir Walter Scott's
"The Tapestried Chamber" (1828) back in volume one. As
noted earlier, Bayly's already morbid song soon had a ghost
added to it on stage. The two stories were received well enough
to garner wider circulation through immediate reprints by
other publications. They received some criticism by bluenoses
afraid of fostering belief in ghosts, but such complaints largely
diminished over the decades.

Scott's story hadn't been written with Christmas reading
specifically in mind; he'd originally planned to include it in his
own *Chronicles of the Canongate*.[3] Nonetheless, the association
was created; a mere month later a writer called it to mind
among a "train of associations" in a letter under the heading
"A Few Ghosts for Christmas-Time."[4]

---

1 "Ghost Frolics," *Weekly Chronicle* [London] (Dec. 1, 1839): 6, cols. 3-4.
2 Edwin Lees, "Signs of Christmas," in *Christmas and the New Year: A Masque, for the Fire-Side* (London: Longman, Rees, Orme, Brown, and Green, 1827): 10-11.
3 David Douglas, ed. *The Journal of Sir Walter Scott: From the Original Manu-script at Abbotsford* (New York: Harper & Bros., 1890): 117.
4 Mem., "A Few Ghosts for Christmastime," *New Monthly Magazine and Literary Journal* (Jan. 1, 1829): 77-80.

Apart from referencing traditional ghosts, the letter mentioned the Scandinavian nix water sprite or Bäckahäst brook horse, "Der Wilde Jäger" by Gottfried August Bürger (1747-1794), *The Fairy Mythology* (1828) by Thomas Keightley (1789-1872), and George Barrington's *History of New South Wales* (1802). Scott's ghost was the only one that had been made available at Christmastime. The inclusion of the others suggested that if one wasn't a natural storyteller then any weird fiction at hand might do. In fact, such a sentiment was expressed in a review of Scott's *Letters on Demonology and Witchcraft Addressed to J. G. Lockhart, Esq.* (1830):

> We are very angry with you, friend Murr[a]y, for publishing this delightful volume in September. Why not about Christmas and the fire-side months, when it would indeed most charmingly entertain the family groups now scattered at watering-places, in country quarters, and on tours of pleasure.[1]

The *Winter's Wreath for 1831* likewise depicted a storyteller turning to a book rather than memory or imagination.

> "On such a night," from tome before him spread,
>   To bright and wondering eyes, some awe-struck wight
> Oft reads how erst have risen the living dead[2]

That same year, a volume of "The Standard Novels" that bound together Mary Shelley's *Frankenstein* with Friedrich Schiller's *The Ghost-Seer* was suggested as one that "might safely and with profit be perused by the young, for whom they are well adapted as cheap and acceptable Christmas Presents, and New-Year's Gifts."[3]

---

1 *Cheltenham Journal and Gloucestershire Fashionable Weekly Gazette* (Sept. 27, 1830): p. 4, col. 3.
2 William Brownsword Chorley, "The Wreath," in *The Winter's Wreath for 1831* (London: Whittaker, 1831): vi-vii.
3 "Standard Novels and Romances," *The Sun* [London] (Dec. 23, 1831): 1, col. 2.

Through the 1830s-40s there would be other ghost stories set or published at Christmas. Aside from Dickens's 1836 "The Story of the Goblins Who Stole a Sexton," examples include "The Green Huntsman, or, The Haunted Villa" (1841) in volume four of this Valancourt series and "The Necromancer, or, Ghost versus Gramarye" (1842) in volume two. References to the tradition in poetry and articles also grew more common.

> The ear of the young most greedily feeds,
> (On nights like thus) upon "Goblin Tale,"—
> Upon SIGNS and KNOCKS, and murderous deeds,
> 'Till the eye looks wild and the cheek turns pale.[1]

If there were any doubts as to the market for Christmas ghost stories by that point, they would have been dispelled by the 1843 publication of Dickens's *A Christmas Carol*.

Even though his *Carol* did not pioneer the genre, it certainly went on to be its biggest success. Dickens can also be credited with adding something to the genre that was entirely new: the anthology. It wasn't unusual for multiple Christmas ghost stories to appear in an annual, Christmas number, or newspaper, but the idea of having them all tied together with a frame story was. Dickens had edited and contributed to anthologies starting in the 1840s, but they did not feature ghost stories. The Christmas number he edited for *All the Year Round*, titled "The Haunted House," combined the idea of the anthology with the idea of ghosts, but without having ghosts *per se*—they were more metaphorical things of imagination and memory. With the 1860 Christmas number, "A Message from the Sea," that changed; the tale "My Brother's Ghost Story" (included here) does feature an actual ghost.

Some monthlies and newspapers copied the idea of such anthologies with editors devising wraparound stories and used them periodically at least into the 1890s. That tradition was

---

1 "Moon-Light Reflections; Induced by the Depopulated Appearance of the Streets of Bury, on Christmas Night!" *Suffolk Chronicle* (Jan. 8, 1842): 4, col. 2.

revived in films, including *Dead of Night* (1945), *Tales from the Crypt* (1972), and *A Christmas Horror Story* (2015). Remarkably, though, very few of the hundreds of Christmas horror movies that have been made[1] have been adapted from published Christmas ghost stories.

As decades passed and the turn of the century approached, complaints about the graphic nature of some Christmas ghost stories began appearing with greater frequency. The lengthiest and most impassioned objection was by George R. Sims in 1893, writing of a Christmas number, "I think I shall take it with me the first time I am invited to a funeral and have to make a long journey in a mourning coach," and cautioning that if the future brought more of the same, "I shall expect next year to open a Christmas number and find that the double-page supplement is a beautifully coloured picture of Hell."[2]

Roughly during the same period of time, a change in Christmas poetry could also be seen. In the latter half of the century, poems that told *humorous* Christmas ghost stories or that had fun with the tradition were multiplying. After the turn of the century, humorous ones were practically the only kind; "Woden, the Wild Huntsman" from 1911 herein is a rare exception.

The genre of the Christmas mystery was also growing, *e.g.* Sherlock Holmes in "The Adventure of the Blue Carbuncle" (1892), Father Brown in "The Flying Stars" (1911), and Hercule Poirot in "The Adventure of the Christmas Pudding" (1923).

Despite such inroads, while the Christmas ghost story in

---

1 See Kim Newman, "You Better Watch Out: Christmas in Horror Films," in *Christmas at the Movies,* ed. Mark Connelly (London: I.B. Tauris, 2001): 135-142; Paul Corupe and Kier-La Janisse, *Yuletide Terror: Christmas Horror on Film and Television* (Toronto: Spectacular Optical Publications, 2017); "Christmas Horror Movies: A History—updated for 2019," *Popcorn Horror,* Christmas Special 2019, available at https://payhip.com/b/bBgE; Richard Mogg, *Giftwrapped & Gutted: The Trashiest Christmas Horror Movies* (RickMoe Publishing, 2019).
2 *The Referee* (Dec. 17, 1893): 7, cols. 2-4.

both its serious and humorous varieties may have declined somewhat, it would never die—and rightly so!

> "Do you—do you believe in—well, in Undying Things?" [asked "The Man Who Read All the Christmas Numbers."]
> "You mean the Christmas Number Thing," I replied. "I have not had the honour of its acquaintance for a good many years. The only one I remember had a habit which, I suppose, is common to all of them."
> "What is that?" he asked, with visible anxiety.
> I stood up and pointed towards a corner of the room. "The Thing—came—slowly—on!"[1]

And they're still creeping on from the Victorian age to ours . . .

CHRISTOPHER PHILIPPO
August 2021

CHRISTOPHER K. PHILIPPO was (it turns out) deeply influenced by Astrid Lindgren's *The Tomten*, Norman Bridwell's *The Witch's Christmas*, and Jane Thayer's *Gus Was a Christmas Ghost* in the 1970s and Dr. Demento's syndicated Christmas broadcasts on PYX 106 in the 1980s. A Trustee of the Bethlehem Historical Society, a former volunteer for the NYS Historian, and a gravestone conservationist, he finds figuratively or literally unearthing and then sharing the forgotten to be intensely satisfying. His future books will examine the complete works of H. C. Dodge, women horror directors' movies, and the early film career of Alfred Hitchcock.

---

1 L.F.A. "The Man Who Read All the Christmas Numbers," *Illustrated London News* (Dec. 23, 1893): 13, cols. 2-3.

John Gibson Lockhart

Little Willie Bell

Both the father and maternal grandfather of John Gibson
Lockhart (1794-1854) *were Scottish ministers, something
germane to the story here. Lockhart was a child prodigy, editor
and contributor to the* Quarterly Review (1825-1853), *a
novelist, and biographer of his father-in-law Sir Walter Scott.
Lockhart's story appeared in early December 1827 in* The
Christmas Box: An Annual Present for Children *and was
immediately reprinted in a number of newspapers and literary
journals. A few monthlies, while not questioning the writing
quality, had misgivings about its potential effect. One worried
it was "likely to impress children with a mysterious fear, and
a groundless terror of ghosts and apparitions"*[1] *while another
assured the young that only good ghosts appeared to good people,
while the bad would be visited by "dreadful ghosts [...] driving
them mad by glaring on them with their eyes, and pointing to
wounds, all streaming with blood, in their side or breast"*[2]—*a
caveat strikingly more graphic than the story occasioning it.*

I N Scotland, at every church door there is a stool and
a broad pewter plate upon it, and every one that goes to
church is expected to put something into the plate, as he passes
it, for the poor of the parish. Gentlemen and ladies put in shillings and half-crowns, or more if they be very rich; but working men and their wives, and any one that is not very poor

1 *The Lady's Monthly Museum* (Jan. 1828): 47.
2 John Wilson, "Christmas Presents," *Blackwood's Edinburgh Magazine* 23
(134) (Jan. 1828): 10.

indeed, would be ashamed to go by the plate without putting in a penny or a halfpenny, to help the old frail people, and the blind and lame, who are not able to work and win money for themselves. It is the custom of good ladies and gentlemen in that country to give each of their children a halfpenny or a penny, or more if they can afford it, every Sunday morning, to put into the plate. And they do this, that their children may learn betimes to think of the hard condition of poor, frail, blind people, and how right it is for us to help them in their distress. I have told you these things, because if you did not know them, you would not be so well able to understand a story which I once heard told in Scotland. Long ago, there was a good worthy clergyman in that country, called Mr. Bell: he was very charitable and kind, and all the poor people loved him exceedingly. One Saturday an old schoolfellow, whom Mr. Bell had not seen for many years, came to visit him. Mr. Bell was very glad to see his schoolfellow, and invited him to stay there for a few days; and he agreed to do so. And Mrs. Bell prepared the best bed-room in the house for this gentleman, whose name was Major Lindsay; and the major had ridden a long journey, so he retired into the bed-room to change his dress before dinner; and this took up some time. He was about an hour in the bed-room by himself. They then dined, and after dinner Mr. Bell asked for the children, and they were brought into the parlour. The major was much pleased with the children, for they were very quiet. There were three of them, all girls, Jane, Mary, and Susan. But Jane was a good deal older than the others. The major took Susan on his knee, and kissed her, and then he looked round, and said to Mrs. Bell, "These are fine little girls, but where is the pretty boy that came into my room while I was dressing!" "These are all the children we have, major," said Mrs. Bell. "I wonder who it could be, then," said the major: "I was sitting by my bed-side, when I saw a little, thin, white hand put through the round hole that is in the door; and it lifted the latch gently, and a very pretty little boy, with long brown curled hair, but rather pale and sickly in his appearance, came in. He did not look at me, but walked across the room very softly, as if he feared to disturb me; and he went into the room beyond mine, and I saw no more of him." The lady, when she heard this, put her handkerchief to her face, and went out of the room with her children. The major was sorry to see Mrs. Bell discomposed, but could not understand the reason of it, until Mr. Bell told him. "I do not know (said he) who this little boy could be; but about a year ago we lost our only son, and what you said brought back my poor little Willie to his mother's mind; for he had a pale complexion, and his hair was very fine, and hung in pretty curls over his neck. He was a beautiful child." These two old friends remained silent for a little while, and then talked of other matters. The major told Mr. Bell about the wars in America, where he had been for many years with his regiment: and Mr. Bell told the major what had happened to others of their schoolfellows, while he was so far away from Scotland. Mrs. Bell was in good spirits again, when the gentlemen went to tea; and they were all very gay and happy the rest of the evening. Next morning, after breakfast, the major took Mr. Bell aside into the garden, and said—"This is a very odd thing: this morning I awoke very early, and presently the same little, thin, white hand appeared opening the latch of the door. The pale boy with the long curled hair came in just as before, and walked through the room into the closet. I was surprised, and got up and entered the closet after him. He was on his knees, scratching, as if he wanted to lift up one of the boards of the floor. I went close to him, and was just going to touch his shoulder, when suddenly, I can't tell how, he contrived to disappear; and I found myself alone in the closet. After a little, I began to examine the board he had been scratching: I found it loose, and lifted it, and here is a sixpence I saw lying on the ground below it." Mr. Bell looked very grave when he heard this. He took the sixpence from the major, and seemed to be vexed with the story. While he was thinking how it could be, the children came running out of the house; Mr. Bell called to them, and, shewing them the sixpence, said, "Come, my dears, can any of you tell me any thing of this? here is a sixpence, which the major has found under a loose board in the floor of the little closet that is beyond his bedroom." Mary and little Susan shook their heads, and said nothing; but Jane, the eldest, blushed; and her papa saw she knew something that she did not like to tell. "Come, Jane," said he, "speak the truth; and I shall forgive you, whatever you have done." "Indeed, papa," said Jane, "it was not I that put the sixpence there." "Then who put it there?" said Mr. Bell. And then the tears came running over Jane's cheeks, and she said, "Oh, papa, I think it was poor Willie: the Sunday before he died, you gave him a sixpence to put into the plate, and he had a halfpenny of his own, and he put the halfpenny into the plate, and kept the sixpence; but Willie did not tell me where he hid it." Mr. Bell shook his head; and the major saw that the tears were standing in his eyes. He said nothing for some time; but at last the church bell began to ring, and then he gave the sixpence to Jane, and bade her put it into the plate the same morning. Major Lindsay stayed some days at Mr. Bell's; but neither he nor any body else ever saw any thing more of the little pale boy.

COMPETITIONS OF THE WEEK.

—

No. 42.—GHOST-STORY COMPETITION.

The telling of ghost-stories, no less than the eating of turkey and plum-pudding, is inseparably connected with Christmas in the popular idea! For the best ghost story— of course, it need not be original, and, still less, need it be true—I will award a handsome book. All stories must reach this office by Monday morning, December 28th. The current COUPON must be enclosed.

Book-Bits (Dec. 26, 1896): i, col 2.

Thomas Haynes Bayly

The Mistletoe Bough

*Popular in Great Britain since its inclusion in an 1829 songbook,
this composition by* THOMAS HAYNES BAYLY *(1810-1856)
has been adapted into plays, stories, and films, as well as widely
parodied over the decades. Edison cylinder recordings from 1904
(excerpted in "Christmas Time in Merry England"[1]) and 1913[2]
survive. A 1904 British short film adaptation was restored and
screened by the British Film Institute in 2013, more than 100
years after its making. That short embellished the tale with a "30
years later" intertitle followed by a ghost's revelation.[3]*

T̲HE MISTLETOE HUNG IN THE CASTLE HALL;
    The holly branch shone on the old oak wall.
The Baron's retainers were blithe and gay,
Keeping the Christmas holiday.
The Baron beheld with a father's pride
His beautiful child, Lord Lovell's bride.
And she, with her bright eyes seemed to be
The star of that goodly company.
               Oh! the mistletoe bough,
               Oh! the mistletoe bough.

---

1 "Christmas on Cylinders." The City of London Phonograph and Gram-
ophone Society. https://www.clpgs.org.uk/concert-no-6---christmas-on-
cylinders-concert---part-2.html
2 University of California, Santa Barbara Cylinder Audio Archive. http://
www.library.ucsb.edu/OBJID/Cylinder6169
3 "Earliest film of Christmas ghost story sees light." British Film Institute.
April 25, 2019. https://www2.bfi.org.uk/news-opinion/news-bfi/announce-
ments/earliest-film-christmas-ghost-story-sees-light

"I'm weary of dancing, now," she cried;
"Here, tarry a moment, I'll hide, I'll hide,
And, Lovell, be sure you're the first to trace
The clue to my secret hiding place."
Away she ran, and her friends began
Each tower to search and each nook to scan.
And young Lovell cried, "Oh, where do you hide?
I'm lonesome without you, my own fair bride."
    Oh! the mistletoe bough,
    Oh! the mistletoe bough.

They sought her that night, they sought her next day,
They sought her in vain when a week passed away.
In the highest, the lowest, the loneliest spot,
Young Lovell sought wildly, but found her not.
The years passed by and their grief at last
Was told as a sorrowful tale long past.
When Lovell appeared, all the children cried,
"See the old man weeps for his fairy bride."
    Oh! the mistletoe bough,
    Oh! the mistletoe bough.

At length, an old chest that had long lain hid
Was found in the castle; they raised the lid.
A skeleton form lay mouldering there
In the bridal wreath of that lady fair.
How sad the day when in sportive jest
She hid from her lord in the old oak chest.
It closed with a spring—and a dreadful doom,
And the bride lay clasped in a living tomb.
    Oh! the mistletoe bough,
    Oh! the mistletoe bough.

Amelia Blandford Edwards

My Brother's Ghost Story

Editor Charles Dickens's 1860 Christmas number of All the Year Round *was an anthology titled "A Message from the Sea," which had for a protagonist Captain Jonas Jorgan of Salem, Mass. In its third chapter, "The Club-Night," the Captain and a fisherman, lost on a Cornish moor, walk into the small King Arthur's Arms and happen upon a club of men telling stories. The one here was written by* AMELIA ANN BLAND-FORD EDWARDS (1831-1892); *she contributed several stories to the Christmas ghost genre, among them "The Discovery of the Treasure Isles" and "The Guard-Ship at the Aire," examples collected in anthologies by the late Richard Dalby in the 1980s-90s. Edwards repurposed "My Brother's Ghost Story" as a segment in her own 1865 volume* Miss Carew, *wherein it became one manuscript among several bought by bored yacht excursionists to read aloud from a butcher who'd acquired a stack of unbound papers from a remaindered book to use for wrapping.*

MINE IS MY BROTHER'S GHOST STORY. It happened to my brother about thirty years ago, while he was wandering, sketch-book in hand, among the High Alps, picking up subjects for an illustrated work on Switzerland. Having entered the Oberland by the Brunig Pass, and filled his portfolio with what he used to call "bits" from the neighbourhood of Meyringen, he went over the Great Scheideck to Grindlewald, where he arrived one dusky September evening, about three-quarters of an hour after sunset. There had been a fair that day, and the place was crowded. In the best inn there was not an inch of space to spare—there were only two inns at Grindelwald, thirty years ago—so my brother went to the one other, at the end of the covered bridge next the church, and there, with some difficulty, obtained the promise of a pile of rugs and a mattress, in a room which was already occupied by three other travellers.

The Adler was a primitive hostelry, half farm, half inn, with great rambling galleries outside, and a huge general room, like a barn. At the upper end of this room stood long stoves, like metal counters, laden with steaming-pans, and glowing underneath like furnaces. At the lower end, smoking, supping, and chatting, were congregated some thirty or forty guests, chiefly mountaineers, char drivers, and guides. Among these my brother took his seat, and was served, like the rest, with a bowl of soup, a platter of beef, a flagon of country wine, and a loaf made of Indian corn. Presently, a huge St. Bernard dog came and laid his nose upon my brother's arm. In the meantime he fell into conversation with two Italian youths, bronzed and dark-eyed, near whom he happened to be seated. They were Florentines. Their names, they told him, were Stefano and Battisto. They had been travelling for some months on commission, selling cameos, mosaics, sulphur casts, and the like pretty Italian trifles, and were now on their way to Interlaken and Geneva. Weary of the cold North, they longed, like children, for the moment which should take them back to their own blue hills and grey-green olives; to their workshop on the Ponte Vecchio, and their home down by the Arno.

It was quite a relief to my brother, on going up to bed, to find that these youths were to be two of his fellow-lodgers. The third was already there, and sound asleep, with his face to the wall. They scarcely looked at this third. They were all tired, and all anxious to rise at daybreak, having agreed to walk together over the Wengern Alp as far as Lauterbrunnen. So, my brother and the two youths exchanged a brief good night, and, before many minutes, were all as far away in the land of dreams as their unknown companion.

My brother slept profoundly—so profoundly that, being roused in the morning by a clamour of merry voices, he sat up dreamily in his rugs, and wondered where he was.

"Good day, signor," cried Battisto. "Here is a fellow-traveller going the same way as ourselves."

"Christien Baumann, native of Kandersteg, musical-box maker by trade, stands five feet eleven in his shoes, and is at monsieur's service to command," said the sleeper of the night before.

He was as fine a young fellow as one would wish to see. Light, and strong, and well proportioned, with curling brown hair, and bright, honest eyes that seemed to dance at every word he uttered.

"Good morning," said my brother. "You were asleep last night when we came up."

"Asleep! I should think so, after being all day in the fair, and walking from Meyringen the evening before. What a capital fair it was!"

"Capital, indeed," said Battisto. "We sold cameos and mosaics yesterday for nearly fifty francs."

"Oh, you sell cameos and mosaics, you two! Show me your cameos, and I will show you my musical-boxes. I have such pretty ones, with coloured views of Geneva and Chillon on the lids, playing two, four, six, and even eight tunes. Bah! I will give you a concert!"

And with this he unstrapped his pack, displayed his little boxes on the table, and wound them up, one after the other, to the delight of the Italians.

"I helped to make them myself, every one," said he, proudly. "Is it not pretty music? I sometimes set one of them when I go to bed at night, and fall asleep listening to it. I am sure, then, to have pleasant dreams! But let us see your cameos. Perhaps I may buy one for Marie if they are not too dear. Marie is my sweetheart, and we are to be married next week."

"Next week!" exclaimed Stefano. "That is very soon. Battisto has a sweetheart also, up at Impruneta; but they will have to wait a long time before they can buy the ring."

Battisto blushed like a girl.

"Hush, brother!" said he. "Show the cameos to Christien, and give your tongue a holiday."

But Christien was not so to be put off.

"What is her name?" said he. "Tush! Battisto, you must tell me her name! Is she pretty? Is she dark, or fair? Do you often see her when you are at home? Is she very fond of you? Is she as fond of you as Marie is of me?"

"Nay, how should I know that?" asked the soberer Battisto. "She loves me, and I love her—that is all."

"And her name?"

"Margherita."

"A charming name! And she is herself as pretty as her name, I'll engage. Did you say she was fair?"

"I said nothing about it one way or the other," said Battisto, unlocking a green box clamped with iron, and taking out tray after tray of his pretty wares. "There! Those pictures all inlaid in little bits are Roman mosaics—these flowers on a black ground are Florentine. The ground is of hard dark stone, and the flowers are made of thin slices of jasper, onyx, cornelian, and so forth. Those forget-me-nots, for instance, are bits of turquoise, and that poppy is cut from a piece of coral."

"I like the Roman ones best," said Christien. "What place is that with all the arches?"

"This is the Coliseum, and the one next to it is St. Peter's. But we Florentines care little for the Roman work. It is not half so fine, or so valuable as ours. The Romans make their mosaics of composition."

"Composition or no, I like the little landscapes best," said Christien. "There is a lovely one, with a pointed building, and a tree, and mountains at the back. How I should like that one for Marie!"

"You may have it for eight francs," replied Battisto; "we sold two of them yesterday for ten each. It represents the tomb of Caius Cestius, near Rome."

"A tomb!" echoed Christien, considerably dismayed. "Diable! That would be a dismal present to one's bride."

"She would never guess that it was a tomb, if you did not tell her," suggested Stefano.

Christien shook his bead.

"That would be next door to deceiving her," said he.

"Nay," interposed my brother, "the owner of that tomb has been dead these eighteen or nineteen hundred years. One almost forgets that he was ever buried in it."

"Eighteen or nineteen hundred years? Then he was a heathen?"

"Undoubtedly, if by that you mean that he lived before Christ."

Christien's face lighted up immediately.

"Oh, that settles the question," said he, pulling at his little canvas purse, and paying his money down at once. "A heathen's tomb is as good as no tomb at all. I'll have it made into a brooch for her, at Interlaken. Tell me, Battisto, what shall you take home to Italy for your Margherita?"

Battisto laughed, and chinked his eight francs. "That depends on trade," said he; "if we make good profits between this and Christmas, I may take her a Swiss muslin from Berne; but we have already been away seven months, and we have hardly made a hundred francs over and above our expenses."

And with this, the talk turned upon general matters, the Florentines locked away their treasures, Christien restrapped his pack, and my brother and all went down together, and breakfasted in the open air outside the inn.

It was a magnificent morning: cloudless and sunny, with a cool breeze that rustled in the vine upon the porch, and flecked the table with shifting shadows of green leaves. All around and about them stood the great mountains, with their blue-white glaciers bristling down to the verge of the pastures, and the pine-woods creeping darkly up their sides. To the left, the Wetterhorn; to the right, the Eigher; straight before them, dazzling and imperishable, like an obelisk of frosted silver,

the Schreckhorn, or Peak of Terror. Breakfast over, they bade
farewell to their hostess, and, mountain-staff in hand, took
the path to the Wengern Alp. Half in light, half in shadow,
lay the quiet valley, dotted over with farms, and traversed by a
torrent that rushed, milk-white, from its prison in the glacier.
The three lads walked briskly in advance, their voices chiming
together every now and then in chorus of laughter. Somehow
my brother felt sad. He lingered behind, and, plucking a little
red flower from the bank, watched it hurry away with the
torrent, like a life on the stream of time. Why was his heart so
heavy, and why were their hearts so light?

As the day went on, my brother's melancholy, and the
mirth of the young men, seemed to increase. Full of youth and
hope, they talked of the joyous future, and built up pleasant
castles in the air. Battisto, grown more communicative, admitted that to marry Margherita, and become a master mosaicist,
would fulfil the dearest wish of his life. Stefano, not being in
love, preferred to travel. Christien, who seemed to be the most
prosperous, declared that it was his darling ambition to rent a
farm in his native Kander Valley, and lead the patriarchal life
of his fathers. As for the musical-box trade, he said, one should
live in Geneva to make it answer; and, for his part, he loved
the pine-forests and the snow-peaks, better than all the towns
in Europe. Marie, too, had been born among the mountains,
and it would break her heart, if she thought she were to live
in Geneva all her life, and never see the Kander Thal again.
Chatting thus, the morning wore on to noon, and the party
rested awhile in the shade of a clump of gigantic firs festooned
with trailing banners of grey-green moss.

Here they ate their lunch, to the silvery music of one of
Christien's little boxes, and by-and-by heard the sullen echo of
an avalanche far away on the shoulder of the Jungfrau.

Then they went on again in the burning afternoon, to
heights where the Alp-rose fails from the sterile steep, and
the brown lichen grows more and more scantily among the
stones. Here, only the bleached and barren skeletons of a forest

of dead pines varied the desolate monotony; and high on the summit of the pass, stood a little solitary inn, between them and the sky.

At this inn they rested again, and drank to the health of Christien and his bride, in a jug of country wine. He was in uncontrollable spirits, and shook hands with them all, over and over again.

"By nightfall to-morrow," said he, "I shall hold her once more in my arms! It is now nearly two years since I came home to see her, at the end of my apprenticeship. Now I am foreman, with a salary of thirty francs a week, and well able to marry."

"Thirty francs a week!" echoed Battisto. "Corpo di Bacco! that is a little fortune."

Christien's face beamed.

"Yes," said he, "we shall be very happy; and, by-and-by— who knows?—we may end our days in the Kander Thal, and bring up our children to succeed us. Ah! If Marie knew that I should be there to-morrow night, how delighted she would be!"

"How so, Christien?" said my brother. "Does she not expect you?"

"Not a bit of it. She has no idea that I can be there till the day after to-morrow—nor could I, if I took the road all round by Unterseen and Frütigen. I mean to sleep to-night at Lauterbrunnen, and to-morrow morning shall strike across the Tschlingel glacier to Kandersteg. If I rise a little before day-break, I shall be at home by sunset."

At this moment the path took a sudden turn, and began to descend in sight of an immense perspective of very distant valleys. Christien flung his cap into the air, and uttered a great shout.

"Look!" said he, stretching out his arms as if to embrace the dear familiar scene: "O! look! There are the hills and woods of Interlaken, and here, below the precipices on which we stand, lies Lauterbrunnen! God be praised, who has made our native land so beautiful!"

The Italians smiled at each other, thinking their own Arno valley far more fair; but my brother's heart warmed to the boy, and echoed his thanksgiving in that spirit which accepts all beauty as a birthright and an inheritance. And now their course lay across an immense plateau, all rich with corn-fields and meadows, and studded with substantial homesteads built of old brown wood, with huge sheltering eaves, and strings of Indian corn hanging like golden ingots along the carven balconies. Blue whortleberries grew beside the footway, and now and then they came upon a wild gentian, or a star-shaped immortelle. Then the path became a mere zigzag on the face of the precipice, and in less than half an hour, they reached the lowest level of the valley. The glowing afternoon had not yet faded from the uppermost pines, when they were all dining together in the parlour of a little inn looking to the Jungfrau. In the evening my brother wrote letters, while the three lads strolled about the village. At nine o'clock they bade each other good night, and went to their several rooms.

Weary as he was, my brother found it impossible to sleep. The same unaccountable melancholy still possessed him, and when at last he dropped into an uneasy slumber, it was but to start over and over and over again from frightful dreams, faint with a nameless terror. Towards morning, he fell into a profound sleep, and never woke until the day was fast advancing towards noon. He then found, to his regret, that Christien had long since gone. He had risen before daybreak, breakfasted by candlelight, and started off in the grey dawn—"as merry," said the host, "as a fiddler at a fair."

Stefano and Battisto were still waiting to see my brother, being charged by Christien with a friendly farewell message to him, and an invitation to the wedding. They, too, were asked, and meant to go; so my brother agreed to meet them at Interlaken on the following Tuesday, whence they might walk to Kandersteg by easy stages, reaching their destination on the Thursday morning, in time to go to church with the bridal party. My brother then bought some of the little Florentine cameos, wished the two boys every good fortune, and watched them down the road till he could see them no longer.

Left now to himself, he wandered out with his sketch-book, and spent the day in the upper valley; at sunset, he dined alone in his chamber, by the light of a single lamp. This meal despatched, he drew nearer to the fire, took out a pocket edition of Goethe's Essays on Art, and promised himself some hours of pleasant reading. (Ah, how well I know that very book, in its faded cover, and how often I have heard him describe that lonely evening!) The night had by this time set in cold and wet. The damp logs spluttered on the hearth, and a wailing wind swept down the valley, bearing the rain in sudden gusts against the panes. My brother soon found that to read was impossible. His attention wandered incessantly. He read the same sentence over and over again, unconscious of its meaning, and fell into long trains of thought leading far into the dim past.

Thus the hours went by, and at eleven o'clock he heard the doors closing below, and the household retiring to rest. He determined to yield no longer to this dreaming apathy. He threw on fresh logs, trimmed the lamp, and took several turns about the room. Then he opened the casement, and suffered the rain to beat against his face, and the wind to ruffle his hair, as it ruffled the acacia leaves in the garden below. Some minutes passed thus, and when, at length, he closed the window and came back into the room, his face and hair and all the front of his shirt were thoroughly saturated. To unstrap his knapsack and take out a dry shirt was, of course, his first impulse—to drop the garment, listen eagerly, and start to his feet, breathless and bewildered, was the next.

For, borne fitfully upon the outer breeze—now sweeping past the window, now dying in the distance—he heard a well-remembered strain of melody, subtle and silvery as the "sweet airs" of Prospero's isle, and proceeding unmistakably from the musical-box which had, the day before, accompanied the lunch under the fir-trees of the Wengern Alp!

Had Christien come back, and was it thus that he announced

his return? If so, where was he? Under the window? Outside in the corridor? Sheltering in the porch, and waiting for admittance? My brother threw open the casement again, and called him by his name.

"Christien! Is that you?"

All without was intensely silent. He could hear the last gust of wind and rain moaning farther and farther away upon its wild course down the valley, and the pine trees shivering, like living things.

"Christien!" he said again, and his own voice seemed to echo strangely on his ear. "Speak! Is it you?"

Still no one answered. He leaned out into the dark night; but could see nothing—not even the outline of the porch below. He began to think that his imagination had deceived him, when suddenly the strain burst forth again;—this time, apparently in his own chamber.

As he turned, expecting to find Christien at his elbow, the sounds broke off abruptly, and a sensation of intensest cold seized him in every limb—not the mere chill of nervous terror, not the mere physical result of exposure to wind and rain, but a deadly freezing of every vein, a paralysis of every nerve, an appalling consciousness that in a few moments more the lungs must cease to play, and the heart to beat! Powerless to speak or stir, he closed his eyes, and believed that he was dying.

This strange faintness lasted but a few seconds. Gradually the vital warmth returned, and, with it, strength to close the window, and stagger to a chair. As he did so, he found the breast of his shirt all stiff and frozen, and the rain clinging in solid icicles upon his hair.

He looked at his watch. It had stopped at twenty minutes before twelve. He took his thermometer from the chimney-piece, and found the mercury at sixty-eight. Heavenly powers! How were these things possible in a temperature of sixty-eight degrees, and with a large fire blazing on the hearth?

He poured out half a tumbler of cognac, and drank it at a draught. Going to bed was out of the question. He felt that he dared not sleep—that he scarcely dared to think. All he could do, was to change his linen, pile on more logs, wrap himself in his blankets, and sit all night in an easy-chair before the fire.

My brother had not long sat thus, however, before the warmth, and probably the nervous reaction, drew him off to sleep. In the morning he found himself lying on the bed, without being able to remember in the least how or when he reached it.

It was again a glorious day. The rain and wind were gone, and the Silverhorn at the end of the valley lifted its head into an unclouded sky. Looking out upon the sunshine, he almost doubted the events of the night, and, but for the evidence of his watch, which still pointed to twenty minutes before twelve, would have been disposed to treat the whole matter as a dream. As it was, he attributed more than half his terrors to the prompting of an over-active and over-wearied brain. For all this, he still felt depressed and uneasy, and so very unwilling to pass another night at Lauterbrunnen that he made up his mind to proceed that morning to Interlaken. While he was yet loitering over his breakfast, and considering whether he should walk the seven miles of road, or hire a vehicle, a char came rapidly up to the inn door, and a young man jumped out.

"Why, Battisto!" exclaimed my brother, in astonishment, as he came into the room; "what brings *you* here to-day? Where is Stefano?"

"I have left him at Interlaken, signor," replied the Italian.

Something there was in his voice, something in his face, both strange and startling.

"What is the matter?" asked my brother, breathlessly. "He is not ill? No accident has happened?"

Battisto shook his head, glanced furtively up and down the passage, and closed the door.

"Stefano is well, signor; but—but a circumstance has occurred—a circumstance so strange!——Signor, do you believe in spirits?"

"In spirits, Battisto?"

"Ay, signor; for if ever the spirit of any man, dead or living, appealed to human ears, the spirit of Christien came to me last night at twenty minutes before twelve o'clock."

"At twenty minutes before twelve o'clock!" repeated my brother.

"I was in bed, signor, and Stefano was sleeping in the same room. I had gone up quite warm, and had fallen asleep, full of pleasant thoughts. By-and-by, although I had plenty of bed-clothes, and a rug over me as well, I woke, frozen with cold and scarcely able to breathe. I tried to call to Stefano; but I had no power to utter the slightest sound. I thought my last moment was come. All at once, I heard a sound under the window—a sound which I knew to be Christien's musical box; and it played as it played when we lunched under the fir-trees, except that it was more wild and strange and melancholy and most solemn to hear—awful to hear! Then, signor, it grew fainter and fainter—and then it seemed to float past upon the wind, and die away. When it had ceased, my frozen blood grew warm again, and I cried out to Stefano. When I told him what had happened, he declared I had been only dreaming. I made him strike a light, that I might look at my watch. It pointed to twenty minutes before twelve, and had stopped there; and,— stranger still, Stefano's watch had done the very same. Now tell me, signor, do you believe that there is any meaning in this, or do you think, as Stefano persists in thinking, that it was all a dream?"

"What is your own conclusion, Battisto?"

"My conclusion, signor, is, that some harm has happened to poor Christien on the glacier, and that his spirit came to me last night."

"Battisto, he shall have help if living, or rescue for his poor corpse if dead; for I, too, believe that all is not well."

And with this, my brother told him briefly what had occurred to himself in the night; despatched messengers for the three best guides in Lauterbrunnen; and prepared ropes, ice-hatchets, alpenstocks, and all such matters necessary for a glacier expedition. Hasten as he would, however, it was nearly mid-day before the party started.

Arriving in about half an hour at a place called Stechelberg, they left the char, in which they had travelled so far, at a châlet, and ascended a steep path in full view of the Breithorn glacier, which rose up to the left, like a battlemented wall of solid ice. The way now lay for some time among pastures and pine-forests. Then they came to a little colony of châlets, called Steinberg, where they filled their water-bottles, got their ropes in readiness, and prepared for the Tschlingel glacier. A few minutes more, and they were on the ice.

At this point, the guides called a halt, and consulted together. One was for striking across the lower glacier towards the left, and reaching the upper glacier by the rocks which bound it on the south. The other two preferred the north, or right side; and this my brother finally took. The sun was now pouring down with almost tropical intensity, and the surface of the ice, which was broken into long treacherous fissures, smooth as glass and blue as the summer sky, was both difficult and dangerous. Silently and cautiously they went, tied together at intervals of about three yards each, with two guides in front, and the third bringing up the rear. Turning presently to the right, they found themselves at the foot of a steep rock, some forty feet in height, up which they must climb to reach the upper glacier. The only way in which Battisto or my brother could hope to do this, was by the help of a rope steadied from below and above. Two of the guides accordingly clambered up the face of the crag by notches in the surface, and one remained below. The rope was then let down, and my brother prepared to go first. As he planted his foot in the first notch, a smothered cry from Battisto arrested him.

"Santa Maria! Signor! Look yonder!"

My brother looked, and there (he ever afterwards declared), as surely as there is a heaven above us all, he saw Christien Baumann standing in the full sunlight, not a hundred yards distant! Almost in the same moment that my brother recognised him, he was gone. He neither faded, nor sank down, nor moved away; but was simply gone, as if he had never been. Pale as death, Battisto fell upon his knees, and covered his face with his hands. My brother, awe-stricken and speechless, leaned against the rock, and felt that the object of his journey was but too fatally accomplished. As for the guides, they could not conceive what had happened.

"Did you see nothing?" asked my brother and Battisto, both together.

But the men had seen nothing, and the one who had remained below, said, "What should I see but the ice and the sun?"

To this my brother made no other reply than by announcing his intention to have a certain crevasse, from which he had not once removed his eyes since he saw the figure standing on the brink, thoroughly explored before he went a step farther; whereupon the two men came down from the top of the crag, resumed the ropes, and followed my brother, incredulously. At the narrow end of the fissure, he paused, and drove his alpenstock firmly into the ice. It was an unusually long crevasse—at first a mere crack, but widening gradually as it went, and reaching down to unknown depths of dark deep blue, fringed with long pendent icicles, like diamond stalactites. Before they had followed the course of this crevasse for more than ten minutes, the youngest of the guides uttered a hasty exclamation.

"I see something!" cried he. "Something dark, wedged in the teeth of the crevasse, a great way down!"

They all saw it: a mere indistinguishable mass, almost closed over by the ice-walls at their feet. My brother offered a hundred francs to the man who would go down and bring it up. They all hesitated.

"We don't know what it is," said one.

"Perhaps it is only a dead chamois," suggested another.

Their apathy enraged him.

"It is no chamois," he said, angrily. "It is the body of

Christien Baumann, native of Kandersteg. And, by Heaven, if you are all too cowardly to make the attempt, I will go down myself!"

The youngest guide threw off his hat and coat, tied a rope about his waist, and took a hatchet in his hand.

"I will go, monsieur," said he; and without another word, suffered himself to be lowered in. My brother turned away. A sickening anxiety came upon him, and presently he heard the dull echo of the hatchet far down in the ice. Then there was a call for another rope, and then—the men all drew aside in silence, and my brother saw the youngest guide standing once more beside the chasm, flushed and trembling, with the body of Christien lying at his feet.

Poor Christien! They made a rough bier with their ropes and alpenstocks, and carried him, with great difficulty, back to Steinberg. There, they got additional help as far as Stechelberg, where they laid him in the char, and so brought him on to Lauterbrunnen. The next day, my brother made it his sad business to precede the body to Kandersteg, and prepare his friends for its arrival. To this day, though all these things happened thirty years ago, he cannot bear to recall Marie's despair, or all the mourning that he innocently brought upon that peaceful valley. Poor Marie has been dead this many a year; and when my brother last passed through the Kander Thal on his way to Ghemmi, he saw her grave, beside the grave of Christien Baumann, in the village burial-ground.

This is my brother's Ghost Story.

Anonymous

Old Hell Shaft

"Will the Editor obligingly spare five minutes to a gentleman who desires to see him on a subject of great importance?" So began the frame story in "The Mysterious Christmas Box, and What Came Out of It," an anthology that appeared in the Christmas Day 1865 Birmingham Daily Post. *The note announced the arrival of an Inventor presenting the titular object to an Editor, a magical box could produce stories or poems upon request and that had done so for* All the Year Round, Chambers' Journal, *and* Once a Week, *among others. The Editor challenged the Box to create poems and stories in various styles, including the comic style of Tom Hood, a mystery with a happy ending, a murder: "Something horrible, you know—appropriate to Christmas", and in the end the story below, "a good downright Christmas Horror to wind up with." Each was in turn sent by pneumatic tube to be typeset by the Printer's Devil (the term for an odd-jobbing apprentice).*

"Copy, Sir, please!" said the Printer's Devil at the door.

"Ah! we must have another, if it's only to keep *that* Demon quiet. So let us have a good downright Christmas Horror to wind up with." And thus it happened that there was added to the list the legend of

Old Hell Shaft.

ALL THE OLD HELL HEATH miners were on strike, but we were drawing water out of Old Hell Shaft. Hearing late at night that the engine had stopped, I went down to know the reason why, and from what I saw, I judged that the tenter, who had been in our service from his boyhood, had at last been induced to leave his work like the rest of the men, and had left it suddenly. The engine had been thrown out of gear with the bucket and chain still down the pit, and the boilers were nearly at red-heat; in another ten minutes they would have burst. I had just put down the damper, opened the valve to its widest, and raked out the fire, when, turning to leave the engine-house, I was seized from behind by a pair of strong arms, and borne swiftly towards the pit's mouth. Being a tolerably powerful man myself, a desperate plunge or two released me from the grasp of my unknown enemy. But not until we were close upon the brink of Old Hell Shaft.

Not a word had been spoken by either of us. By the glare of a distant furnace I saw that my antagonist, though haggard in appearance, as if hunger-pinched or worn by long illness, was a much larger built man than I was, and that upon his blackened face—blackened, as I imagined, for purposes of disguise—there was a dangerous scowl of mingled hatred and despair. His dress was that of a miner. This was all I had time to see. Hardly had I turned upon him when with a yell he flung his whole weight against me. Seizing him by the arms, I saved myself by a hair's breadth from the yawning gulf behind me, when, grinning horribly, he tried to close with me. It was a fearful struggle. I was something of a wrestler; he was evidently an adept at it. Already I felt his iron hand nervously gliding down the back part of my thigh, when, assured that that grasp would be a death grasp, I by an almost superhuman effort jerked myself on one side, and we stood at arm's length—both on the brink of the pit, but I no longer with my back to it.

Then we grappled—still in silence, a silence broken only by our own heavy breathing and the scuffling of our feet among the brittle waste on the bank. There seemed to be no time to speak, much as I longed to do so—my adversary's movements were so agile, his wiles so various and so many. I also stood at this further disadvantage—I knew not how to shape my course of action. His plan was evidently a well-defined one. He had determined to fling me down the pit, no matter at what risk to himself. Great as was my danger, I shrunk with horror from the thought of throwing him down, and was deterred from taking the attack as much by the fear that I might in self-defence be compelled to do so, as by the fear that I might be thrown down myself in the attempt. Once or twice, when his rapid feinting had left him for a moment unguarded, I felt strongly tempted to close with him at all risks, in the hope of getting him away from the pit's mouth, and so transferring the struggle to ground less dangerous. But I was always held back by the phantom of two bodies locked in their death embrace, pitched headlong into the shaft, and tumbling over and over until they fell smashed to pieces upon the surface of the black water, seven hundred feet beneath. So that I stood upon the defensive, constantly harassed by indecision—by a desire to attack, restrained as much by fear for my antagonist's life as for my own.

He tried to trip me with his heel, to trip me with his hand—first right, then left. He attempted a hug, and we came so near the edge of the shaft that we started the brickwork, and heard the fragments rattling hideously down—now clanking against the chain, now striking against the walls of the pit, until they finally fell with a dull plash into the water. Then I got him away a few yards, but he dragged me back with the grasp of a giant. We were still at arm's length, grappling. I held his arms by the biceps, he held mine a little higher up. We were looking fixedly into each other's eyes, both watching for the next movement, when a feeling of intensest horror crept through me as I noticed what I had not before had time to notice—a strange, wild glare in the man's eye. He was a maniac—I felt as certain of it as I did of my own existence. I think he must have partly seen what was passing through my mind, for he grinned a frightful grin, half defiant, half triumphant, and I felt his fingers closing in upon the muscles of my arm with the grasp of a vice. I saw that he meant mischief, and summoning the courage and the strength of despair, I awaited his assault. With a sudden twist that almost wrenched my arms from their sockets, he flung me to the right, away from the pit, and then, before I had had time to recover my balance, to the left, towards the pit; and for one brief moment I again hung over the chasm. Still clinging to him, I felt that the time had now come to abandon fear both for myself and for him, and to fight only for the mastery. No sooner, therefore, did I feel the terrible fingers once more tightening around my arms, than with one blindly furious swirl I flung my adversary off his feet into the shaft, and held him there—his body half out, resting upon the ruinous brickwork, his legs dangling helplessly over the frightful depth beneath.

"Now, tell me," I demanded, half breathless, and still struggling to keep his knees below the kerbing of the shaft, "tell me why you have made this murderous attack upon me? What have I done? How have I injured you? Why do you thus risk your own life in an attempt to take mine?"

The hideous malice which had previously shone through his every look disappeared at once; his jaw dropped, his every muscle fell flaccid, and he hung a loose dead weight upon my arms.

"God help me, Master George," he gasped, "I daint know it was you—I daint know it was you. I—I—I. Drop me down—drop me down. It's safest."

I knew the man then. He was one Sangream, who had worked in our pits for years—for my brothers and myself for the last twelve, and for my father long before then—so long that he knew us all, though one or two of us were growing grey, as "Master George," or "Master Tom," or "Master William," as the case might be.

"Surely Sangream," I said, horror-struck at the discovery that it was he, "surely you are not the man to do murder, because you can't get the rise. Besides, we offered you work at the advance as long as you lived."

"'Taint that," he moaned, "'taint nothin' to do wi' strike," and then cringing and glaring fearfully, he hissed out, "ish-ish—*he'll* hear."

"Whom?" I asked, following the direction of his shuddering glance across the heath—weird, lonesome, desolate, with nothing to relieve its barrenness but the gaunt windlasses of a dozen shafts, standing out in the fitful furnace-light like skeletons.

"*Him,*" he screamed, "*him;*" and wrenching one of his arms from my grasp, he stretched out his forefinger until it trembled with the muscular power thrown into it. "*Him,*" he shrieked again, following some imaginary phantom, with eyes and finger half way round the heath, his whole body the while contracted by terror, and quivering like an aspen leaf. "*Him,* wi' his eyes a-fire! Let me loose—let me loose—I'm dangerous." And he grasped at my legs with his disengaged arm, which, by a dexterous movement, I once more laid hold of.

The old light was in his eyes again, and the old malice upon his face. In a few moments he struggled desperately to pull me over—so desperately that more of the brickwork gave way, and clattered down ominously into the abyss.

"Come Sangream," I said, soothingly. "It's Master George, remember. Be a man, be a man." And I made an effort to drag him on to the bank.

"Let me go," he screamed, "let me go;" and then, sinking his voice to a hoarse whisper, "*he* told me to do it. He comes to my bed just as I was gettin' well of the typhus, and says he, 'black yourself, and be one of us; jump into Old Hell Shaft, and be immortal; but you must throw two in first,' he says. "I've throwed one in—Jem Luckin, the tenter. If you don't leave go, you'll be the next—leave go, Master George; leave go, I say!"

Horrified at the man's revelation, I was debating what to do for the best, when the shriek of a distant engine-whistle broke in upon the momentary silence.

"There it is," he yelled, "*he's* said it."

In an instant—while uttering the words—without a hint as to his hellish design—he planted his feet firmly against the wall, flung himself back to his full length, and—we both fell headlong into Old Hell Shaft.

Is "time fleeting?" Or is it that, being unconscious of its flight, we only think it is fleeting? An hour of suspense seems as long as a day of activity—five minutes of agony, as long as a week of enjoyment. Are they so? Does the mind measure time as the eye measures objects—never out to its full vastness? The simile sounds strange, perhaps; but let us consider. You see a speck at sea. Take your telescope, and it is a full-rigged ship. A moment ago it occupied not an inch of space—now it occupies a hundred feet. What is its true size? A hundred feet, you say—the telescope has only "brought it nearer." Stay. Here is a drop of water—clear, pellucid. There can be no mistake about that. It is close to the eye. Put it beneath the microscope, and you find living creatures in it. You did not see these living creatures before, but, inasmuch as the microscope did not create them, they must have been there. To the naked eye they were too small to be perceptible; under the microscope they are so large that you are able to count their limbs. What size are they? Does the eye, then, measure objects aright; and does the mind measure time as inaccurately as the eye measures objects? Is it, as I asked at the outset, that "time is fleeting," or that being unconscious of its flight, we only think it fleeting? I am strongly inclined to think the latter, and I will tell you why.

As I fell into Old Hell Shaft, the memories of years and the reflections of an age were crowded into one brief moment of time—measured as the clock travels. I saw the gloomy depth into which I was plunging—every winding of the bottom workings as I had myself dialed them out years ago. I remembered the explosion which took place just afterwards, and how two of Sangream's sons were blown to shreds, Sangream himself being buried alive, and rescued a raving madman. I attributed his lunacy now to the injuries he then received. I remembered how I had come away from home without saying where I was going, and this carried me back to my courting days, and still further back to the time when I was as young and as happy as the little ones who were sleeping the sleep of childhood yonder, all unconscious of their father's fate. Then I wondered how the firm would come out of the strike, for it was as ruinous to us nearly as it was to the men. Presently I saw the tenter flung down the pit as I had been, and mentally I again made my journey down to the engine-house, again finding the engine out of gear, the boilers at red heat, and—the chain down the pit.

And here came my first impulse. Hitherto all had been passive reflection. But now—could I but grapple the chain!

It was at somewhere about this point—it is impossible to fix the time more accurately, for by the clock a second had not elapsed: my feet were barely off the kerb—that with a demoniacal peal of laughter that rung round the cavernous shaft downwards, and seemed to be flung dully back from the stagnant pool at the bottom, the madman relaxed his hold upon me, and parted company.

Then, stretching out my hand frantically, I grappled for the chain.

I caught it; I grasped it with both hands—with a grasp of despair—a grasp so fearfully tenacious that, though carried down forty feet or more by my own momentum—though my hands were rent open by the irregularities of the rough links, and seared to the bone by the terrible friction of the descent—I still held on. At length I came to a dead stop.

At the same moment, a dull dead blow resounded up from the depth, followed by a wild shriek of agony and a plash that froze my very heart's blood. A slight tremor ran through the chain, and then, to my horror, it began to swing to and fro. In my then state the wildest theory found acceptance. Could it be that the devil was really at the bottom of the mischief—that Sangream was *not* the subject of a horrible delusion—that the chain was being shaken by some hideously malicious demon with the one object of shaking me off it? For a moment I felt paralysed. Reason returned as it flashed across me that the huge bucket had been left, not in the water, as I had supposed, but dangling above it. The dull blow and the shriek, before the final plash, had told me that; and, as the slight oscillations of the chain grew fainter and fainter, I was confirmed in my judgment.

Then came the terrible question, "What is to be done now?" Thus far I was safe—I had grappled the chain. But what of that? It was forty feet to the top. With hands lacerated as mine were, how could I hope to climb there? And even if I succeeded, what was I to cling to until help came? Calling for help was hopeless. I must find some place of repose where I could wait till help came. At the top of the pit there was no place of repose. It was idle to think of springing from the chain on to the bank—more idle to think of climbing over the pulley on to the small pent-house that covered it from the weather—lunacy to dream even of crawling between the pent-house and the pulley out on to that part of the chain running into the engine-house.

Meanwhile the strain upon my arms and legs was rapidly becoming unbearable. For present exigencies I drew out my pocket handkerchief, passed it through one of the links of the chain, knotted it with my teeth, and thrusting one foot into the loop, stirrup-wise, first tried its strength, and then, throwing my whole weight upon it, gained a moment's rest. Instantly another danger threatened. Released thus suddenly from their tension, my muscles lost their strength, and a clammy perspiration exuding from every pore, I began to tremble so violently that I scarce knew whether I was holding on to the chain or still falling down the shaft. Then my handkerchief gave way beneath me.

Perhaps it was fortunate that it did so, for the moment it became necessary to cling once more for life, all my old energy returned, and I held on with the vigour of a giant refreshed. Suddenly it occurred to me that my best plan would be to slide down by easy stages to the bucket, and there await the help

which I felt certain must come. No thought of ultimate starva-
tion, or indeed of death in any shape—except by an accidental
slip—had yet entered my mind. So true is it that, while we
believe all others must die, we refuse to entertain the thought
that we must die ourselves. Difficulties obtruded themselves,
however, even upon the comparatively simple plan of sliding
gradually down into the bucket. There was no fear of foul
air—Sangream's last shriek had told me that. But there were
the dangers of getting down so far; and there was this further
danger—the bucket must be full of water, and it was eight feet
deep. Still there was the chance of bestriding it, and holding
on to the bail.

So I began the descent—cautiously, but firmly—pausing
every twenty or thirty feet, and knotting my handkerchief
into the links as I had done before, to take a short rest by this
way. In this manner I had accomplished, I suppose, some four
hundred feet of my perilous journey, when, pausing awhile to
get breath and renew my strength, my frail support once more
gave way beneath me. I was gazing upward out of the mouth
of the shaft at the time, wondering when I should again live in
the strange light that played across it. But in an instant I had
increased my relaxed grasp on the chain. I was feeling for the
under part of it with my legs, when a fearful crash awoke the
slumbering echoes below. It was not my handkerchief that had
given way.

The chain had broken between my legs—I hung dangling
from the end of what remained of it.

A furious blind scramble upward, and once more I was
clutching the links between my knees. What was now to be
done I knew not. For the first time in that dread fight for existence, I could have wept hot tears. All was so hopeless. For the
last half hour—half year it seemed to me—I had been labour-
ing, as it now appeared, to remove myself from my one chance
of escape. And now, worn out by fatigue, maimed, bleeding,
exhausted, I must retrace the fearful journey in face of the
dreadful disadvantage of having to climb upwards instead of

downwards. It crossed my mind once, and only once, to solve the terrible problem by dropping voluntarily into the abyss below. The remembrance of the loved ones at home banished the thought, and it did not return.

Suddenly I remembered me. When the men struck work, they were running out a new level some distance up the shaft. Where was it? Could I by any means give myself momentum enough, by swinging backwards and forwards, to drop into it? If the new level was only near enough to the end of the chain, my new-formed plan would be just practicable. If not, the dangling weight beneath would prevent my swinging, and render it impracticable. I tried to peer through the gloom to discover the new workings; but all was dense darkness—I failed even to define the walled boundaries of the shaft. Tearing my neckerchief from my neck, I once more made good my foothold, and then began to swing.

At first my design worked to perfection; but gradually the oscillations of the chain fell out of the straight line, and I found myself graduating helplessly towards a circular motion which was both useless and worse—I was no nearer my object, the exertion fatigued me, and I was growing giddy. Letting the chain swing listlessly for a time, however, I by a desperate effort righted myself, and then, exerting myself to the utmost, increased my motion rapidly until I struck the side of the shaft. There was no opening on that side for twenty yards up—of that I was certain. The brief but intense glance I had hastily flung upward assured me of it. Nor on either hand for at least a third of the circumference of the shaft could I discern any opening in the brickwork. Now for the other side. I failed to touch it. This was strange. Could it be that I was once more deviating from the straight line? If so, farewell hope. I should fall giddy and drop—I was as certain of it as that I still breathed. No—again I struck the shaft on the same side as that on which I had struck it first, and harder than before. So, planting my disengaged foot against the wall, I impelled myself backward with a force that I thought could not fail to carry me across. This time I struck.

But not the wall of the shaft. I lay almost horizontal when the blow came, and my shoulder struck first. I concluded therefore that I had not only hit upon the very spot where the new level had been opened out, but that I had swung absolutely within it, and had struck the roof of the workings. Still it was only an inference; and my life depended on the accuracy of that inference. Should I risk all and release my hold on the chain when next I swung in; or should I explore further and run the danger of the dreaded rotatory movement? There was but brief time to weigh risks, however. Already I had struck the opposite wall—already I had impelled myself back again with disengaged foot—once more I felt the roof of the new level, and—I dropped.

Thank Heaven, upon a hard floor! Scarcely had I touched ground, however, before I became conscious that I was being tugged out into the shaft again—I had forgotten to release my foot from my neckerchief.

Crooking my fingers to lay hold of any obstruction that might come into my way, I for the first time gave myself up for lost, when, crossing a piece of timber, I clung to it, and, by one final exertion of the strength of despair, arrested the dead weight—increased by impetus—of the chain.

And I was saved. Sangream, it seems, had, during the delirium of fever, raved incessantly about Old Hell Shaft; and, missing him from his bed, his wife came down in the early morning to look for him. With what little strength remained to me, I shook the chain till her attention was drawn to it; and, my position being made known, the lads, strike or no strike, soon found means to rescue me. Sangream's body was got out and decently buried. The tenter was no more heard of until he looked in upon me one day in the full uniform of a lieutenant in the army of the United States, and explained that after leaving his work that fatal night he felt so ashamed of himself that he went direct to Liverpool and emigrated. Sangream he had not seen. We have never used Old Hell Shaft since.

John Pitman

Ejected by a Ghost

This story appeared in the 1869 Belgravia Annual, *edited by Mary Elizabeth Braddon, a publication and a woman both known for ghost stories. Information about John Pitman has proved elusive; not so the reception of "Ejected By a Ghost." Praise for it extended across the British Isles. Newspapers in Ireland called it "a really thrilling and highly dramatic narrative, the power of which makes one overlook its extravagance"[1] and "a specimen of the grimmest side of the Annual."[2] A paper in England wrote, "notwithstanding—indeed in consequence of—its horrors, it is sure to attain a very extended circulation."[3]*

I HAD TAKEN MY CHAMBERS in Gray's-inn-square, and was inclined to like them. They were on the second-floor, and consisted of three rooms. The door on the landing opened on to a narrow passage, at the end of which, on the right, was the door of the sitting-room, the three windows of which looked on to a dingy green expanse, where stood a few tall gaunt London trees. In one corner of the sitting-room was a door leading into the bedroom, which communicated with a dressing-room. This dressing-room had a door leading into the end of the passage, to the left of the main entrance from the landing. Thus I could make the complete circuit of my premises: from the sitting-room, through the bed- and

1 *Saunders's News-Letter and Daily Advertiser* [Dublin] (Nov. 18, 1869): 2, col. 2.
2 *Cork Examiner* (Nov. 23, 1869): 4, col. 1.
3 *Leamington Spa Courier* (Dec. 18, 1869): 3, col. 3.

dressing-rooms into the passage, and through the passage into the sitting-room again. I am anxious to be understood on this point, as a realisation of the topography of the place is necessary for the comprehension of the incidents I have to relate.

I will premise by assuring my reader that at the time of which I am speaking I was in thorough physical health. As is the case with most sucking barristers, I rather prided myself on cultivating a habit of mind that should not permit me to be unduly impressed by causes unwarranted by calm reflection. I had been accustomed to a sedentary, to some extent a solitary, life, and in moving to Gray's-inn-square had determined to apply myself unremittingly to legal studies.

My new chambers had been unoccupied for some months, and after making sure that they had been well cleaned and scrubbed, I sent in my furniture, and took possession. It was on a chill dark October evening that, after dining at an accustomed eating-house, I wended my way to my new quarters. I shall never forget that evening: there was a heavy clammy feeling in the air of the streets; and as I turned into the dreary square the air seemed heavier and clammier. On arriving at my chambers, I found the deaf spirit-sodden old creature who had attached herself to me as laundress and charwoman in the act of setting out the tea-things. The lamp was lighted, and a bright fire burned in the grate. On my coming in, the old woman mumbled a few words, the meaning of which I did not catch; however, well pleased with the air of comfort she had imparted to the place, I wished her a cheery good-night as she went out.

Having closed and locked the outer door, I returned down the passage into the sitting-room. I can perfectly call to mind its appearance on that night. The polished furniture was gleaming and glistening in the light, the windows were veiled by thick curtains, and the door leading into the bedroom stood ajar. I congratulated myself on my possessions, and having poured myself out a cup of tea, and lighted my pipe, settled myself with a volume of Hallam in an arm-chair by the fire. I had been reading for some time, my attention had somewhat wandered to a vague sleepy consideration of matters not strictly relevant to constitutional history, when I became aware of a strange all-pervading sensation of cold. The sensation was so sudden, so acute, that I rose from my chair shivering, in the expectation of finding one of the windows open. But no; they were all closed and fastened. Through the panes I could discern the gaunt branches of the trees, unstirred by any gust of wind. On glancing round the room, I noticed the flame of the lamp, which, though somewhat dim, did not flicker or seem agitated by the icy stream of air which chilled me to the bones. The bedroom door, as I have mentioned, was ajar; and thinking the draught might proceed from one of the inner rooms, I lighted a candle, with the intention of looking through them. But the instant I entered the bedroom the candle went out; not suddenly, as from a current of air, but quietly, instantaneously, as though it had been introduced into an atmosphere of carbonic-acid gas. At the same moment the sensation of cold again came over me with ten times greater intensity than before. The gaslight in the square shone feebly into the rooms, and I was able to find my way through them into the passage, and back into the sitting-room. My sensations appeared to me somewhat unaccountable; but attributing them to some draught, of which I could ascertain the cause in the morning, I closed the doors and resumed my place by the fire. After a little while I fell again into my interrupted train of dreamy thought, and gradually fell asleep. Now, before proceeding further, I may state that I had never been a victim to nervous fancies. Nothing had ever occurred to me bearing in the remotest way on the events I am about to relate,—events so utterly inexplicable by natural causes, and yet so fantastically real, that even after a lapse of many years I call them to mind with a shudder of horror.

I remember, as though it were yesterday, the appearance of the room as I mused lazily in my arm-chair before going to sleep. The sound of an organ, which was playing in some neighbouring street, came to me fitfully, at times seeming to be almost close to me, at times, again, seeming to proceed from some great distance. The fire had burned low, occasionally cracking and ticking; the lamp, as I have mentioned, was burning dimly, and a large portion of the room was in deep shadow. I do not know how long I had slept, when I became conscious of my own being. I cannot say that I awakened; for though all my mental faculties were struggling painfully into life, my vital action seemed suspended, and I was unable to move hand or foot. A cold perspiration burst from all my pores as I made tremendous but vain efforts to shake off the incubus that was upon me. My feeling was not one of impotence: it was as though I had been frozen into a solid block of ice. I endeavoured to call out; I had no power over my voice, and could not utter a sound. But as I gasped and panted, there stole into my nostrils a deadly, terrible, overpowering stench, unmistakable in its penetrating sickliness to me who had frequented hospitals. It was the dread odour of decomposing mortality that was suffocating me as I sat. I felt that I must break the spell, or die. With one terrific exertion that strained every nerve and muscle, I burst from the chair, and fell cowering on my knees before the fire. The lamp had gone out, a faint gleam from the fire afforded the only light in the room. I relighted the lamp, and having swallowed a glass of brandy, endeavoured to collect my thoughts. My first idea was, that a dead body must be somewhere concealed in the room. The hideous odour still clung to my nostrils, and the absurdity of such a supposition did not strike me. I searched the room, but of course found nothing; though, to my astonishment, the bedroom door, which I had carefully closed, was wide open. As I advanced towards it with the intention of shutting it again, my lamp was extinguished in the same unaccountable manner as before; I locked it, however, securely, and again struck a light.

By this time I had sufficiently recovered to endeavour to reconcile my sensations to natural causes, or at any rate to a formidable attack of nightmare. I lighted my pipe, in the hope of neutralising the terrible stench that still pervaded the room.

Leaning on the mantelpiece, I actually smiled at beholding my
own pale scared-looking face in the mirror. As I looked, suddenly every pulse in my body stood still. I beheld the reflection
of the bedroom door, which gradually, noiselessly, opened of
itself. I tried to command myself, and turned round towards
the door. The same intense thrill of cold, but not a soul was
there. I considered for an instant, and cross-examined myself
as to my own condition. It was evident that my nerves were
completely unstrung, and I decided, as I saw reflected in the
looking-glass my own ghastly-looking face, that I was not in a
condition to investigate the matter any further for that night.
A dread was upon me that I could not shake off; so, hastily
putting on my great-coat and hat, I hurried out of the room,
through the passage, found myself on the landing with a sigh
of relief, and locking the outer door, walked to the rooms of a
friend who lived in the neighbourhood.

S——, who was reading for the Indian Civil Service, was
glad to see me, and offered me a shake-down for the night. I
informed him at once of the cause of my ignominious flight
from my own rooms. My experiences had been too unmistakably real for me to dread ridicule in the relation of them.
So, confessing unreservedly that I had been almost frightened
out of my wits, I sat patiently enough as he endeavoured to
prove satisfactorily that my sensations were entirely due to
nerves or indigestion. Before retiring to rest, however, we
agreed to spend the following night together in my chambers.
In the morning we each went to our respective duties, with
an arrangement to meet at dinner in the evening. I did not call
at Gray's-inn-square during the day; and what with attending
to lectures and reading tough law, had not only overcome any
idea of supernatural agency in the events of the preceding
night, but, as the evening drew near, entirely ceased to think
of the matter.

It was about eight o'clock as we entered the rooms
together. The old laundress had evidently been at work, as
on the preceding evening. The fire was burning brightly,

the lamp was lighted, and the tea-things were set out on the table. We walked through the rooms, and found everything in perfect order. S—— laughingly envied me my comfortable quarters, showing by his manner that he was more than ever convinced I had been the victim of an exceedingly bad attack of nightmare. After a little while we agreed to play at chess, and arranged a small side-table in front of the fire. I sat in the arm-chair with my back to the bedroom-door, as on the previous night; S—— was seated opposite to me, consequently facing the door, which I had closed, locked, and bolted, on completing our tour of inspection; S——, who was in high spirits, joking at me the while. I remembered, however, the uncomfortable tendency it had to open on its own account, and determined that it should be as securely fastened as a good lock and bolt would admit of. We were both fair chess-players, about equally matched.

Two hours, perhaps, had elapsed, when the interest of the game culminated, and we were considering it with an intentness known only to chess-players. The move was with me. Knowing it to be a critical one, I was considering it at length, in all its aspects; my decision was just formed, and I was on the point of moving a piece, when gradually, surely, I became aware of the same extraordinary sensation of cold as on the night before, just as if the surrounding atmosphere were becoming iced into solidity. I felt that the bedroom-door behind me was opening. I looked up with the intention of calling S——'s attention to the phenomenon, but my movement was unnecessary; he was equally conscious of it with myself. He had risen from his chair, and I can never forget the expression of his face, which was livid and distorted. His eyes were wide open, and turned full on the door that was behind my chair. All his features were convulsed, and his appearance, as he bent forward, as if in an intensity of horrified expectation, was perfectly terrific. I actually saw his hair lift from his head, and the great beads of perspiration burst from his forehead. He took not the slightest notice of my movement, but slowly raised one hand, as if pointing to something in the room behind me; then suddenly, and without giving me a moment's warning, with one loud yell of agonised terror, he dashed to the door leading into the passage, through the passage, and out of the main door, which slammed heavily behind him. I hurried after him into the passage. Then I remembered that the outer door closed with a spring-lock, and that the key was in the pocket of my greatcoat, which was hung up in the bedroom. We had inadvertently left the door open on coming in, and thus S—— had been enabled to escape. It would be impossible for me to describe my feelings at finding myself alone in the passage. How long it was before I mustered up sufficient presence of mind for reflection I cannot tell, but at last I realised to myself the fact that to leave my chambers it was necessary to get the key. With a desperate courage, I returned to the sitting-room. The lamp was extinguished; the fire was burning with a sickly glare. With closed eyes I advanced into the bedroom. I quickly felt my way to the peg on which my coat was hanging, when something happened that caused my very heart to stand still, and my blood to freeze. I heard a movement in the passage,—a strange, heavy, shuffling sound, as of a body dragging itself along the floor. An impulse seized me, unaccountable as all the other events of that memorable night. I felt impelled to follow *the thing* that was painfully, slowly dragging itself down the passage. I stepped through the dressing-room; and as I moved, I heard it move on before me, keeping at the same relative distance from me. I quickened my pace, I ran; but still I could not overtake that which I still heard dragging itself along.

After three or four headlong rushes from room to room, I stopped in the middle of the sitting-room to recover breath. As I stood, a revulsion of feeling came over me. My eagerness to confront and discover the cause of the sounds I still could hear gave way to horror. I felt my life and reason to depend on my escape. As I moved to the bedroom-door, it closed in my face. I frantically endeavoured to force the lock. The *thing* was dragging itself along the passage into the room in which I was. Again the nauseating stench of the night before rose into my nostrils; I rushed to the window with the intention of throwing it open and jumping into the space beneath; but it was too late. I turned my eyes downwards. It was close to me, and I beheld it. A man writhing on the floor, his features blue, bloated, and decomposed, the eyeballs turned up, yet bearing full upon me, dead and glassy, an impure phosphorescent light emanating from the body itself. As I gazed, one discoloured hand was raised to the throat, in which I perceived a hideous gash. It drew itself gradually closer to me. . . . . . I became insensible. When I was discovered in the morning, my friends, who were telegraphed for, removed me to the country, where, amongst cheerful scenes and people, I soon recovered. S——died of brain-fever within three days of the night on which he sat and watched with me.

I have never cared to make any inquiries as to the previous inmates of the chambers. It is true I have heard that an inmate of one set cut his throat under peculiarly horrible circumstances; but I was never curious to identify the scene of the suicide's death with the chambers I occupied for so short a time; indeed, nothing would induce me ever again to enter Gray's-inn-square.

The Christmas party that has just listened to a ghost story would rather go on all night, drinking in fresh horrors, than separate to their cold and gloomy chambers.

Evening Mail [London] (March 27, 1846): 8, col. 2.

Mrs. S. R. Townshend Mayer

The Netherstone Mystery

When it appeared in the Illustrated Sporting and Dramatic
News *of December 14, 1878, the author's other works were
noted as the novel* Sir Hubert's Marriage *and the collection of
stories* The Fatal Inheritance. *Among the later books of* GER-
TRUDE MARY DALBY TOWNSHEND MAYER (1840-1932)
was Women of Letters, *a collection of biographies including
one of Mary Shelley. Many of her stories remain uncollected,
including 'The Netherstone Mystery,' along with other several
Christmas ones, some supernatural, some ghostly, some neither,
but evidently all seasonal stories containing a darkness of some
kind.*

CHAPTER I.

A CORPSE-CANDLE.

"WHAT! EXILE MYSELF FROM TOWN at this time of year
of all others? Give up the Christmas parties, and
shut myself in a lonely country house where I don't know a
soul, and work hard all the holiday time! Hang it, the thing's
preposterous. I won't do it."

"Very well, dear boy. Take it or leave it. The loss is yours.
Only remember, it's the last time *I'll* exert myself to do a
fellow a good turn. I cracked you up to the skies to the old
man, and said you were the best hand in England—in fact, the
only one—at what he wanted. It's the sort of thing you've
been always wishing for, and I thought you would jump at

it. However, please yourself and you'll please me. I must tell
him I made a mistake, and he can look for somebody else. Of
course I shall seem a howling idiot."

"That will be nothing new, old boy," I observed pleasantly.
"But don't be rash. I suppose I must go. I only had my grum-
ble—it's an Englishman's privilege. I may not find it so bad,
after all. Of course, in a house like that there will be some sort
of family gathering."

"I never heard that there was any family to gather."

"By Jove! There ought to be an opening, then. Is the Squire
a genial old card? The sort of fellow to take a fancy to a good-
looking youth, of engaging address, and adopt him as his
heir?"

"You'd better try," said my friend Frank, drily; "I never
asked him to adopt *me*. The only thing he seems to care about
is keeping up his place. I was there six weeks sketching all the
points, and I daresay you will be twice as long over this new
whim. Well, good-bye. Look me up before you go."

I was serving my apprenticeship as a literary man-of-all-
work, ready to undertake anything, from *The Times'* money
article to a triolet on Lady Blanche Broadacres. But in my
secret soul I believed I had a specialty, and that it was for family
history, enriched by historico-poetic-antiquarian lore.

I started for Netherstowe, resolved to return with fame in
one pocket and money in the other.

I arrived there on a very "drear-nighted December" indeed.

The Priory loomed vast and gloomy through the gathering darkness. A responsible-looking elderly gentleman,
afterwards revealed as Mr. Belton, the Squire's butler and
personal attendant, received me, and told off a son of Anak in
hair-powder and calves, to conduct me to my room. A bright
comfortable room, boasting of Morris's wall-papers, and the
latest improvements in lounging-chairs and writing-tables.

"The gong will sound in about ten minutes, sir," observed
James, as he withdrew; and I forthwith plunged madly into
an elaborate toilet, wondering how large the party would be,

and trusting that a conversible, pretty-looking girl would fall to my share.

James was in attendance to conduct me through a labyrinth of corridors and stairs, richly carpeted, crimson lined, relieved here and there by a statue, a painting, a stand of evergreens; well-lighted, warmed, decorated—and empty.

At last he threw open the doors of a huge dining-room, with enough plate on the sideboard for a civic guild, and enough room round the table for a staff corps. It was carefully laid for—one.

The sight came upon me like a shower-bath on a January morning: the shock, the chill, but not the after-glow. I hesitated a moment before taking my seat.

"Am I not to have the pleasure of seeing Mr. De Morgue?" I asked the solemn butler.

"My master never dines, sir," was the reply.

"Never dines! Good heaven," I thought, "how does he get through the winter evenings?"

I shall never forget that dinner—its length, its solitude, its splendour.

If the dining-room was bad, the drawing-room was worse —a glittering solitude, with its gilt mouldings and azure panels, its one fire in remote perspective, its one small chandelier lighted, its slender-legged, high-backed furniture in pinafores of delicate chintz, looking like Doré's *drôles* about to perform a weird and ghostly dance.

My lonely figure, reflected in many mirrors, looked indescribably absurd. I soon grew tired of contemplating it, and requested to be reconducted to my room.

While James was making up the fire, I drew aside the window curtains, to see how the park looked by moonlight. But the night was pitch dark, and the view a gulf of blackness. Only on the dim horizon gleamed something too large, and bright, and steady for a star.

"What is that light in the distance?" I inquired. "Surely the station cannot be seen from here?"

"That is the family Mausoleum, sir," was the cheering reply. "There is always a light burning there, day and night, all the year round."

CHAPTER II.

MY MYSTERIOUS VISITANT.

"Colours seen by candlelight," says Mrs. Browning, "do not look the same by day." But the morning impressions made by Netherstowe in no way contradicted the evening. The whole house, so far as I saw it, was handsome, admirably kept up, and deserted. It should have been bright with happy faces and loud with merry voices. In four-and-twenty hours I found its luxurious loneliness more depressing than the wildest ruin.

Breakfast, like dinner, was prepared for me alone. Mechanically I made the same inquiry about my host.

"My master never breakfasts, sir," replied Mr. Belton, with the same portentous gravity.

He never breakfasted, and he never dined! What did he do? Did he live on grains of rice and midnight visits to graveyards, like the uncomfortable woman in the "Arabian Nights"?

At lunch, at dinner, when the dinner-hour at length arrived, I was still alone. The day seemed interminable. At last I said desperately—

"If this sort of thing goes on, I shall go mad. I'll see the crazy old curmudgeon to-morrow, if I break into his room by violence, and tell him——"

"I could not think of giving you so much trouble," said a cool sarcastic voice behind me.

I jumped up and faced round, with an involuntary apology for the peculiar form of expression I had made use of.

"Pray do not mention it," replied the apparition. "Recluse though I am, I know too much of the manners of the present generation to expect verbal courtesy from the young. May I inquire what you so particularly wished to say to me?"

Mr. De Morgue was tall and spare, with a slight stoop, thin aquiline features, an obstinate mouth, and dark eyes peering maliciously from beneath shaggy eyebrows. He had a wizard look, increased by the black velvet cap which partly covered his thin white hair, and the long dressing-gown whose crimson folds waved behind him.

His *tout ensemble* did not tend to relieve my embarrassment. But I managed stammeringly to explain that anxiety to enter on my duties had betrayed me into undue emphasis. And that I only desired instructions as to the work for which I was there.

"If you will have the goodness to follow me," said my host, "I will give you all that you require. You must pardon my entering on business details at this unseasonable time, for I do not keep the usual hours, and you will probably not see me to-morrow."

And he preceded me through the smaller drawing-room by which he had entered, to a large neighbouring apartment of a sombre and severe aspect.

Seating himself at the head of the table, Mr. De Morgue pointed to several large packets of letters before him, and a formidable array of tin boxes ranged along the floor.

"Here you will find the archives of my house for many generations," he said with a sort of icy satisfaction. "Title deeds and documents of every description, private correspondence, and records of public services. These I wish you in the first place to classify chronologically, throwing aside all you consider unimportant, and retaining such as may in your opinion be woven into an interesting history. When you have done so I shall be able to judge approximately of your capacity for writing that history."

Having spoken thus, he vanished; that is to say, he went out through a small door concealed by heavy hangings. I wondered how the household in general liked their lord and master to move in such eccentric orbits.

Next morning saw me fairly launched on my chosen career and beginning to feel an absorbing interest in my work.

About a week after I began my acquaintance with the ancestral De Morgues, as I was going away to dress, a door at the further end of the dimly-lighted room opened, and a figure glided with slow and noiseless steps to just beyond the circle of light made by my shaded writing lamp; and seating itself in one of the antique carved chairs, rested a fair cheek on a fairer hand.

It was the figure of a girl of seventeen, slender and tall, with the resolute mouth I had learnt to know so well in those long rows of family portraits, with a mass of fair hair piled high above her shapely head, with pale cheeks and dark shadowy eyelashes, which hid the downcast eyes. Her dress was some white shining stuff of antique fashion, and the lamplight kindled the secret fire of rubies glowing in her ears and on her breast.

I was not more surprised than delighted by this visit. The young lady's extreme beauty, and the manner of her entrance, supplied just the element of romance which had been wanting at Netherstowe. Who could she be? I never heard that Mr. De Morgue had a daughter. But then I had heard nothing about his family.

Presently she turned over some of the papers which strewed the table, and asked in a low voice:—

"Do not you find it very lonely here?"

"Not at all," I said, enthusiastically. "I am too much interested in my work."

"Your work? Ah! you are writing a history of the family, are you not?"

"I am preparing the materials for one."

"You have papers—letters—from most of the family?"

"From almost all, I believe."

"Have you got very far—say, to the last generation?"

"Oh! not half way. The papers are so numerous, and, you see, the earlier ones take so much longer to decipher and arrange."

She scarcely seemed to heed my explanation.

"Will you have to search so far?"

"I suppose so—yes, undoubtedly."

"Have you the late letters here?" she asked, looking lingeringly, wistfully at the piles that heaped my desk.

"Most probably; but unexamined as yet, of course. I am working chronologically."

"I detain you," she said, with gentle courtesy, as the gong sounded. And she rose, with a slight inclination of her lovely head.

"Pray do not hurry," I urged, eagerly, blunderingly, unwilling to lose a moment of her presence. "It is such a pleasure —such a rare pleasure—to see, to speak to anyone here."

"Oh, we shall meet again," she replied with a faint smile. And as she did not resume her seat, I left the library.

We did meet again—often, often. Not at dinner, as I had ventured to hope. Not at all that evening; but afterwards, "between the daylight and the dusk;" or later, in the large rooms whose partial lighting made a twilight of its own, I used to see her constantly. And the day became a lost and dark day to me on which I did not see her.

I never met her with others, never saw her in a full light, never close by my side. We shared none of the every-day pursuits which throw people together, no rises, or walks, or songs, or laughter. Yet this shadowy distance seemed a bond rather than a barrier between us, for it made her more exclusively my own.

Yes, my own, I learnt to call her in my heart, though I did not even know her name. As the days grew into weeks I began to watch for her with feverish eagerness. Sometimes she did not come, and then the world was a blank.

This feeling, this infatuation, if you will, ripened fast in an atmosphere of silent mystery.

One evening when I entered the drawing room I saw the gleam of her white dress in the smaller room beyond, and advanced eagerly. But as I approached she retreated beyond the radius of the furthest light, and seated herself within the perfumed dusk of the conservatory. Then she returned to the subject which had occupied her on our first meeting.

"How do you progress with your work?" she asked.

"Slowly, I am afraid."

"You have not come to the recent letters."

"No; not yet."

She sighed.

"To tell the truth—may I—will you be angry if I tell the truth?"

"Why should I be angry?"

"To tell the truth, then, I fear I am not very anxious to get to those recent letters."

"Why not?"

"Because—I cannot tell why—I have a fancy, an impression, that then I shall lose you—I shall see you for the last time."

There was a moment's silence. Then she asked, in a voice which, unless my hopes deceived me, faltered a little—

"And what if it were so?"

"If it were so!" I repeated, a sudden impulse mastering me, and driving prudence and reason to the winds. "It must never be so! I cannot lose you—I will not. My words may sound madly presumptuous, but it is the madness of love. I love you with all my soul."

She gave a low, incredulous, half-scornful laugh.

"Love *me?* Ah! you know not what you are saying. Love a shadow—a nameless vision?"

"I said it might seem madness, but it will be lifelong madness—longer than life, and stronger than death. Only give me the smallest hope! I will wait—I will work—I will endure any probation you may require, submit to any test you may propose."

I thought she wavered. I took a hasty step forward, but a warning gesture restrained me. She paused, and seemed thinking deeply. Her brows were knit, her eyes fixed on the ground.

"You are brave?" she asked, at last.

"Try me."

"You *wish* to be tried? You would do anything to prove your—what you call your love?"

"Anything in the world—or out of it."

"Meet me, then, alone, at midnight, on Christmas Eve, in the Mausoleum."

CHAPTER III.

LOST TO NAME AND FAME.

"Mrs. White," I said to the good-natured old housekeeper, the cheeriest and least abnormal member of Mr. De Morgue's establishment. "Mrs. White, are you particularly busy just now? I should like to speak to you."

I had grown desperate. Since that strange tryst was plighted I had seen nothing of my mysterious visitor; and if I could not see her I must hear of her. If I could not talk to her I must talk of her.

"Mrs. White, has Mr. De Morgue a daughter?"

"A daughter! Dear, no, sir, he has never been married."

"Then who is the young lady staying in the house?"

"Young lady, sir? There's no young lady—there's no one in the house but master and you."

"That is nonsense," said I sharply, "when I see her almost every evening."

Mrs. White looked as if she thought me out of my senses.

"Indeed, sir, you are mistaken," she repeated earnestly. "There has been no young lady in *this* house for more than twenty years."

"She is here, I assure you, nearly every evening," I said, with forced composure. "I have seen her in the library, the drawing-rooms, and the conservatory. She wears a white dress, with ruby ornaments. She is slender and fair, with heaps of golden hair, and dark eyes. She is pale—but, pooh! words are absurd—hundreds of girls look like that. See here!"

I had drawing-pencils and water-colours before me. In a few seconds I produced a rough, but recognisable sketch of my beloved, and gave it to Mrs. White, who turned pale, and trembled so violently that she leaned against the table for support. She held the sketch for a moment with shaking hands and a look of terror; then dropped it with a loud cry—

"Lord have mercy upon us, sir! That's my poor young mistress—master's sister. And she died eighteen years ago!"

I could not believe it—I would not believe it. I laughed at her and at myself. I said the sketch was not a likeness, that her memory deceived her. In a breath I reasoned with, ridiculed, and reviled the terrified woman. I know not what absurdities of gesture and exclamation I was perpetrating when Mrs. White laid her shaking hand upon my arm.

"What I've told you is the simple truth, sir, as true as that I'm standing here! Come to my room, and I'll prove it to you."

I followed the housekeeper to her room, and on its threshold I stood transfixed. There, on the opposite wall, hung a life-size portrait, whose likeness was unmistakable—from the pensive curve of the red lips, the proud grace of the small head, the pearly paleness of the colourless cheeks, even to the ruby cross on the slender throat, and the shining folds of the white robe.

But right across that delicate face was a cruel mark, as though some sharp instrument had been violently thrust at it.

Mrs. White stood beside me, crying quietly.

"What is the meaning of *that?*" I asked her, pointing to the scar.

"My master did it in his anger, sir, and when I begged him to stop, he tore the picture from the wall, and bade me have it destroyed. But I could not do that. I brought it here, when I knew he would never see it again. It is rather heavy; can you lift it down, and look behind it?"

I did so. On the back was inscribed—"Adela Endsleigh

De Morgue, born 18—," and below, in a trembling woman's hand, "Died December 186–."

I set the portrait tenderly against the wall, then threw myself on the floor beside it. I was stupefied, miserable. Only one idea was clear to my bewildered brain. I must learn all I could about her. Her! Whom? A picture—a vision—a dead woman!

"Why did he want to destroy the picture?"

Mrs. White paused—hesitated. But my strange interest in the portrait overcame her scruples.

"Because—because she had disgraced his name, sir. They were orphans, and when he came into the property, he would have his sister home, without a governess or any one to look after her, though she was but a child. He worshipped her, and her whim was law. They were always together, riding and rowing, and skating and fishing. Whatever he did she would do; and he never seemed to care for any other companion—but one. There was a Captain Clifford who had been at College with my master, though he was much older; and one Christmas he came here to stay, and then there were three, for Miss Adela was with them just the same. I soon saw how it was, sir; but I'm sure my master never guessed, till one day her room was empty, and so was the captain's. They had gone away in the night—together; and my master knew, and Miss Adela knew too, what I did not—that Captain Clifford was a married man."

She stopped a moment, to steady her trembling voice.

"His sister was the only human being my master ever loved. But there was one thing he loved better—the good name of his house. And they were swept away from him at one blow. It well nigh turned his brain. He took a dreadful oath that neither Miss Adela nor anyone belonging to her should ever cross his doors again. And after that he never saw daylight, and never had a visitor. He lives entirely in his own rooms, with the windows blocked up, and he only goes out at night. It is an awful life, sir!"

I had risen, ashamed of my violent outbreak of feeling,

and was replacing the poor, marred, lovely face, symbol of a ruined life, in its place in the wall.

"And she—Adela—was she ever heard of?"

"Oh, sir, that was the worst of all! She came back one bitter December night, four or five years after she ran away—she came back, sir, with scarcely clothes to cover her—and my master with his own hands put her out into the darkness and the snow.... We servants would have followed and helped her, for we loved the very ground she trod on. But her brother went round the house from door to door and bolted and locked them all, and took the keys up into his own room. It was awful, sir! Well, three weeks after, by the last post on Christmas Eve—and a wretched Christmas it was for all of us—there came a black-edged letter for my master; I saw that Belton's face was as white as ashes when he took it upstairs, and I lingered in the hall, feeling uneasy, when my master came downstairs in his dressing-gown with nothing on his head, and dashed out at the hall door into the storm, with the letter in his hand. We all stood horror-struck at first, and then Belton and I followed him; for we thought he'd gone raving mad at last; and we saw him flying through the park, over the wet grass and brambles, never waiting for the path till he got to the Mausoleum. As we came up with him the door was locked in our faces, and there he stayed all night long. Belton was the only one that dared to sit up for him. When I saw him again he was as cool and sharp as ever, as if nothing had happened. My dear young lady's name was never mentioned again in this house, but I know the letter was to say she was dead, and that cruel night had killed her. But I never heard," asked Mrs. White, in lowered tones of awe and terror, "that she *came again*. And why, sir, should she have come to you?"

I cannot describe the days that followed. They were a waking nightmare haunted by one unnatural, incredible, intolerable idea. I, who had all my life ridiculed the theory of supernatural presences. I, to have seen and *loved* a phantom!

Yet as every evening came round I listened and longed for

that strange presence which, if unearthly, was dearer to me than anything on earth. I knew that we should not meet again till that appointed meeting to which I had pledged my word. I knew I should go. I knew that the next, and perhaps the last, time I should see that strange and lovely vision would be at the Mausoleum in the park.

CHAPTER IV.

THE SECRET OF THE TOMB.

Christmas Eve arrived. To my part of that melancholy house the anniversary brought no change, except an added sense of gloom. The occasional opening of a distant door betrayed some festivity in the servants' regions, though Mrs. White's frightened face and Belton's increased sternness showed that they took no part in it. My lonely dinner was a mere show, which I sat out impatiently. When at last in the drawing-room, I opened one of the windows that the icy night air might blow on my heated face, and stood watching the distant glimmer of that sepulchral light, visible from almost every window of the house. Hour by hour I watched it, unable to avert my eyes or my thoughts.

Then, as the cupids on the mantelpiece chimed half-past eleven with their silver bells, the light drew me like a magnet out of the silent house, across the wet and clinging grass, and up to the more silent dwelling of the dead. The door was ajar, and I entered with a beating heart, expecting I knew not what revelation of horror. But the mausoleum was empty, and my hurried step was the only sound that broke its echoes. In the centre was a richly-carved marble tomb, where the bodies of Mr. De Morgue's father and mother rested, while their ancestors slept below. At its foot stood a large ebony cabinet, which supported an open funereal lamp. A larger lamp, pendant from the roof, gave the light I had so often watched.

I leaned against the side of the tomb, and waited—chilled, burning, awe-struck, incredulous—with every conflicting sensation rending mind and body. Twelve tolled from the great clock of the Priory, and the mausoleum door slowly opened. I started up, expecting to see *her* again; but it was Mr. De Morgue who entered, dressed as I had last seen him, and unprotected from the winter night. His white face had the fixed, unseeing expression of a sleep-walker, and his whole being seemed absorbed by one thought.

He stopped before the cabinet, unlocked it, and took out a large black-bordered packet; paused a moment, then held it over the lamp. But before the flame touched it, his hand dropped powerless by his side, as from behind the tomb glided the figure so well known to me—the white-robed girlish figure of her who had lain in the grave for eighteen years.

The old man shrank and cowered at its approach. "Adela!" he cried, wildly, "forgive me—leave me; I will not destroy it. I will acknowledge your child. His voice died away in a choking sob, and he fell senseless on the ground.

As the old man fell, a woman swiftly passed me, with pale, resolute face and gleaming eyes—not to lift the grey head or summon help for the dying, only to snatch the letter from the loosening grasp of the cold fingers, and cry, with a low laugh of bitter triumph, "I have found it at last!"

★ ★ ★ ★ ★ ★

I regret to say that I did *not* marry the heiress of Nether-stowe, as, after so romantic an introduction to her, I ought to have done. She had all the pride of the De Morgues—perhaps a double allowance, because of the wrongs of her youth. She married a rich baronet, whose name I will not mention, lest you should stare too hard at her ladyship's victoria when next you see it in the Row.

The supernatural part of the matter had been easily managed. When Adela was turned away from her brother's door that night, she went to a little farm belonging to Belton's mother, and died there, leaving her infant daughter in the woman's care. On her death-bed she told Belton that she had been married to Mr. Clifford in India after his first wife's death. He left the army soon after the elopement and went in search of some small Indian appointment which he failed to obtain. Their child was Mr. De Morgue's legal heir. This was the news contained in the black-edged letter, together with the certificates of marriage and baptism. But Mr. De Morgue did not consider that his sister's shame had been blotted out, and in his unsettled brain he resolved to keep his oath. So the younger Adela was brought up by the Beltons, who sent her to school in a distant town. When she learnt her history she determined somehow to obtain possession of the documents, without which she would not have had a tittle of evidence in support of her claim. The scheme was all her own, and Belton, who kept the keys of the rooms, did not hesitate to give her the clothes and ornaments her mother had left behind in her flight. The conspirators had been baffled in effort after effort to obtain the papers. Miss Clifford's interviews with me were to try to obtain some clue to their hiding-place, which Belton himself did not know. The scene at the mausoleum was planned to work on her uncle's feelings. She knew he had visited it every Christmas Eve since his sister's death. Why she had drawn me thither I hardly know—perhaps she feared violence, and thought she might need help.

I don't suppose she ever contemplated the fatal result of her plot—but I am sure she did not regret it.

I left Netherstowe on Christmas Day, and have never seen nor wished to see it since. A very handsome cheque was sent me for the time I had wasted over that family history, which never went to press, and I was fool enough to light my cigar with it. But I am unchanged in my conviction that my forte *is* Family History, and I am open to any handsome offer to try my hand again.

Florence Marryat

That Awful Face!

Florence Marryat may be familiar to Valancourt readers from the round-robin The Fate of Fenella (1892) *or her novel* The Blood of the Vampire (1897). *She published dozens of books, including novels, story collections, and nonfiction works on Spiritualism, yet despite that—as is the case with several of the authors herein—some of her prolific output hasn't been seen since it originally appeared. "That Awful Face!" was printed in several newspapers across England and Wales, including the December 19, 1885 Cardiff* Times. *Marryat was a Spiritualist, though her "authentic" tales were weak sauce compared to her fiction, provoking the same wonder as Arthur Conan Doyle having been taken in by photos of cutout fairies on sticks.*

A VISITOR FOR THE Right Reverend the Lord Bishop of Gorhambury.

The Bishop is seated in his study, puzzling his brains how best to settle certain clerical disputes that have been submitted for his arbitration. He is a spare little man, dressed in a long black coat and gaiters, with very white hair, and a nose like a chilblain; a little man indeed, of so frosty an appearance, that he looks as if he had been expressly got up to ornament a Twelfth cake.

But the frostiness is all on the outside. His lordship's heart is in the right place, and brimming over with kindly feeling for his fellow-creatures.

"Who is it, Matthews?" he demands of the dignified creature who has been kind enough to bring the intelligence to him.

"Mr. Ryle, my lord."

"Oh, show Mr. Ryle in, show him in at once," replies the Bishop with sudden interest, for Mr. Ryle is a wealthy land-owner in the diocese of Gorhambury—a munificent man, moreover, who spends his money liberally on charities for the good of the county; a friend and neighbour whom even the Bishop of Gorhambury cannot afford to despise.

In another moment Mr. Ryle has entered the room, and is shaking hands with its Right Reverend occupant. He is a stout, florid, genial-looking fellow, also dressed in gaiters, but of quite a different cut to those of the Bishop, and the splashed condition of his velveteen suit, no less than the crop he carries in his hand, shows that he has ridden for some miles through the muddy lanes that lead to the episcopal residence.

"Well, Mr. Ryle, and what brings you out this wet morning?" demands the little Bishop, when they have shaken hands.

"Business, my lord, business!" replies the other with a twin-kle in his eye; "I have come to ask a favour of you on behalf of a friend of mine."

The Right Reverend screws up his little chilblainy nose, and laughs.

"A favour! Well, Mr. Ryle, if there is anything I can do for a friend of yours that you cannot do for him yourself, you may command me. But I am afraid substantial benefits are more in your line than mine."

"It is not a benefit, but a benefice I come to ask at your lordship's hand. The fact is, my friend Darrell, an excellent fellow—first-class man at Cambridge, and been working like a horse ever since—has suddenly conceived an ardent desire for matrimony. They all do it, you know, my lord, sooner or later! The shepherd's crook is all very well for a while, but it stands no chance against a four-post bedstead."

The little Bishop chuckles softly to himself. He also com-menced life with the intention of dedicating it to the good of suffering humanity, but there is a little Bishopess and more than one episcopal olive shoot in the upper storey, that look as if his thoughts had, at some time or other, wandered sadly out of the beaten track.

"Yes," he admits, after a judicious pause; "it is certainly true that a helpmeet has a wonderful effect in sweetening the path of duty."

Mr. Ryle laughs aloud.

"So my friend Hugh Darrell thinks, and he has found the helpmeet if he had only the means of marrying her. But he is half starving by himself somewhere down at the East End of London, and it is useless trying to do a division sum with nothing but oughts. So I have come to you, my lord, to see if you can assist me. Is there no cure in this big diocese of Gorhambury into which you could pop my friend and his wife, and let them begin a pastoral life together?"

The Bishop knits his brows.

"How sorry I am to be obliged to say 'no.' But I have really nothing to offer you—nothing! except indeed the curacy of Sarcelett, and that Mr. Darrell would not thank me for. Indeed I am just considering how I can unite it with that of Payne."

"But why? What objection is there to Sarcelett?"

"Have you not heard?"

"Indeed no! These parish disputes and scandals are not at all in my line."

The Bishop glances round to see if the door is closed and lowers his voice.

"We don't like to speak of these things," he says mysteriously, "but I am afraid this story has been too much talked about to be a secret. Have you not heard the reason that Mr. Sheepshanks left Sarcelett?"

"Not a word of it, my lord. I did not even know he had gone till you told me."

"He could not stay there, Mr. Ryle; no one will remain in that parsonage after a few months' trial. I have been Bishop of this diocese now for ten years, and during that time I have put as many men into the cure of Sarcelett."

"But what's the matter with it?" demands Mr. Ryle again.

"*It is haunted!*" whispers the Bishop.

His visitor bursts into a loud and unseemly laugh.

"Is that all, my lord? Well, then, give Darrell the chance of exorcising the ghost! He is the man to do it if anyone can. He is not a pale-faced, white-livered creature like poor Sheepshanks, who would tremble at the falling of a leaf, but a stout-hearted muscular man, with the wisdom of a serpent and the courage of a lion. *He'll* clear Sarcelett of its ghosts, I warrant you, and you'll never hear another word about them after he has taken up his residence there."

"It is all very well to laugh at such things, Mr. Ryle, but do you think I should be justified in allowing him to accept the cure? Remember Sheepshanks is not the only one who has found life impossible at Sarcelett. Everyone has told the same tale, and given up his means of subsistence sooner than remain there. I could not justify it to my conscience to instal another man in that parsonage without telling him the truth."

"Let us tell it to him then," cries Mr. Ryle. "I know my friend better than you do, and an obstacle in his way will only make him the more eager to fight and overcome it."

"You can do as you choose in the matter, Mr. Ryle. The cure is vacant, and Mr. Darrell is welcome to it, on condition that you fully explain its disadvantages. The parsonage is a charming old house, and the stipend is four hundred a year. But these facts only prove how much its former holders must have been annoyed before they consented to resign so good a curacy."

"Darrell will not resign it," says Mr. Ryle, confidently. "I will make out the case to him as black as I can; and in another month you will see him and his pretty little wife as happy as two birds at Sarcelett. And now all I have left to do is to thank you cordially, my lord, for your kindness in the matter."

"I hope you may see cause to thank me as cordially three months hence," replies the little Bishop, with a perturbed countenance, which only causes the irreverent and unbelieving Ryle to break out laughing afresh. And his ridicule seems at first to be justified. Hugh Darrell is as ready as himself to pooh-pooh the idea of so paltry a thing as a ghost—even could it exist—having the power to oust him from a curacy that he is to share with lovely Bessie Lympton; and his gratitude both to his friend and the Bishop of Gorhambury is in proportion to his anticipation of coming matrimonial bliss. Only he says, as he parts with Ryle—who has made a journey to London to convey the good news to him—

"I think, perhaps, that all things considered, it will be as well to keep this story from Bessie's ears, Ryle. She's an awfully clever girl, you know—plucky and full of common sense; still, women are more timid and superstitious than men, and this idea of a ghost to be looked out for might mar the pleasure of our honeymoon. So, we will keep it to ourselves for the present, and it will go hard with me if the first time it appears in Sarcelett Parsonage after I am installed there, I don't hit it such a crack over the head as will transform it into a ghost in earnest."

He is brimming over with happiness at his unexpected good fortune, this merry Hugh Darrell. He has no thought but for his pretty Bessie and his four hundred a-year, and a few weeks afterwards he goes up to the altar with as firm a step as ever bridegroom bore, and signs himself away for life as cheerfully as if he were merely putting his hand to a receipt for five shillings. Everyone is contented and satisfied, and before long the villagers of Sarcelett hear that their new parson has arrived and taken up his residence in the haunted house. Of course the furniture is of the plainest and most modest description, although good Mr. Ryle has sent many a pretty ornament and useful article over to Sarcelett. But Mr. and Mrs. Darrell are in the seventh heaven as they arrange their various possessions, and Hugh varies the monotony of labour with unclerical kisses.

The first difficulty arises on the question of servants, and Bessie cannot imagine why none of the rosy-cheeked girls of the village will consent to be her housemaid. However, she has a useful married sister in London who she makes a referee on all domestic matters, and who soon despatches her a couple of servants procured from the registry office in the next street.

Then all goes merry as a marriage bell.

The little household gets into perfect working order. The Reverend Hugh Darrell has become a first-class favourite with his parishioners, and Bessie has but one complaint to make, that the village people take up his time so fully he has hardly a moment to bestow on herself—that is, until after his afternoon rounds are concluded, and the delightful tea-time comes, when she can bring him his slippers and his lounging coat, and sit at his feet to hear all that he has to tell her of the events of the day.

But one morning, at breakfast, the Rev. Hugh proposes to his wife that they shall take a ramble together.

"The summer is nearly over," he says, "and we shall not have many more opportunities of spending the day out of doors. This morning, for a wonder, I am free. Let us walk over to Gorhambury, Bessie, and explore the beauties of the cathedral."

Bessie's face falls! "How tiresome," she says, "that it should have happened so, but I have engaged Mrs. Brown to come to-day to alter my winter dresses, and if I do not superintend her she will not do a quarter of the work. I cannot put her off if I would. What shall I do?"

"Never mind," replies her husband cheerfully, "the dress is of the more importance of the two, and it is right you should attend to it. I will write my Sunday sermon instead, and we will put off our little jaunt till the end of the week." So saying, he rises from table, kisses his wife, and walks into his study.

As he is writing his sermon, however, an hour afterwards, and raises his eyes mechanically to look for ideas amongst the roses in the garden, he is rather surprised to see Mrs. Darrell going down the gravelled path towards the gate. She is attired in a blue dress which he has not seen before, but he admires its shape and fashion, and thinks how well it becomes her, as

Bessie goes steadily through the garden and out upon the village road. Yet he cannot help wondering where Mrs. Brown can be, and why his wife did not tell him she had broken her appointment. The incident, trifling as it is, disturbs him, and he does not make much way with his sermon during the rest of the morning. And when he meets his wife at the early dinner-table his first words revert to the subject.

"Why didn't you tell me, my dear, that you had changed your mind about going out this morning? I should have liked to accompany you."

"I have not been out," says Bessie, indifferently.

"*Not been out?* Why, I saw you go with my own eyes."

"Nonsense, Hugh! I have been upstairs the whole morning working with Mrs. Brown. I have had no time for walking, worse luck! It is quite a penance to be kept in such a lovely day."

Hugh Darrell regards his wife with the utmost astonishment.

"My dear, you must have forgotten. Do you think I am blind? I tell you I saw you leave the house, and I can tell you what you wore into the bargain. A blue dress——"

"I haven't a blue dress in my possession," cries Bessie, in a tone of annoyance, "and do you think I would tell a falsehood for such a trifle? I repeat, Hugh, I have not been out this morning."

"It is very strange," replies her husband; "who can it have been, then? I made sure it was you."

But inquire as he will, he can hear no further tidings of the lady in blue, and an uncomfortable suspicion that his wife has, for some reason or other, deceived him remains on his mind.

A few days afterwards, however, Mrs. Darrell, having a question to ask her husband, steals downstairs with the view of knocking at his study door. As she comes in view of it she sees the figure of a woman dressed in blue standing on the threshold, who, as she catches sight of her, enters the study door and disappears.

"That must be the lady whom Hugh mistook for me," she thinks to herself; "but she is not a bit like, in figure or style, and I am sure he will never catch me wearing such a hideous blue dress. I wonder what her face is like, and what she can want to see Hugh for?"

Bessie is too sensible to be suspicious or jealous, so she goes down to her kitchen for half-an-hour, and at the end of that time returns, and gaining admittance to her husband's study, finds that he is alone.

"Where is the lady?" she asks inquisitively, "and what did she want with you?"

"What lady?" demands Hugh, looking up from his writing.

"The lady in blue, who was here half-an-hour ago."

"There has been no lady here, Bessie."

"Oh! Hugh, what a story! I watched her go into your study, with a hideous old-fashioned dress on."

"What was she like, Bessie? young or old?"

"I'm sure I don't know. I only saw her back. But she came in here."

"That I'll swear she didn't. No one has entered this room but yourself."

"I can't see the good of denying it," pouts Bessie. "One would think there was something wrong in the matter to hear the way you go on."

"My dear, you cannot mean what you say. You *know* I would not deceive you. But wherever your lady friend went, it was not into my study.

"I tell you I *saw* her," cries Bessie, "and you are not infallible, you know, Hugh. You declared you had seen *me* in the garden last Tuesday, when I had been upstairs with Mrs. Brown all the time, and now I believe it was this lady you saw, because of her blue dress."

At this reminder Mr. Darrell looks visibly disturbed. What was the story Mr. Ryle told him, and they had both laughed at, about some apparition at the parsonage, and was it possible that this phantom in blue, which had appeared to both Bessie and himself, had anything to do with it? A chilly feeling seems to creep down his back as he reflects upon the possibility of such a thing, notwithstanding his serpent brain and lion heart. And he does not know whether to tell his wife the truth, or to leave her to cope with her suspicions as she best may. But as he is deliberating with himself, the cook appears in the passage and approaches the open study door.

"Hearing the mistress upstairs, sir, I make bold to say a few words to you. I don't know the way as they go on in the country, but as a London woman I consider it's a tempting of Providence to leave a Christian house all on the latch, as this be."

"Why, cook! What on earth do you mean?" said Mrs. Darrell.

"Why, ma'am, there isn't a door as fastens, not to say properly; and 'Liza and me have been frightened out of our wits more than once since coming here, by strangers hanging about the premises."

"You need be under no alarm, cook," interposes her master. "No one in Sarcelett would come up to the parsonage with a dishonest intention, and I don't suppose there is a house in the village that is bolted at night; so I should not like to be the first to set an example of distrust."

"Well, that must be as you choose, sir," grumbles the woman; "but t'aint pleasant to have strangers a-coming and going at all times."

"What strangers, cook? What do you mean?" repeats Mrs. Darrell.

"Well, ma'am, there's a woman—a lady I s'pose she calls herself—always a-prying and peeping about the place. Wherever we go, 'Liza and me, we're pretty sure to come across her blue back, peering into a cupboard or a door."

"*Her blue back!* Do you mean to say she wears a blue gown?"

"Yes, ma'am, an old-fashioned concern of 20 years back. I guess she's some prying old maid out of Sarcelett; but she don't pry into my pantry, and that I'll tell her before she's many days older."

"I know who you mean, cook. I have seen her too, and so has the master—that is, her back. But what is her face like?"

"I can't tell you that, ma'am. I've only seen her back and her ugly blue gown."

"How strange! and so have we. Oh, Hugh! who *can* she be? This must be inquired into."

The look of alarm in his wife's eyes makes the husband decide that honesty will be the best policy.

"Come with me, my darling, and we will talk the matter over together. And as for you, cook, I will see that proper bolts and bars are placed upon the outer doors, so that Eliza and you may sleep in peace for the future."

He draws his wife within the study as he speaks, and then and there makes a clean breast of all that Mr. Ryle told him. He is very uncertain how Bessie will take his intelligence, but he tries to soften it by reminding her that (except for the parsonage being haunted) they might never have been married to each other.

"I feared the shadow it might cast upon our first married days, my darling, but I hardly believed that it was true, and I hoped if it were so that my love might have the power to remedy the evil. You trust in God, Bessie, and you trust in me. Will not these two trusts—human and Divine—help you to cast our your natural dread of the supernatural?"

He is terribly afraid of the effect his words may have upon her, but to his delight she seems as fearless as himself.

"A ghost, Hugh?" she explains, with a rapidly changing colour. Do you really think it is a *ghost* that we have seen? How very strange! But do not be anxious about me. I am not in the least afraid of it. Why should I be? Poor thing! Next time she comes I will speak to her—see if I do not, and ask her what she wants in our beautiful parsonage."

Even as she speaks the evening shadows seem to gather in the little study, and through them gleams the blue dress of the phantom woman.

"See, there she is!" cries Bessie, clinging to her husband.

"How strange and weird it seems that she should stand there, yet never show her face. Are you afraid of us?" she continues, addressing their ghostly visitant; "you need not be. We are your friends. Show us your face; tell us if we can serve you by our sympathy or our prayers, and we will do all in our power to give you rest."

But the only answer she receives is conveyed by a backward waving of the phantom hand as the spirit melts into thin air.

"Let me go after her," says Bessie, struggling in the clasp that would detain her.

"No, dearest; do nothing rash," replies Hugh Darrell. "I am thankful beyond measure to find how little this story has affected you, but there is no necessity for you to court the mystery that surrounds us. Let us hope it may die out as it has arisen."

But the parson's hope is not realised.

The lady with the blue dress is seen oftener than ever after that day, and the occupants both of the kitchen and drawing-room become so familiar with her appearance as to mind her no more than if she had been one of themselves. They meet her everywhere; upstairs and downstairs her blue back goes before them, and the servants, discovering at last that she is an apparition, make almost as much fun out of it as their mistress. Yet they never see her face. They know exactly how her dress is made and how her hair is worn, but no one has had the good or ill fortune to view her features. It has become a regular custom to follow the phantom and banter her on her modesty respecting her charms; but no jesting has induced her to turn and look at her pursuers, until one day, as Mr. and Mrs. Darrell are downstairs together, a fearful scream calls them to the upper storey, where they find their housemaid, Eliza, foaming on the ground in a fit. Restoratives are freely applied, and as soon as the woman has recovered her consciousness, she is eagerly questioned as to the cause of her illness.

"Oh! ma'am," she exclaims, "I have seen the Blue Lady, and I must leave you at once. I can't stop in this house another night."

"What nonsense, Eliza! Why, you have seen the Blue Lady as often as you have seen me. Why should you be frightened of her now?"

"Oh! but I have seen her face, ma'am. I was turning down your bed, when she came round the other side, and looked at me; and I wouldn't sleep under this roof another night, not for all the wealth of the Indies."

"You saw her face!" cry her listeners, simultaneously. "What was it like?"

"Don't ask me, sir! Don't ask me, ma'am, not for the love of Heaven," screams the housemaid, as she goes off in another fit.

Mr. and Mrs. Darrell are very much annoyed, but they attribute the girl's fear to her illness rather than to the phantom with which she is so familiar. Nothing, however, will induce her to remain in their service, and she leaves the parsonage the same evening, having told nothing further of her adventure with the Blue Lady.

The cook is disposed to resent Eliza's departure as a personal injury. Had they not weathered the storm together, and is she to be left to ride into port alone? She calls the poor housemaid all sorts of hard names for being such a timorous fool, and swears that twenty ghosts may come and grin in her face before they'd persuade her to give up a good service and a kind master and mistress. Notwithstanding her boasts, however, not more than a fortnight has elapsed since Eliza's departure, when a very similar scream is heard from the basement, and Bessie, running down in consternation, finds the cook struggling on the floor, black in the face, and with distorted features. The usual remedies are applied, and in a few minutes the servant is sitting on the hearth rug trembling in every limb.

"Cook—cook! What *is* the matter?" cries Bessie Darrell.

"O! ma'am! that face! that awful face!" returns the servant, sobbing.

"What! Have *you* seen it too?"

"The Lord help me—yes, ma'am. I've seen it for the first

and last time in my life. No power on earth shall make me sleep under this roof another night."

"What! are *you* going to desert us also? I thought you always wanted to see the Blue Lady's face. What is the matter with it? Why are you so frightened?"

"Don't ask me," exclaims the cook, as she regards her mistress with a look of terror. "I couldn't describe it to you, not if you was to kill me for it; but I must leave you this very night ma'am, or I shall be a dead woman before the morning."

"This is becoming serious," says Hugh, when his wife confides the cook's intentions to him. "We shall be unable to keep a servant at this rate. However, my dear, you must send for old Martha Scragg, to help in the work, and your sister will find us a new cook and housemaid as soon as she can."

Notwithstanding the inconvenience to which they are subjected, Mr. and Mrs. Darrell contrive to make themselves very comfortable until the morning that Bessie receives a letter from her married sister in London to say that she has found her some fresh servants.

"It is all right, Hugh," she says, cheerfully, as she brings the letter to her husband to read. "Maggie has found two charming servants for us, and only wants to know when she shall despatch them to Sarcelett. But what is the matter?" she continues, as she observes his downcast countenance, "has anything gone wrong? You look as if there was a death in the family."

"Bessie," replies Mr. Darrell solemnly, "write and thank Maggie for her kindness, but tell her we shall not require the servants, for we cannot remain in Sarcelett."

"Not remain in Sarcelett! And for what reason?"

"My dear! I have seen the Blue Lady's face."

"And are you going to be as ridiculous as the servants?" cries Bessie. "Upon my word, this is too absurd, and for a brave man too."

"You may laugh at me as you like, Bessie, but we two must leave the parsonage to-night. I would not sleep here again to save my life. I am going to ride into Gorhambury at once, and tell the Bishop of my resignation."

"Oh, Hugh! this is most disappointing, and after all the trouble we have taken to make the house comfortable. And how are we to live if you give up the curacy?"

"Don't ask me! I have not the courage to think," replies the unhappy man.

"And all because you have seen the Blue Lady's face when you have seen her back fifty times. I wish *I* could see it. What *is* she like?"

Hugh Darrell groans, and buries his face in his hands.

"Merciful heavens!" he exclaims, "preserve me from dwelling on or remembering it, or I shall go out of my mind!"

Not all the persuasions of his wife will prevent his riding into Gorhambury to see the Bishop; but he insists upon her leaving the parsonage when he does and putting herself under the protection of a neighbouring farmer's wife. He is to be away for a night, and he enjoins Bessie to remain at the farm until he can fetch her away, and starts on his journey, very downhearted, but serene in the idea that his beloved wife will be safe during his absence. But Bessie is a very courageous and independent little woman. She does not like being treated like a child, and she is curious on the subject of the Blue Lady's face. She is even anxious to confront it. Old Martha Scraggs sleeps in the house, and why should not she? So, when evening arrives she makes some lame excuse to the farmer's wife and slips back to her old house. The deaf and blind Martha hardly knows she has returned and she steals up to her bedroom, and lays herself down to rest. At noon the following day Hugh Darrell presents himself at the farm-house and demands his wife.

"Mrs. Darrell ain't here, sir," replies the farmer's helpmate, "she went home to sleep last night, and haven't come back yet. I've been wondering all the morning if she've got her breakfast."

He makes no answer, but setting spurs to his horse, gallops as fast as he can to the vine-covered parsonage.

"Where is your mistress," he demands breathlessly of old Martha.

"The mistress, sir! I'm sure I don't know. She came in last evening, but I haven't seen her since. I thought she had gone back to the farm."

He leaps to the ground and dashes upstairs with one bound. The curtains are drawn closely round their nuptial bed. He tears them open and reads the awful truth at a glance. Bessie is lying on the pillows, white as marble, with her eyes open and fixed with horror, but dead—dead beyond all hope of recall! There is no need to tell the wretched husband what has caused his loss. He knows that she has been brought face to face with the Blue Lady!

* * * * *

Doubtless my readers will imagine that I have invented this little story for their Christmas mystification, and lay it down again with a smile of superior wisdom. Will it interest them more if I tell them that it is no fiction built on my own fancy, but the relation of facts that happened in our own country, and not very long ago.

The parsonage of Sarcelett is still vacant. No one has ventured to inhabit it since Bessie Darrell came by her death there, and the chances are that now this story is becoming more freely circulated, the Blue Lady will remain unmolested for evermore.

Howell Davies

Two Christmas Eves

HOWELL DAVIES (*c. 1840-1893*) *was manager for the London and Provincial Bank in Tenby, Wales and active in his community. News items show him as an amateur theatrical stage manager, reciting for the Workingmen's Club Rooms' entertainments, president of a Baptist church's annual tea, joint treasurer of the Tenby and County Horticultural Society, etc.* "Two Christmas Eves" *appeared in* Diprose's Annual *for 1885, followed by reprints in the U.K., Australia, and New Zealand. Stories by him include* "The Huntsman's Leap: A Story of South Pembrokeshire," "The Haunted Hansom," *and* "A Storm-Waif: or, Two St. David's Days," *and he also had poetry in the* Red Dragon: The National Magazine of Wales.

CHAPTER I.

C HRISTMAS EVE in the quaint little town of Cliffside; and a good old-fashioned Christmas too. Not one of those miserable remnants of November which are, alas, too common in modern experience of an English Christmas, but a downright hard season, such as our grandfathers love to talk about when they laud the superiority of the "good old days." There had been sharp frost for a week, but on the day on which my story opens, the sky was overcast with heavy clouds which betokened a near snow-storm, and not a light one either, if appearances went for anything.

I had a great deal of work to do that season in the little town and its neighbourhood, for although but a young surgeon, I bore a name that stood well by me in my native place, when, on my father's death, I succeeded to his practice.

Some of my old patients were beginning to feel that a continuance of north-easterly winds and advanced age were not the most harmonious companions imaginable.

I very well remember the feeling of gratitude with which I dismounted from my gig—for we were old-fashioned folk at Cliffside, and the possession of a comfortable gig was the acme of medical respectability—at my own door, that Christmas Eve. I had the consciousness of having got through a long day's work and earned some little rest at any rate, which I devoutly hoped I should get. As a bachelor, I was greatly attached to the snug old house which had come to me with the practice. It was my childhood's home, and every nook and corner had its sad or sunny memories. Entering it that afternoon just as the grey shadows were wrapping themselves round it, my mind reverted to the joyous Yuletides I had spent there in days of yore, and I could not shake off the feeling of melancholy which those recollections, awakened with unusual force to-night, threw around my spirits. It hung upon me when, half-an-hour later, I sat in my snuggery with my slippered feet upon the fender, a pet meerschaum in my mouth, and a new medical treatise in my hand.

Have you ever experienced this hopeless struggling against some indefinable misery which seems ready to pounce upon you? It may come only once in a lifetime, but there is no mistaking its hideous power when once it lays hold of you. Reason, laugh, sneer as you will, you can't shake off its grip, nor turn its shadow aside. It holds you with a relentless tenacity, and vampire-like, sucks hope and ease from your heart.

I felt its thraldom that Christmas Eve, and in the light of after events I read its weird secret. Would that I had died first! I say so now, deliberately, after the lapse of many years, and should you trouble to read my story, you will appreciate the fervour of that wish.

On the morrow I was to dine at the vicarage with my dear old godfather, the Rev. Dr. Forbes, and ———. But I must tell you a secret now. At the vicarage lived the sweetest and loveliest girl in all the country round. Even now as I think of her exquisite beauty of form and feature, her grace of carriage, her low sweet voice, and all the thousand and one charms with which Heaven had endowed her, the dull, cold tide in my old veins leaps to life again, my withered cheek flushes, and all the passionate love of the intervening years concentrates itself upon that unburied past.

I loved Violet Forbes the first moment I saw her on her return from the continental school, where she had spent most of her young life.

I loved her on that fatal Christmas Eve which seems so far away now; loved her madly, fervently, with all that strength of passion which a strong man gives once and for ever to the being whom Destiny has ordained to rule his life for good or evil.

Are you a psychologist? Then you will understand me when I say that when the deep grey eyes of Violet Forbes looked into mine on the sunny August evening on which she returned home from her long exile, I felt that her soul and mine had gone out, each to the other, and like two streams of molten metal become instantly commingled beyond all power of future separation.

Men lightly call this thing "love at first sight." It is more than that. It is Fate! Inscrutable, if you will; irrevocable surely.

The Vicar's daughter came thus into my life, never to leave it again. I love her still! Ah, you will wonder, perchance, at that when I have told you all, and some of you will call me mad. Be it so. I am mad enough to speak the truth.

Just a week before the commencement of my story, I had won from Violet her promise to be my wife as soon as the first of her pretty namesakes peeped forth in the woodland ways around Cliffside. The vicar had given us his blessing, and on Christmas Day I was to dine with them.

The great Festival was a time of strange associations at the old vicarage. It was Violet's birthday and the anniversary of her mother's death; for almost at the moment that my darling's eyes opened on the light of this world, the sunshine of a better swept over the mother's face.

CHAPTER II.

To return to the incidents of that memorable night. I had finished my solitary dinner without interruption, and had once more ensconced myself in my easy arm-chair, with my pipe and book, when that horrible feeling of impending evil suddenly deepened around me and would not be put away. Not even the sweet thought of my little Violet's delight when I should call later on at the vicarage "to watch Christmas in" with her, was strong enough to lift the dead cold weight that lay upon my heart.

But something came to rouse me from my despondency, and that something was a voice. It spoke to me as distinctly as ever human lips did; and yet, if you had asked me at the moment whence it came, I could not have told you for the life of me. There was no knock at the snuggery door, no myste-rious tap on the window; neither door nor window had been opened, and yet as I sat there in my chair, broad awake and on the alert, a voice *somewhere in the room* said, "You are wanted at the vicarage at once."

I started from my seat and looked instinctively towards the door. It was bolted on the inside as was usual when I did not want to be disturbed. I drew the bolt and opening the door looked along the passage. Half-way down towards my dispen-sary I saw the retreating figure of Dr. Forbes. A sudden chill struck me, and almost unconsciously I cried out, "Heavens! there is something the matter with Violet! I know there is!" Then shouting to the vicar (who was evidently hurrying away), "I'll be with you in a moment, sir," I hastened to get on my boots and hat. As I did so, Dr. Forbes turned, as if in answer to my call, and looked at me for an instant. Ah, me! when shall I ever lose sight of that face as it met my gaze beneath the full blaze of a swing-lamp? There was the pallor of death on it; anguish, fright, and horror were there, as I have never seen them in a human face before or since, amid all the strange experiences of my profession. From the drawn lips there issued a word that I did not seem to hear so much as feel, and that one word was—"Violet."

It was as I feared then. She, my love, my beautiful one, was ill, perhaps dying, and had sent for me. How serious it was, I judged at once by her father not daring to trust a messenger to summon me.

You may be sure I did not take long to get into my boots, coat and hat, and to rush down the passage after the vicar, who had apparently passed through the dispensary into the street.

"Did Dr. Forbes say what was the matter?" I asked my assistant as I passed through.

"Who, sir? Dr. Forbes?" queried the youth, looking a little puzzled.

"Yes," I snapped, with a glance at the surgery clock which stood at 9:22. "Dr. Forbes, the vicar. He passed out this way a minute ago. Did he say anything?"

"He has not been here to-day, sir," replied the young man very firmly.

"Not been here to-day," I repeated. "What rubbish you are talking! I spoke to him in the passage, not two minutes since, and he must have come through this door."

My assistant stared at me in astonishment, and I did not wait to hear his reply. I bounced into the street, mentally resolving that young Mr. Howardson and I must part company. A young man who could sleep at his post, and then brazen it out in that way, was hardly the sort of assistant I cared to have about me.

From my home in the High Street, Cliffside, to the vicarage was a distance of nearly a mile and a half, along an exposed but not a difficult road by the cliffs. As I emerged from my surgery,

I became aware that heavy snow was falling, and I soon found that this impeded the progress I was so anxious to make. When I had got within half a mile of the bright, pleasant parsonage, I discerned a figure on the white and silent road in front of me, and could not help feeling astonished at the pace at which the aged vicar had outstripped me. The next instant showed me I was mistaken. It was a younger and more active man running to meet me. I stood rooted to the spot by the most awful sensation of terror. A great horror, which no words can describe, overwhelmed me. I knew, I felt, that these swift but noiseless footsteps hastening towards me bore tidings that would break my heart and wither up my life. I was right in my surmise, although I did not know it until many years had come and gone.

Breathless nearly, and with a scared face, the vicar's groom rushed up to me, and exclaimed:—

"O, Doctor Hepworth! pray be quick! come at once, sir! The poor old master 'ave been murdered, and Miss Violet is goin' from one fit into another. Heaven help us, sir; it's a dreadful night's work, and Christmas Eve, too."

Even as the meaningless tones of the man's voice (for my mind was too paralysed to grasp on the instant their full intent) fell upon my ear, there came mingled with them the solemn but happy music of the bells. This recalled me, and the words were on my lips to say, "Why, I've just seen your master," when discretion, even in that moment of supreme excitement, bade me hold my peace. Quickening our footsteps, we soon reached the dear old parsonage where Violet and I had spent such delightful hours together.

It was a lonely spot on the slope of a considerable hill, facing the south and the broad, blue, ever-restless sea. In summer-time it was embowered in roses, honeysuckles, and every other sweet creeper that grew in those sheltered nooks along the coast. In the wintry months the faithful ivy clung to it, and kept it warm and snug.

CHAPTER III.

As I passed through its portals that night, a voice within me whispered that a vague something worse than death had been there before me. How little did I guess what it was.

In the well-ordered household, whose placid home-life was proverbial, all was now confusion, horror, and dismay.

In the library lay the body of its master, the life-blood still oozing from a ghastly cut across the throat, which I soon discovered had been inflicted by someone who must have stolen up behind him as he slept in the easy chair, where he had taken his after-dinner nap for nearly forty years. I saw from the nature of the wound, that death must have been instantaneous, without time for a prayer or a cry.

I could do him no good, so I turned all my attention to my beloved, who lay on the couch in a swoon as deep, silent, and impenetrable as death. I ordered her instant removal, for I knew that if she recovered consciousness amid those awful surroundings, her reason would probably give way. She had always been highly sensitive and delicate, and absolutely idolized the fond parent whom she had found in that room cruelly murdered.

I gathered from the servants that Miss Violet, as they all called my pet, had gone to the study to read with her father for an hour, as was her regular custom. A minute or two later her shrieks brought them to her side, and their terrified eyes beheld the sight which had unmanned me when I came later on. One thing was evident, although the world, I knew, would laugh at my story, or look at me in ill-disguised pity. *I had seen the vicar and heard his voice in my house at the very time when he lay murdered in his own.* There is the fact. You may make what you will of it.

Subsequent enquiries failed to elicit anything beyond the discovery of one of the murdered man's dinner knives (all stained with blood) just outside the half-opened library window. Whatever footsteps had passed that way, all trace of them was obliterated by the snow, which continued to fall heavily all through the long hours of that horrible night. There was no apparent motive for the crime, as not a single paper had been disturbed, not a drawer ransacked, nor a pocket rifled.

An inquest held two days later threw no fresh light upon the awful tragedy, and went no further than returning a verdict of "Wilful murder against some person or persons unknown." The ablest detectives took it up with a zest, for it was enshrouded in terrible mystery, but they could do nothing with it, and finally relinquished it in despair.

All this time Violet had hovered between life and death, passing from delirium to unconsciousness, but never in her wildest moments making any reference whatsoever to the awful circumstances which had placed her in this condition.

She talked of her father constantly, but ever in her mind was he associated with the days preceding his tragical end, and mostly with the events and thoughts of her early childhood.

Happily for her, the tablets of memory retained no traces of that frightful Christmas Eve and its gruesome work.

But I need not linger over this part of my story. I must hasten on. The sequel has yet to be told.

When Violet was sufficiently recovered to be removed, I packed her off in charge of a nurse to a mild little place on the west coast, where there was plenty of cheerful society, but no dissipation, and where her maternal aunt managed to subsist on the pension of an Indian colonel's widow.

Here I frequently visited my affianced bride, and spent many a delicious hour in her presence.

Ah, me! what days of intense uninterrupted happiness those were. As I sit with my pen in hand to-night, setting down this record of a blighted, broken life, I cannot believe that I am the same man who thirty years ago found the mere habit of existence an absolute felicity, because "Love took up the glass of Time, and turned it in his glowing hands."

At my heart's fireside I brood over the ashes of a past which is terrible to contemplate even at this long interval in time, until I find myself wondering how I lived through it all? And why?

In the second springtime after her father's tragical and mysterious death, Violet Forbes became my wife, and I honestly believed myself to be the proudest and happiest man in all this universe. Then commenced a life of pure, calm, delicious happiness which my own heart, and my knowledge of life, ought to have told me was far too great and good to last. But the wisest of us in this school are veritable fools.

CHAPTER IV.

Smoothly the years sped on, dimmed only by one cloud. A little child had been given us within a year of our marriage, but in less than six months after, there was a sad sore place in our hearts, and a little mound in the quiet churchyard at Cliffside. I remember how bitterly I railed against Fate, which had left us childless. There came a day when I thanked Heaven it was so.

* * * * *

Once more it was Christmas Eve, and just seven years since that fateful night when the disturbed shade of dear old Dr. Forbes had come to me and had reawakened all the dormant superstition of my nature.

I sat in my snuggery almost precisely where I had sat seven years before, in the same chair certainly, and with that same faithful old meerschaum pipe in my mouth.

It is surprising that memory's giant strides stepped back across the intervening years and called up every incident of that harrowing past? Are these emotions which sometimes we woo in vain, and at other times cannot suppress, mere accidents of digestion, mere volitions of will? I think not. The step from coincidence to predestination is much shorter and easier than some people think.

My wife and I had often and often talked over the inexplicable mystery in which her father's sun had gone down, but neither of us could penetrate the secret.

Why did that deathly chill, which had never visited me but once, steal over my senses that night for the second time?

I only know that it did.

As I sat there fighting against what I had the arrant conceit to call my weak and feeble superstition, the door behind my chair was opened suddenly but quietly, and I heard a stealthy step on the thick carpet approaching me. Another moment and the sound of panting, excited breath was close to my ear.

With a nameless terror at my heart, I started from my chair, and turning round, beheld a sight which made my pulses forget their function for the nonce.

My wife stood before me, a long glittering knife in her right hand, her left pressed tightly to her bosom as though to stop the wild throbbing of her heart. In her beautiful eyes, that had never looked on me but with infinite tenderness, gleamed the awful light of madness!

Great Heaven! what a lifetime of anguish was compressed into the brief moment it took me to realize the fearful purpose with which she had crept to the back of my chair!

As I write down the words now, I seem to live it all over again.

She, whom I loved with all the fervour of my being, better, far better than my own poor life. *She had come there to murder me!*

Scarcely had the fearful thought entered my mind, ere she made a wild spring towards me, and tried to plunge the knife in my heart. By a dexterous movement I avoided the blow, and seized my wife in my arms. A dreadful struggle then ensued, for her madness gave her superhuman strength.

"Let me go," she cried. "I came to kill you and I *will* do it! I must! I killed my father years ago, and why should I spare *you?*"

Then she broke out into wild, hysterical laughter, which froze my blood with horror.

Oh! the change that insanity wrought in that sweet voice, and those plaintive tender eyes. Her loveliness was as the beauty of some splendid wild beast, thirsting for blood.

"Ha! ha!" she shrieked, "I killed him, and you must die too!"

My soul sank at those fiendish words, words which I felt (although they were uttered by a mad woman and that woman my wife) offered the clue to the old vicar's murder, which had hitherto baffled all attempts at solution.

Having secured the knife, I placed a chloroform pad to her face, and in a second or two she lapsed into unconsciousness.

How I dreaded the awakening from that stupor! In my own arms I bore my beloved to her own room and laid her down to sleep, that unnatural sleep which could do her no good, but gave me time to think.

Why need I prolong my story, and torture myself by recounting all the incidents of that hideous nightmare of my life? Let it suffice me to say that as the sun of that Christmas Day sank to rest, my wife, the light and beauty of my home, found her repose in the deep strong arms of death.

But little remains to be told.

By dint of patient and protracted inquiry I discovered that in the family of my dear, dead wife (on her mother's side) there was the accursed taint of insanity. Her mother had escaped it, but she transmitted it to the child on whose face she had never looked.

That child had suffered twice, and twice only, from its most terrible development—homicidal mania. The first time it came upon her she slew her father, whom she had idolised; but with the unconsciousness that supervened, had passed away all recollection of her crime. The second time she attempted my life, and then came the end.

Only those who have suffered as I have, will understand the gratitude to Heaven which filled my breast as I laid my treasure away from her burden of sorrow and madness, in that quiet graveyard where, "after Life's fitful fever, she sleeps well."

Mabel Collins

A Tale of Mystery

An author of more than forty books, MINNA MABEL COLLINS
COOK (1851–1927), *had learned of Helena Blavatsky's occult
Theosophy religion in 1881, and met Blavatsky herself in 1884.
That same year, Mabel Collins began writing* Light on the
Path, *published in 1885, a book she claimed was dictated to her
by some mystic source and moreover that it was "written in an
astral cipher, and can therefore only be deciphered by one who
reads astrally." It quickly became a Theosophical classic, and
Collins would go on to be co-editor with Blavatsky of* Lucifer:
A Theosophical Magazine. *One of her lovers was Robert
Donston Stephenson, one of a number of men suspected of having
been Jack the Ripper. She would also become an acquaintance
of poet and occultist William Butler Yeats and the notorious
Aleister Crowley. Her uncanny story "A Tale of Mystery"
doesn't appear to have ever been reprinted after its appearances
in the December 19, 1885* Cardiff Times *and* Northampton
Mercury.

ALARIC GADDESDEN WAS MY MOST INTIMATE FRIEND. We
met at college, became chums, and after that were always
together until a certain incident, which I am bound to relate,
separated us for a long time. We were friends, but something
else besides. Gaddesden had the peculiar gift, held by some
few men, of influencing those about him to an extraordinary
degree. He was a born leader of men and of thought, and
I sat at his feet, as did many others, like a disciple. His abil-
ities were great, and he had distinguished himself at college,

where his friendship was much sought, so that even in the
early days I had realised his preference for me as an honour.
Later on, when he made his mark on the world, I was scarcely
more proud of it than quite at first. Gaddesden was an eager
student of philosophy and of metaphysics, and scaled heights
of thought and speculation to which I could not follow him;
I was compelled to sit afar and wonder. His philosophic tendency was so strong that it practically preserved him from the
usual experiences of a young man's life. So far as I knew, when
I first met him the word love had no meaning for him, and it
never entered his vocabulary during the years of our acquaintance until he encountered Clotilde Francillon. It was at a
large evening reception that I first saw her; she was singing.
The big drawing-rooms were crowded with people standing
so close that it was hardly possible to move; and just before
there had been a buzzing of conversation in every direction.
The moment Clothilde's voice was heard, the moment the
first note of it sounded through the rooms, there was silence.
That voice took hold of a man so that he could not choose but
listen. Yet it was not beautiful, and although it was evidently
trained to the utmost perfection, yet it was used in a mode
almost barbaric. I saw Alaric standing near her, his eyes fixed
on her face; and once or twice she threw her dark eyes on his.
He was absolutely spell-bound; the strange voice, the extraordinary face of this girl had evidently caught and influenced
his swift imagination.

It was winter, and very dreary weather. When we went
out of the house, I proposed to get immediately into a cab;
but Alaric strode off down the wet street, and I followed him,
wondering much what this new vagary might mean. He did
not tell me; and when, after we got home, I tried to get him
to speak a little, all I could gather was that he had been talking
to Miss Francillon, and had discovered that she had not only
a poetic, but a philosophic mind. I began then to have a faint
inkling of the truth, and to guess that all was lost; that my
friend was in love. A man of the world would have known it at

once; when a philosopher discovers the philosophic tendency in the mind of an attractive woman, it is a pretty sure sign of the worst.

As the days passed on I could no longer blind myself to the fact; evidently Alaric was in love. He was constantly at Miss Francillon's house. Sometimes I went also, and I found it not exactly amusing but very instructive to be there when he was. For Miss Francillon played what seemed to me the most patent of games; but still, it was played with quite sufficient skill to deceive the philosopher. She sat at his feet, metaphorically, as the pupil sits at the feet of his master. She drank in his words, and declared his thoughts to be her own; that she had entertained them since her early youth, but had never been able to express them. She made Alaric feel that he had found the wonder of the world, a woman actually thoughtful and philosophic at heart, and that she had only waited for the touch of his brilliant mind to kindle the fire in herself. It was the profoundest and subtlest form of feeding his vanity. If he had not been blinded by this he must have seen through it all, for Miss Francillon simply used the tricks of a clever conversationalist to make him believe she understood him. In reality, she was a shallow and frivolous creature, though with a strange depth of something which seemed to me more like passion than anything else; something which was heard in the notes of her voice and seen in the fire of her eyes.

The great mystery, the profound puzzle, which ceaselessly perplexed me was why she devoted so much trouble, so much art and subtlety, to the obtaining of Alaric's admiration. She was a favourite in a large circle, and had many admirers, and evidently some lovers. She was rich, and able to gratify every fancy or whim that seized her. Why should she seize upon Alaric Gaddesden to his destruction? For I was troubled from the first with a dim yet certain foreboding that it was to his destruction that Clothilde Francillon should love him. How or why I could not tell.

She was singularly isolated, living alone, and having apparently no relations. With most girls this would have seemed strange, and must have excited comment. But Miss Francillon was bizarre and unlike other people; and, moreover, she had a powerful influence which, when she chose to exercise it, made others judge her kindly. She calculated on this power evidently, and did daring things no other girl could do: for instance, she encouraged Alaric in coming daily to her house and spending hours talking to her. True, she always contrived to have something in the shape of a chaperon, but that something was one of the women who were completely under Clothilde's influence and thought that all she did was right, whatever it might be.

I was obliged to see all this, and bear it with as much resignation as might be, only wondering a little how Alaric could be so blind, and marvelling very much at his taste. For Miss Francillon was palpably very far from being that ideal creature which one would have expected Gaddesden to love. In fact, from the ordinary point of view, and in the slang of the day, she was "bad form." But Gaddesden evidently thought her perfect, and, stranger still, found life a burden when away from her. This state of things grew daily more intense. He lounged wearily about till the hour for going to her house, and came home dejected and broken spirited, plainly with but one thought in his mind, and that was the thought of to-morrow, when he might again go to her. Of course all this I put up with heroically, as needs must; every man is liable to the boredom of his chum falling in love. But the affair wore a different aspect when it suddenly dawned on me that Alaric was getting very ill. Once having seen the fact I wondered that I had been so blind hitherto. There was no doubt about it; every day he grew paler and weaker and more languid, till at last all the spirit and fire faded from his face, and I looked at him in wonder, for it seemed to me that the Alaric I had known was fast vanishing from sight. Where had he gone? Was his soul always with this woman who had fascinated him, and was his body fading from the strain of overpowering love? I could not tell; but one night, when he came home looking more like a corpse than a living man, I determined I would save him from this baleful passion at any hazard.

Why did he not marry her? I supposed he was afraid to speak, for he was poor; but from what I knew of her I thought her quite capable of proposing if she wished to.

I had been avoiding the house; I determined to visit there more and study the state of things.

I soon saw that Alaric was as lifeless and weary when at Miss Francillon's side as when away from her. A faint glow of animation came into his face when he first met her, but it soon died away. But she grew brighter and more full of life with every moment he spent in the room.

The whole thing was inexplicable to me, until one day, as I watched them, an idea came into my mind which I rejected at first as absurd, but, spite of that, it took hold of me. My friend had all the air and appearance of a man who was simply being vampirised. Was this girl one of those fiends?

The vampire is a creature we have all met with in modified form one time or another; old people draw strength from the young, weak people from the strong. I had seen some ordinary everyday instances of this in my life, but I had never come across the actual thing before. As I watched Miss Francillon, with this idea in my mind, I felt I had met with it now.

If I was indeed right—and I momently became more confirmed in my conviction as I watched the brightness and colour steadily wane in Alaric's face and wax stronger in hers—then at all hazards must I save my friend. I had vowed to do so in any case; now more than ever I felt certain that I must act, and act immediately.

The only question was, how? To speak to him would evidently be worse than useless. He was in that state when every word and act of Miss Francillon's must be right, simply because they were hers. No other reason was needed. And this man was a philosopher!

Should I appeal to Miss Francillon, and beg her to spare

a man who had power in him, and who was of too fine and valuable a stamp to be sacrificed in this way? No; I rejected that idea immediately. No doubt if his magnetism was stronger and purer than that of other people, she had already found that out, and was rejoicing in it. It was absurd to suppose an appeal would induce her to give up that which fed her very life.

I came at last to the conclusion that there was only one thing to be done. I must fling myself between these two; I must offer myself as a sacrifice instead of my friend. In short, I must feign a profound passion for Miss Francillon, and take Alaric's place with her. There was no other chance of saving him.

I walked my room nearly all night thinking about this hateful course; at one moment rejecting it utterly, at the next entering into it with the energy of despair.

When I emerged from my cold bath in the morning, the idea seemed like a nightmare, and I put it aside altogether; I felt fresh and wholesome, and could not help regarding the thoughts of the past night as mere visions of the darkness.

But when I met Alaric at breakfast his face woke me up to the reality of the thing with a shock. It was blanched; it was like the face of a corpse. He ate nothing; but I had grown used to that. It was his ghastly colour that startled me; and another fact, that he was not working. He had written nothing, he had read nothing for weeks. Had this girl power to kill his soul and his brain as well as his body? It was too horrible.

That afternoon I called at Miss Francillon's house early, before the hour when Alaric usually went there. When he came I was in his accustomed place. Miss Francillon was a shivery mortal, and the weather was bitterly cold. In her drawing room she had a couch drawn right in front of the fire, and a screen behind it which hid it from the rest of the room. She spent her afternoons in the corner of the couch, and Alaric sat beside her. But to-day when he came I was there; and I made no sign of giving up my place to him, as a day or two ago I might have done. On the contrary, I sat aggressively still, and regarded my friend with a triumphant smile; played the puppy, in fact.

I saw plainly the fierce spasm of jealousy which passed through him and shook him. But he controlled himself by an effort, and sat down at a little distance, trying to take his deposition quietly, and as a matter of course. I felt Miss Francillon look from him to me, and I turned to meet her eyes; they had in them a wild, hungry look that made me shudder. I shuddered, yes, but I did not hesitate, for my mind was made up to save my friend. I saw now that I had come at the right time, and should succeed. Alaric's strength was almost gone. I was a fine strong fellow full of health and vigour. She was quite ready to let me step into his place.

In fact, as I had anticipated, my difficulty was not with her but with him. In his present state he was not a reasonable being. He became mad with jealousy. I tried my utmost to bear it all, and to remember that he could not possibly realize the situation. To him it simply seemed that he was madly in love, and that his best friend was deliberately and treacherously taking his love from him. The situation was an insupportable torment to him; to me, even with my strength, it was scarcely bearable.

And that strength began to lessen. In a very few days I began to feel the drag, the grip as it sometimes seemed, that came from Miss Francillon. I knew that I was being held and wrapped up magnetically by a thousand sucking mouths, like those of the hideous octopus. I was suffering as Alaric had suffered before me, and many another before him. It must have been so, for evidently this girl could not live without such food.

The odd thing about it was that she could not, try how she would, take hold of my reason or my heart. This made my experience unique. I had gone into the position I filled with my eyes open, knowing what I did, and knowing her. She could not make me love her; in fact, my hate and loathing for the creature who was sapping my strength and feeding on my life grew stronger in me every day.

How was it all to end?

I could not guess. Had my very life to be sacrificed for a

friend who regarded me as his worst enemy? It seemed hard, and I rebelled bitterly against it, but so it was.

Alaric was mad with jealousy.

He regarded me gloomily and with a covert glance, which sometimes made me wonder to what lengths his madness might carry him. I was not afraid, for even if he took my life it had become of very little value to me now. I, too, began to feel the loss of all interest in work, the dying out of all ambition, the inability to care for anything which was not directly connected with Miss Francillon. Although I hated her, still she was the centre of my existence. I could think of nothing else; I lived in nothing else. In fact, though with such different feelings, I was suffering the same direful fate as that from which I had saved Alaric; and that without the consolation of imagining that I loved.

On Christmas eve Miss Francillon went to a large party, to which neither Alaric nor I were invited. Whenever this happened we both passed the hours in misery; the only difference was that his misery was active and mine dull. He was tormented by raging jealousy; I by a weary sense of pain and a longing for death to release me from it. We always avoided each other. To-night I sat doggedly by the fire to pass the evening and the night as best I might. Anything in the shape of amusement or society seemed to me intolerable. Alaric went out; I neither knew nor cared where.

That evening was as long as if every minute had been an hour. Dull and absolute despair settled on my soul, and I sat there gazing into the fire without power to think; I was only capable of suffering.

The night was half through before anything roused me from this wretched stupor. Then it was with a start and a thrill of something like horror that I found there was someone besides myself in the room—someone who had entered without noise, and who was of so strange an appearance that that alone was enough to startle me.

In a corner of the room stood a man so small and slight that he was in fact a dwarf; his complexion was very dark, and his face marked in strong lines as if from hunger or suffering; the face was extraordinary, and was made doubly so by the eyes that looked out from it. They were so piercing in their gaze that I almost trembled as I met them. A wild mass of black hair surrounded this strange face; the whole effect was almost fantastic. But there was an air of resignation and something not unlike despair in the way in which this mysterious figure stood in the corner, leaning against the wall as if in weariness, and with one thin arm thrown up over his head. As my gaze met his, the strange face gradually lit up with the most wonderfully sweet smile I have even seen.

"Do not fear me," said a voice, so low, so hoarse and deep in note, that it startled me more than any other feature of the apparition. "I am come as your friend. You are unhappy. I mean to help you."

"To help me!" I echoed. "No one can do that. I am lost."

"No," he answered, "you are not lost. I have travelled from the other side of the world to help you."

"What are you?" I said, overcome by the profoundest curiosity as I heard the tone of confidence and power in which this strange creature spoke.

"I am an ascetic," he answered. "One of the religious mendicants of India. If you saw my body you would see but a poor shrivelled dwarf, with very often scarcely power of breath."

"If I saw your body!" I exclaimed, suddenly realising what these words implied. "Where is it?"

"Asleep, hidden beneath the undergrowth of a deep forest, where no men dwell or pass."

"You have escaped from the society of men, in the body!" I exclaimed, "and yet your wraith comes to me here, in the heart of civilization. What does this mean?"

He answered in a profound tone of mournfulness—

"I come to conquer my prejudices. I have learned that asceticism alone cannot liberate the soul. The eyes of my spirit have become clear while I have lived away from men; and all across the world I have looked and seen your suffering and seen that I can help you. Therefore I am here. In my solitude I have become possessed of knowledge of magic, and I will use it for you. Take of cooked rice enough to make a ball with your hands, and mix it with the blood of some slain animal; and put this ball upon the stairway in the house of the devil who is devouring you. Do this for seven nights, each night putting less and less blood, till on the seventh the rice is mixed only with water; and on that night—the last—you must watch by the rice till the devil comes for it, and then catch tight hold of him, and command him to leave that place for ever. If you grasp him firmly you can command him; and a command given to him on that night must be obeyed. Do as I bid you, and you and your friend will be freed. Farewell."

I started up as if to prevent his leaving me, for my terror had all gone, and I desired to ask innumerable questions. But the apparition had grown fainter and fainter while he spoke; and now, as the last word was uttered, it vanished altogether.

The state of mind in which I found myself was one of the profoundest bewilderment. I tried to persuade myself I had been dreaming, but that was useless. I started up and walked about the room; I went and dipped my head in cold water—all with the idea that I might succeed in waking myself up. But no, I was awake now, and I had been awake all the time. In fact, I began to feel as if I should never sleep any more. All that night, at all events, I passed in walking restlessly to and fro, and thinking about my extraordinary adventure. As soon as it was light I went out of doors. I continually expected the remembrance of the apparition and its words to become faint like the memory of a dream. But no; if anything they became stronger and more positive.

This only left me with one question to decide. Was I to carry out the prescription I had received or not?

It seemed utter folly to carry it out; sheer superstition. Yet I knew, the moment I began to think about it, that I must and should do so, and do so faithfully. Absurd as the whole thing seemed, yet I could not avoid carrying out my instructions. No ordinary efforts could save me; perhaps something so extraordinary might.

And so that very evening, when I went to Miss Francillon's house, it was with a fearful compound secreted in my pocket; a ball of rice mixed with blood which I shamefacedly bought at the butcher's. Fortunately for me, I had passed the stage of affairs in which Miss Francillon expected me to talk. She was content if I sat beside her. Otherwise I could hardly have acted my part. I could think of nothing but this ball of rice and the object with which I was to use it. Was there some devilish power driving this wretched girl on in her hideous career? And was there any hope of my release from her clutches? There was a faint dim stir of hope within me, but I dared not listen to it yet.

Every night throughout the week I contrived to leave the ball of rice on the stairs. What puzzled me was that I never heard anything of its being found there. It was not until the third or fourth day that it flashed into my mind that if there were devils in the affair, these devils were intended to carry the rice away, tempted by the blood, and devour it; and that it began to look very much as if they actually did so.

New Year's eve came; the seventh night; the night on which I had to try my experiment. I had begun to regard it in good earnest now, and I was full of dread lest I should be unnerved and fail.

Miss Francillon had a musical party that evening; she sang herself several times, and produced, as it seemed to me, a stranger and more startling effect with that fascinating voice of hers than ever. One could not choose but listen—even I, who hated her, was compelled to yield to the spell; but there were notes in the voice that made me shudder, that made my flesh creep.

My whole mind was occupied with the effort to contrive how to remain and complete the final ceremony. I could think of no means but that of feigning passion which would no longer endure delay. I must outwait the other guests and then make love to her. What a masquerade! But a wild fancy that deliverance was at hand gave me courage and new strength—I had a strange light-headed feeling, as if I were intoxicated with excitement.

I outstaid all the other guests but Alaric. He would not go. I saw that he was wild with jealousy. He eyed me moodily. I felt a sudden dread, that if I went too far with the masquerade of love I might have a madman to deal with. Mine was a strange position! It seemed to me that it was by some sort of miracle that I kept my coolness and sanity.

The large drawing-room was very hot with the fires and lights. A little sitting-room of Miss Francillon's was just across the landing.

I determined to risk suggesting to Miss Francillon that we should go there, giving the heat as my reason, and leaving her and Alaric to infer that I wanted to be rid of his presence. This would enable me to put the ball of rice on the stairs; and I must trust to my own adroitness to watch it.

Alaric was sitting on a couch at the other end of the room watching us under his hands. I risked a great deal in thus openly daring his jealousy; I knew it, but I saw nothing else to be done. He was my enemy already; it would not make matters much worse if he sprang at my throat.

I asked Miss Francillon in a low voice to come to the cooler room. She agreed at once, and we rose and crossed the drawing-room to the door. Alaric started up, but did not follow us immediately. A faded friend of Miss Francillon's, who was playing chaperon that night, was sitting near him, but she was so sleepy that she hardly noticed our movements.

The landing was dark; the servants had put out the gas thinking everyone was gone. This favoured my purpose. I hastily took the ball of rice from its hiding place, and deposited it as near the accustomed corner as I could. Something seemed to rush past as I did so, and I heard Miss Francillon utter a cry of terror. Instantly it flashed into my mind that it was some hours later than the time at which I usually placed the rice. If some thing had indeed been tempted by the blood, no doubt it was waiting hungrily for its accustomed food. I resolved to act at once, for if this were so the demon would be waiting for me, and I should not have to wait for it. I kept my hand upon the ball of rice, and almost immediately I felt a touch that made my blood boil with horror and rage like fire, and then turn, as it seemed, to ice within me. I did not hesitate, despite the horror; I quickly clutched at the thing and cried out, "I command you to leave this place for ever!"

Another wild shriek of agony came from Miss Francillon; Alaric burst open the drawing-room door and rushed out. But in spite of the confusion I heard, and heard distinctly, a hoarse voice chanting unknown words in a marvellous musical cadence. I knew that voice, and my heart leaped with gladness. My mysterious friend had not left me alone to fight the awful battle.

Alaric found Miss Francillon on the floor. He hurried back to the drawing-room and fetched a light. As he did so Miss Francillon's sleepy chaperon rushed past him. She was wide awake now, and utterly terrified.

I glanced round hastily. The rice was gone; nothing of any sort was visible on the stairway; and now there was complete silence.

Alaric was bending over Clothilde, and now suddenly raised himself with a faint cry and staggered back. I rushed to where she lay, and in my turn looked in her face and touched her. And I, too, knew instantly that she had not fainted. She was dead!

Dead! Had there been nothing but the loathsome demon, then, to animate that fascinating body?

The thought was hideous even to me who had always shrunk from her with horror. For after all she had seemed like a woman.

I know not how long, whether it was many hours or no, that we remained motionless, overcome by the horror. The daylight streamed in at the high staircase window, and mingled in a ghastly fashion with the gas-light from the shuttered drawing-room. I sat couched on the stairs like one stunned; all my strength was spent. And Alaric remained leaning against the wall, as he had staggered back against it.

At last I felt a touch. It was Alaric's hand on my shoulder. I looked up into his face, and knew that my friend had come back to me in that awful hour. We rose, and went slowly out of the silent house into the morning sunshine, carrying with us the memory of a horror which must go with us all through life.

A CHRISTMAS GHOST HOAX

Some remarkable scenes were witnessed late on Tuesday night and in the early hours of yesterday morning outside St. Mary's Parish Church, Islington, in consequence of a rumour which had gained credence that a ghost was haunting the churchyard.

Towards twelve o'clock a large crowd, the majority of whom were of the rougher class, assembled in Church Lane and the vicinity, and by shouts and cat-calls managed to attract unwary passers-by, with the result that some of them lost their watches. Some police-constables tried to dissuade people from attempting to see the "spook," but the crowd instead of getting smaller, grew bigger. As many passers-by were molested a larger force of police were requisitioned to prevent a serious disturbance. The scene originated in a letter to a local paper, in which the writer said, "On Christmas night, while passing the old parish church, I was startled by seeing a figure in white standing in front of me. I stopped, when it seemed to vanish towards the church."

Yorkshire Telegraph and Star (Jan. 5, 1899): 4, col. 1.

Phœnix

The Ghosts of the Bards

A Legend of Anglesea

The pseudonymous contribution to the South Wales Echo *of December 24, 1886 is heavily rooted in national history. The Roman historian Tacitus'* Annals *recorded the 1st century A.D. attack led by Suetonius Paulinus on the island of Mona, as the Romans called it, or Anglesea, as the Vikings called it, in northern Wales. Written information on the Druids and Bards is scarce, though archaeological sites—standing stones, cairns, circles, tombs—are numerous.*[1]

CHAPTER I.

THE MURDER OF THE BARDS AND DRUIDS.

MANY HUNDRED YEARS AGO the sacred isle of Anglesea, or Mona, was the scene of a terrible massacre. The Roman sway had been established in Britain, but the natives had never submitted. No sooner was a rebellion overcome in one part of the country than it broke out in another. The Roman generals had, one after another, adopted the most brutal means to quell the warlike ardour of the Britons, but in vain. At last, the inhuman Nero sent to Britain a man after his own heart—the cruel, relentless Suetonius Paulinus, who was,

---

1 "Ancient Druids of Wales." National Museum Wales. https://museum. wales/articles/1016/Ancient-druids-of-Wales/

however, a very shrewd man and possessed of great foresight, but far more savage than the people he had come to subdue. Finding that the rebellious spirit of the Britons was being continually roused by the Druids, their priests, and by the stirring songs of the Bards, he determined to break the heart of the people by exterminating their leaders, their minstrels, and their priests. Accordingly he crossed over to Mona—the home of the Druids—with his army and found the shore lined with British warriors, both male and female—for even the women had taken up arms to protect the sacred isle from the ravage of the invaders. So furious was the assault of the Britons that the Romans would most certainly have been defeated had it not been for the bravery of their commanders and of Paulinus himself, who taunted his soldiers with wavering before "the barbarians." Incensed by these taunts the Romans fought more desperately and succeeded in winning the battle. Then ensued a tragedy such as Mona's isle had never before witnessed. The Druids and the Bards were burnt alive, and men women, and children were thrown upon the pyre. Tradition has it that not a cry of mercy or of pain came from the lips of either the Druids or the Bards, but that they died bravely, cursing their conquerors with their last breath and vowing the vengeance which afterwards overtook Paulinus and his murderous soldiery. A long time was spent by the Romans in the work of exterminating the Druids and the Bards in Mona, and they had ultimately to leave the island on account of the rebellion of noble Buddug or Boadicea. So well, however, had Suetonius accomplished his work that very few of the Druids and Bards remained on the island after his departure. But we will not follow the story of brave Buddug's victories, defeat, and painful, though heroic death, for the scene of our story is laid in Mona itself.

About three miles from the shore a great forest was situated and extended for many miles into the interior of the island. Running parallel with the edge of the forest was a chain of mountains stretching almost to the sea-shore—very steep in some places and containing a number of caverns at the base. Between the mountains and the forest was a beautiful valley.

It was night. The moon shed its peaceful rays down upon the valley which was now so silent. Now and again the cry of some wild animal in the forest or a night-bird on the wing would break upon the calm air and find an echo among the mountain boulders a mile or so distant, and anon the wind would wail thro' the forest as if bemoaning the loss of the brave hearts that had been stilled by the ruthless spear of the invader. Suddenly from one of the caves in the mountain side a tall figure was seen approaching, and as it crossed the valley it could be distinguished as that of an old man, whose snow-white beard fell low upon his breast. He was enveloped in a long blue robe which completely covered his body and hid his feet from view. On his head he wore a cap made of the skin of some wild animal. In the folds of his robe he carried something, though what could not be seen, for the robe completely covered it. As he passed some ruined huts he paused for a short time, muttered something to himself, looked up to the sky and then proceeded on his way. On reaching the edge of the forest he boldly entered it, being evidently well acquainted with the place. Really, he was walking into the forest by a well-worn footpath. Once in the heart of the forest he did not pause until he came to, what the Americans call, "a clearing." This open space was perhaps about forty yards square and was for the most part a natural break in the forest, for scarcely a root could be seen. In the corners, however, several stumps of trees attested the fact that the hand of man had been employed to accomplish what nature had omitted to do, viz., to make the opening as far as possible a perfect square. In the centre of the square was an enormous boulder, and round about it were a dozen similar boulders, every one of them, however, being smaller than the central one. The latter looked black in the moonlight and a fire had evidently been lighted upon it, for the embers were plainly visible. This, however, was not the worst, for the circle formed by the boulders was completely filled with charred bones, showing unmistakably that some persons had been burnt alive on the central stone. Outside the circle more than twenty bodies lay in every conceivable position—some with their glassy eyes turned up to the peaceful heavens, as if appealing for assistance or vengeance from the unknown world. In one place, near the western side of the circle, was the corpse of an aged Briton whose long beard swept his breast. His bony fingers were clasped at the throat of a Roman warrior who lay dead at his side. The body of the aged man was fearfully mutilated; the grassy plot was soaked with his blood and showed signs of a fearful struggle having taken place between him and his murderer. The spear of the Roman, red with blood, lay shivered at the side of the dead combatants. With this exception only two Roman bodies were visible, for the unarmed and unprepared Britons, bravely though they had fought, could do little against their armed enemies, and were consequently cut down to a man.

Such was the scene which met the gaze of the aged man as he entered the "clearing." For a moment he appeared to be stunned: then he silently bent forward and gazed long and earnestly at the faces of the dead. Proceeding to the circle he looked at the bones which the fire had not consumed, but as might have been expected he failed to recognize any body in that horrible place, so well had the fire done its work. Standing on the rough boulder which stood in the centre, with his anguished face turned full on the calm autumn moon, the old man remained for some time in deep reverie and his aged form trembled anon with the bitterness of his grief. Placing his hand in the folds of his robe he drew forth a small harp of exquisite workmanship, and instinctively his fingers wandered along the strings. As if unconscious of the place or the time, he broke forth into a soul-affecting lament, his voice being extremely sweet and musical for one so old. The harp seemed to feel the spirit of the minstrel's grief, for the sounds it gave out were low and solemn, and harmonized with the plaintive melody that was being wafted on the night breeze.

Descending from the stone, the aged man again entered the forest, but shortly afterwards he returned with a younger man than himself, who carried a flaming torch. "Iorwerth," said the minstrel, "we will light a fire here to keep the wild beasts away from the corpses of my brothers, and to-morrow we will return and bury them." He kept his word.

CHAPTER II.

CHRISTMAS EVE.

The shriek of her tortured children no longer resounded through the lovely isle of Mona, and her fair fields were no longer over-run by the foreign enemies of Britain. Romans, Saxons, Danes, and Normans had successively invaded Prydain, though comparative tranquillity reigned in Mona. But if the wars which had taken place in other parts of the kingdom had not reached the little island, the story of the massacres of the Bards and Druids had been handed down from father to son, and from generation to generation, and though hundreds of years had passed away, it had not been forgotten.

Once more it was night in the Isle of Mona, but a very different night from that on which the old minstrel had sung his lamentation over the bodies of his slaughtered countrymen. It was Christmas Eve, and the wind howled fearfully through Mona's forest. The snow fell in heavy flakes, and was whirled about by the raging wind. Altogether it was just such a night as would induce anyone to stay at home, and, indeed, rendered it extremely dangerous for anyone to venture out. Every footpath in the valley had been covered with snow, and the mountain side appeared like some unearthly white monster. The waves of the sea tossed about by the heavy wind swept along the shore, and were occasionally driven hundreds of yards up the valley. Towards midnight, however, the wind moderated, but the snow continued to fall. Suddenly a tremendous crash was heard from the direction of the sea, and almost directly afterwards the shrieks of women and the cries of strong men broke upon the comparative quietude of the night.

In less than half an hour a form was seen wending its way up the snow-covered valley with great difficulty. The stars above threw a fitful light upon the scene, and as the form of the traveller stood for a moment, as if contemplating the desolation which appeared on every hand, it could be seen that she was a woman. She continued to trudge along the valley for some time, and it soon became apparent that she had lost her way, for she wandered about from one place to another, retracing her steps when she found that the path she was making ended abruptly at the edge of the forest or the base of the mountain. Again she paused and from her lips escaped an agonising cry which pealed out strangely on the midnight air. "My God!" she wailed, "have I escaped the terrors of the sea only to die in the snow in this strange place?" The voice which uttered this piteous wail was extremely musical although the lady was evidently on the verge of despair.

Scarcely had the words left her lips than she heard a peculiar sound behind her. A hand was laid lightly on her shoulder. She turned, and there close beside her stood the figure of a man. She uttered a loud shriek as she beheld the strange object, but a strange fascination prevented her from seeking flight. The man was of enormous stature, standing close upon seven feet. He wore a long robe of some dark colour, which could not be distinguished in the sombre light afforded by the stars and the snow. This robe covered the whole of his body from his neck to his feet. On his head he wore a peculiar kind of cap, which was rendered hideous in appearance, through being adorned with the head, including the shining teeth, of some wild animal. His face was that of a very aged man, and the furrows of time could be easily distinguished. His eyes were large and seemed to blaze with fire. His white beard swept his breast for about two feet, and completely covered the upper part of the front of his robe, whilst his hair hung in profusion down his back. The eyes of this strange being were fixed upon the lady with a peculiar stare, and she trembled with fear when he addressed her sternly.

"What does the strange woman want in the land of Mona?" demanded the old man, and his eyes blazed with anger.

"O, sir," moaned the terrified lady, "I was wrecked on the coast, and am now seeking a place where I may rest for the night. Surely you will not refuse to help a poor girl, although you may not know her."

The old man vouchsafed no reply, but beckoned the maiden to follow him. With this he started up the valley, but immediately stopped until the girl came beside him. As he moved along his companion noted the strange fact that his feet made no noise, but she at once attributed this to the snow storm, although it seemed strange that her own foot did not move silently over the earth. The pair stopped before what appeared to be a mound covered with snow—the place where the ruined huts had stood hundreds of years ago. The right hand which the man had placed upon the female's shoulder was now pointing towards the ruins, and in a few seconds more was buried in the folds of his robe. The hand, when withdrawn, held a small harp. Standing in front of the ruins, the old man's thin, long bony fingers wandered over the strings of his instrument, and he proceeded to sing in a low voice a very mournful melody. His companion could not comprehend the strange actions of the old man, but continued to gaze upon him with a feeling of dread. At last the song was ended. The harp that had sounded so strangely in the hands of the remarkable old man was placed away, and the minstrel once more turned to his terrified companion, who followed him mechanically. The harper proceeded up the valley for some distance farther, and suddenly turned in the direction of the forest. He never spoke a word to the maiden meanwhile, but beckoned her to follow him. As they approached the forest he caught her by the hand, and she felt with a shudder that his hand was as cold as the snow itself, and that it seemed to have no flesh upon it.

They entered the forest by a path which seemed to be quite familiar to the old man, who did not pause to look about him, but boldly entered and led the unresisting girl along with him. After a few yards the passage through the wood was a tolerably wide one, so that there was no danger, their way being obstructed by overhanging branches. As they proceeded into the heart of the forest a low, peculiar sound was heard issuing from what seemed to be the depths of the wood; a low, sad sound which could not be defined. The old man did not seem in the least surprised to hear this curious sound, but hastened along the pathway with his companion making directly for the place whence the sound proceeded.

Gradually the strange sound grew louder, but when, as it appeared to the young lady, they were close to the place from which it emanated, her companion stopped suddenly and laid his hand on her shoulder as if commanding her to do the same thing. The pale December moon just then peeped out from behind the snow clouds. The girl observed an open glade, where twenty men were standing, some bearing torches and others playing upon small harps. The number was increasing gradually, as from various parts of the wood a figure emerged and took up a position near his fellows. Most of the figures had long, white beards, which covered their breasts, and all were clad in long robes stretching to their feet.

The scene was weird beyond description, and the frightened girl looked upon it with eyes that were almost bursting from her head. The sound which the lady heard in the forest was no longer a mystery, for she now knew that it proceeded from the harps in the glade. As the strange company continued their music they moved about over the snow-covered earth and the girl saw with horror that their feet made no imprint in the snow. A horrible fascination held her spell-bound, so that she could neither scream nor run away. But her nerves were destined to be more rudely shaken still. As she gazed in horror upon the scene before her, she heard some of the figures mutter some words she could not understand, pointing meantime to what seemed like deep wounds in their body from which the blood flowed copiously. Every arm was lifted towards heaven, as if each person was taking a solemn vow. Immediately she heard a peculiar sound close to her and she turned to behold her companion playing on his harp, as he had done before. Instantly every one of the figures listened intently, and then they moved straight to the place where she stood. She could now see the same blaring eyes that she had noticed in her companion.

She had little time for reflection, for no sooner were all the figures close around her than she was seized by her companion, and the chilly hands of other figures were also laid upon her. Almost dead with terror, she was dragged into the centre of the glade, and securely held by her former companion and another. The other retired for a moment and returned with what seemed to her to be long knives and daggers. They moved once more silently towards her. Then nature, which for so long had seemed dead, returned for a moment, and uttering a succession of shrieks which resounded through the forest she rushed from her captors and ran away. The terrible figures followed her, and caught her just on the edge of the forest. She shrieked and fell senseless to the earth.

CHAPTER III.

CHRISTMAS DAY.

When the poor girl awoke she found herself in a comfortable room with everything at hand that could assist in her recovery. A kindly old woman bent over her, and smiled with satisfaction when the blue eyes of the beautiful girl opened (for it could now be seen that she was endowed with more beauty than falls to the lot of the majority of human beings). A score of questions were put to the old woman before she had time to answer one. When the latter perceived that her patient was getting along as satisfactorily as could be expected she went to the door, and almost immediately a young man of fine physique entered the room. Explanations were then given on both sides. The young lady said, "My name is Millie Aintree, and I was on my way to see some friends in the North of England when our ship—the Agnes—was wrecked, and all the crew and passengers were drowned except myself. I clung to a large empty barrel, and was blown ashore by the gale of wind. The place was covered with snow, and I was wandering about when I encountered what seemed to be a very old man." She trembled violently as she narrated to the young man and the old nurse her terrible experience of the previous night. The former, however, did not seem to be very much surprised, and the old woman, too, looked at the young girl with eyes which seemed to say, "I could tell you all about it, but not until you are quite well will I do so."

"And now," continued Millie, "will you not tell me where I am, and how I came here?"

The young man replied, "About twelve o'clock or so last night I heard a succession of screams in the forest, and at once took Bill (that is the name of my big bloodhound) with me to see what was wrong. We journeyed on until Bill found you lying in the snow, and I brought you here. You are now in Castell Orthrwn, one of the ancient buildings in the island of Anglesea, and here you shall stop, if you have no objection, until I communicate with your friends and relatives."

The young girl thanked him for his kindness, and enquired his name. "Owain Ap Meigan" was the reply of the young man. "My parents died several years ago, and left me an orphan to manage the castle and the surrounding villages."

Having obtained the addresses of Millie's relatives Owain pressed the outstretched hand warmly, and left the room, first telling Gwen to take care of the young lady, but poor old Gwen did not require to be told that. She acted as a mother to the sufferer, and in a couple of days the latter was able to leave her room. Not only had Owain communicated with the parents and friends of Millie, but on the evening before New Year's Day they all arrived at the Castle. That evening was one of general rejoicing to all the company, especially as Owain had not forgotten to invite some of his own friends, including Idris ab Joan, his old harper, and the oldest bard in Anglesea. Idris played on his good harp a selection of old Welsh airs and pieces he had composed on the spur of the moment.

After several hours had been spent thus merrily Millie approached Owain and said, "Now, won't you tell me all about that strange scene I witnessed in the forest on Christmas eve?" Owain was on the point of telling her all he knew when he suddenly remembered that there was at least one person present who knew the tale far better than he did.

So he called upon old Idris to tell his friends the story of Suetonius Paulinus's massacre of the Bards and Druids, of the vow of the last of the Bards made over the bodies of his murdered friends, as related in the first part of our story, and all the other incidents that had been handed down by tradition from the time of Boadicea.

The English guests seemed greatly interested in the story, and old Idris was the hero of the evening. Owain insisted that the company should remain at the castle for several days, and his request was granted. It became evident to all he had been smitten by the charms of the beautiful, honest-eyed Millie, and that the feeling was reciprocated. On New Year's Day Owain showed his guests "over" the old castle, which stood not far from the entrance to the forest on the opposite side of the valley. The scene of the massacre of the bards and Druids was also visited, and all the other places of historical interest.

★ ★ ★

Once again it was Christmas Eve. Numerous guests had assembled at Castell Orthrwn. Great preparations were made for an event which was to take place on the following day. This was nothing less than the marriage of Owain ap Meigan and

Millie Aintree. Everybody appeared in the best of spirits, and old Idris had brought his bardic dress with him, for he intended donning it on the following day, and was going to sleep at the Castle that night. Just before midnight a low sweet sound was heard outside the Castle on the side next to the forest. Old Idris was the only one who heard it at first, but subsequently it was heard by all. Millie knew the sound well; it was the same beautiful sound of harps that she had heard on that terrible night just a year ago. But the melody was no longer sad and solemn; it was light and gay.

Old Idris noted this fact, and after communicating it to the others (some of whom, like himself, had heard the ghostly music before, and now wondered at the change), he said, "The spirits of the murdered bards rejoice at the union of their race with another mighty nation, and those who have haunted yonder glade will haunt it no more."

He was right. The wedding took place on the following day, and in after years Millie was wont to say that she thanked the ghostly bard whom she had first met on that fearful night long ago, for if he had not led her into the "Haunted Glade" she would probably never have met her darling Owain.

HOW TO MAKE A CHRISTMAS STORY.

Take an old country house, and sprinkle in it two or three well-worn ghosts; add a lost will, an old murder, and a rascally guardian. Take, then, a little moonlight, frosty weather, and a happy party; mix all together thoroughly, and keep stirring the ingredients over and over through five chapters till the orphaned, defrauded heiress and the good young man come to the surface. Marry them to the accompaniment of Christmas bells; then serve in pale yellow covers, bordered with holly berries.

Teignmouth Post (Dec. 23, 1904): 6, col. 3.

Jessie Saxby

Hel-ya-water

A Shetland Legend of Yule Time

Author, folklorist, and suffragist JESSIE MARGARET EDMON-
STON SAXBY (1842-1940) *particularly specialized in adventure
stories for boys, in no small part because she had been widowed
with five sons. This poem appeared in* The Boy's Own Paper's
*special Christmas issue for 1886, the same year she also published
an article on "The Folklore of Yule in the Shetland Isles" in the*
Leisure Hour Monthly Library. *The poem was later incorpo-
rated into in her 1892 novel* Viking-Boys, *and that year she
also gave an inaugural address at the Viking Club in London
on "Birds of Omen in Shetland," a topic upon which her poem
touched. So significant was the era's interest in the subject that the
BBC has stated, "it was Victorian Britain that really invented
the Vikings as we now know them."*[1]

WHERE the sod is seldom trodden,
    Where the haunted hillocks lie,
Where the lonely Hel-ya-water[2]
    Looks up darkly to the sky;
Where the daala mists forgather,[3]
    Where the plovers[4] make complaint,

1 Andrew Wawn, "The Viking Revival." BBC. Feb. 17, 2011. http://www.
bbc.co.uk/history/ancient/vikings/revival_01.shtml
2 Holy lake.
3 Lowland vapours meet each other.
4 Shorebirds. [CKP]

Where the stray or timid vaigher[1]
    Calls upon upon his patron saint.

Where the waves of Hel-ya-water
    Fret around a rugged isle,
Where the bones of Yarl Magnus
    Lie below a lichened pile,
There the raven found a refuge,
    There he brought his savage brood,
And the young lambs from the scattald[2]
    Were the nestlings' dainty food.

Year by year the Viking's raven
    Made that mystic spot his rest,
Year by year within the eyot[3]
    Brooded he as on a nest.
And no man would ever venture
    To invade the lone domain,
Where, in solitary scheming,
    The grim bird of doom did reign.

It was Yüle-time, and the Isles folk
    Sained[4] the children by their fires,
Lit the yatlin,[5] filled the daffock,[6]
    As of ealdon[7] did their sires.
There was wassail in each dwelling,
    And the song and dance went round,
And the laugh, the jest, the music,
    Rose above the tempest's sound.

1 Wanderer.
2 Common.
3 Little island. [CKP]
4 Guarded by Christian rites from evil spirits, who are supposed to have great licence at Yüle.
5 Candles used on festive occasions.
6 Water-bucket, which was always required to be full of *clean* water at Yüle.
7 Olde. [CKP]

Ho! the winds are raging wildly,
　　Ho! the thunders are awake,
'Tis the night when trows[1] have licence
　　Over saitor,[2] hill, and brake.[3]
Power is theirs on land and water
　　While the Yüle-star leads the night:
For where trows may trace their circles
　　There they claim exclusive right.

Yelling round the Hel-ya-water,
　　Sobbing by its eyot drear,
Screaming with the tempest-furies,
　　Over hillock, over mere.
On the wings of silent snow-flakes,
　　On the bulwands[4] from the rill,[5]
By the haunted Hel-ya-water
　　Flit those heralds of all ill.

There the dismal bird of boding
　　Is exulting with the storm.
Who will dare to-night, and conquer
　　The old raven's sable form?
Who will venture to the vatn[6]
　　Where the phantoms of unrest
Set their weird and magic signet
　　On each knoll and wavelet's crest?

See, young Yaspard's eye is blazing
　　With the fires so fleet and free:
Come of Magnus, yarl and sea-king,

1 Trolls.
2 Plains or pasture land.
3 Thicket. [CKP]
4 Bulrushes, which trows are supposed to use as aerial horses.
5 Brooklet. [CKP]
6 Fresh-water lake.

Son of Norland scald[1] is he:
Well he knows the gruesome story
    Of that evil-omened bird,
And of trows and vengeful demons
    He hath dreamed and he hath heard.

But his heart is hot and steadfast,
    And his hands are strong to try;
He will dare with fiends to combat,
    He will dare, and he will die.
Forth against the howling tempest,
    Forth against each evil power,
Wild and reckless, went young Yaspard
    In a dark unguarded hour.

Cold the surf of Hel-ya-water
    Breaks around the Norseman's grave,
And the boy is lifted rudely
    By each charmed and chafing wave.
Now he struggles boldly onward,
    Now he nears the haunted isle,
Where in grim and boding silence
    Waits the bird of woe and wile.

Fain is Yaspard to encounter
    That fierce harbinger of gloom—
Fain to dare the spells of magic.
    Fain to foil the wrath of doom.
Hark! the solitary raven
    Croaks a note of death and pain,
And a human call defiant
    Answers from the flood again.

Morning breaks,—a snowdrift covers
    All the drear deserted earth.

1 Bard. [CKP]

In young Yaspard's home is weeping,
    Quenched the fire upon his hearth.
But he broke the spells of evil,
    And he found a hero's grave.
When you pass the Hel-ya-water
    Cast a pebble to its wave.[1]

'TWAS EVER THUS!

On Christmas Eve, twenty-five years ago, the same as to-day, the unsophisticated rustic was being startled out of his wits by the brilliant light of

SALSBURY'S LAMPS,

and more than one farmer of those days saw Christmas ghosts riding on pitchforks with cart wheels between their legs and Salsbury Lamps blazing in the middle.

Cycling 20 (519), Dec. 29, 1900

---

1 When passing any haunted water people cast therein a stone, to appease the troubled spirits.

Barry Pain

The Undying Thing

BARRY ERIC ODELL PAIN (1864-1928) *was primarily known as a humorist, but his 1893 story featured here was decidedly not that. "The most striking item in the excellent Christmas number of 'Black and White' is undoubtedly the weird and not too pleasant tale 'The Undying Thing,'"*[1] *wrote one contemporary reviewer, while another called it "a story which no one should tackle after eating a plum pudding"*[2] *A slightly edited version reprinted in Pain's 1901 collection* Stories in the Dark *caught the attention of H. P. Lovecraft, who marked it for future inclusion in his survey* Supernatural Horror in Literature, *and it was the first of 100 stories included in John Pelan's* The Century's Best Horror Fiction *(2011).*

CHAPTER I.

UP AND DOWN the oak-panelled dining-hall of Mansteth, the master of the house walked restlessly. At formal intervals down the long severe table were placed four silver candlesticks; but the light from these did not serve to illuminate the whole of the surroundings. It just touched the portrait of a fair-haired boy, with a sad and wistful expression, that hung at one end of the room; it sparkled on the lid of a silver tankard. As Sir Edric passed to and fro, it lit up his face

---

1 "'Black and White' Christmas Number," *Northern Whig* (Nov. 27, 1893): 6, col. 3.

2 "Some Christmas Numbers," *Glasgow Evening Post* (Dec. 12, 1893): 2, col. 2.

and figure. It was a bold and resolute face, with a firm chin and passionate, dominant eyes. A bad past was written in the lines of it. And yet every now and then there came over it a strange look of very anxious gentleness, that gave it some resemblance to the portrait of the fair-haired boy. Sir Edric paused a moment before the portrait, and surveyed it carefully, his strong brown hands locked behind him, his gigantic shoulders thrust a little forward.

"Ah, what I was!" he murmured to himself. "What I was!"

Once more he commenced pacing up and down. The candles, mirrored in the polished wood of the table, had burnt low. For hours Sir Edric had been waiting, listening intently for some sound from the room above, or from the broad staircase outside. There had been sounds—the wailing of a woman, a quick abrupt voice, the moving of rapid feet. But for the last hour he had heard nothing. Quite suddenly he stopped, and dropped on his knees against the table:—

"God, I have never thought of Thee. Thou knowest that—Thou knowest that by my devilish behaviour and cruelty I did veritably murder Alice, my first wife, albeit the physicians did maintain that she died of a decline—a wasting sickness. Thou knowest that all here in Mansteth do hate me, and that rightly. They say, too, that I am mad. But that they say not rightly, seeing that I know how wicked I am. I always knew it. But I never cared until I loved—oh, God, I never cared!"

His fierce eyes opened for a minute, glared round the room, and closed again tightly. He went on:

"God, for myself I ask nothing. I make no bargaining with Thee. Whatsoever punishment Thou givest me to bear, I will bear it. Whatsoever Thou givest me to do I will do. Whether Thou killest Eve or whether Thou keepest her in life—and never have I loved but her—I will from this night be good. In due penitence will I receive the holy sacrament of thy body and blood. And my son—the one child that I had by Alice, I will fetch back again from Challonsea, where I kept him in order that I might not look upon him, and I will be to him a father in deed and very truth. And in all things, so far as in me lieth, I will make restitution and atonement. Whether Thou hearest me or whether Thou hearest me not, these things shall be. And for my prayer, it is but this, of Thy loving kindness, most merciful God, be Thou with Eve and make her happy; and after these great pains and perils of childbirth, send her Thy peace! Of Thy loving kindness, Thy merciful loving kindness, O God!"

Perhaps the prayer that is offered when the time for praying is over is more terribly pathetic than any other. Yet one might hesitate to say that this prayer was unanswered.

Sir Edric rose to his feet, once more he paced the room. There was a strange simplicity about him—the simplicity that scorns an incongruity. He felt that his lips and throat were parched and dry. He lifted the heavy silver tankard from the table and raised the lid; there was still a good draught of mulled wine in it with the burnt toast, cut heart-shape, floating on the top.

"To the health of Eve and her child," he said aloud, and drained it to the last drop.

Click, click! As he put the tankard down he heard distinctly two doors opened and shut quickly, one after the other. And then slowly down the stairs came a hesitating step. Sir Edric could bear the suspense no longer. He opened the dining-room door, and the dim light strayed out into the dark hall beyond.

"Dennison," he said, in a low, sharp whisper, "is that you?"

"Yes, yes. I am coming, Sir Edric."

A moment afterwards Dr. Dennison entered the room. He was very pale; perspiration streamed from his forehead; his cravat was disarranged. He was an old man, thin, with the air of proud humility. Sir Edric watched him narrowly.

"Then she is dead," he said, with a quiet that Dr. Dennison had not expected.

"Twenty physicians—a hundred physicians could not have saved her. Sir Edric. She was——" He gave some details of medical interest.

"Dennison," said Sir Edric, still speaking with calm and restraint, "why do you seem thus indisposed and panic-stricken? You are a physician—have you never looked upon the face of death before? The soul of my wife is with God——"

"Yes," murmured Dennison, "a good woman, a perfect, saintly woman."

"And," Sir Edric went on, raising his eyes to the ceiling as though he could see through it, "her body lies in great dignity and beauty upon the bed, and there is no horror in it. Why are you afraid?"

"I do not fear death, Sir Edric."

"But your hands—they are not steady. You are evidently overcome. Does the child live?"

"Yes, it lives."

"Another boy—a brother for young Edric, the child that Alice bore me?"

"There—there is something wrong. I do not know what to do. I want you to come upstairs. And, Sir Edric, I must tell you—you will need your self-command."

"Dennison, the hand of God is heavy upon me. But from this time forth, until the day of my death, I am submissive to it; and God send that that day may come quickly! I will follow you and I will endure." He took one of the high silver candlesticks from the table, and stepped towards the door. He strode quickly up the staircase, Dr. Dennison following a little way behind him.

As Sir Edric waited at the top of the staircase, he heard suddenly from the room before him a low cry. He put down the candlestick on the floor and leaned back against the wall, listening. The cry came again—a vibrating monotone, ending in a growl.

"Dennison, Dennison!" his voice choked, he could not go on.

"Yes," said the doctor, "it is in there. I had the two women out of the room, and got it here. No one but myself has seen it. But you must see it, too."

He raised the candle and the two men entered the room—
one of the spare bedrooms. On the bed there was something
moving under cover of a blanket. Dr. Dennison paused for a
moment and then flung the blanket partially back.

They did not remain in the room for more than a few seconds. The moment they got outside, Dr. Dennison began to
speak.

"Sir Edric, I would fain suggest somewhat to you. There
is no evil, as Sophocles hath it in his *Antigone,* for which man
hath not found a remedy, except it be death, and here———"

Sir Edric interrupted him in a husky voice. "Downstairs,
Dennison. This is too near."

It was, indeed, passing strange. When once the novelty of
this—this occurrence had worn off, Dr. Dennison seemed no
longer frightened. He was calm, academic, interested in an
unusual phenomenon. But Sir Edric, who was said in the village to fear nothing in earth, or heaven, or hell, was obviously
much moved.

When they had got back to the dining-room, Sir Edric
motioned the doctor to a seat.

"Now then," he said, "I will hear you. Something must be
done—and to-night."

"Exceptional cases," said Dr. Dennison, "demand exceptional remedies. Well, it lies there upstairs and it is at our
mercy. We can let it live, or placing one hand over the mouth
and nostrils, we can———"

"Stop," said Sir Edric. "This thing has so crushed and
humiliated me that I can scarcely think. But I recall that while
I waited for you I fell upon my knees and prayed that God
would save Eve. And, as I confessed unto Him more than I will
ever confess unto man, it seemed to me that it were ignoble to
offer a price for His favour. And I said that whatsoever punishment I had to bear, I would bear it; and whatsoever He called
upon me to do, I would do it; and I made no conditions."

"Well?"

"Now my punishment is of two kinds. Firstly, my wife,

Eve, is dead. And this I bear more easily because I know that now she is numbered with the company of God's saints, and with them her pure spirit finds happier communion than with me; I was not worthy of her. And yet she would call my roughness by gentle, pretty names. She gloried, Dennison, in the mere strength of my body, and in the greatness of my stature. And I am thankful that she never saw this—this shame that has come upon the house. For she was a proud woman, with all her gentleness, even as I was proud and bad until it pleased God this night to break me even to the dust. And for my second punishment, that too I must bear. This thing that lies upstairs, I will take and rear; it is bone of my bone and flesh of my flesh; only, if it be possible, I will hide my shame so that no man but you shall know of it."

"That is not possible. You cannot keep a living being in this house unless it be known. Will not these women say, 'Where is the child?'"

Sir Edric stood upright, his powerful hands linked before him, his face working in agony; but he was still resolute.

"Then if it must be known, it shall be known. The fault is mine. If I had but done sooner what Eve asked, this would not have happened. I will bear it."

"Sir Edric, do not be angry with me, for if I did not say this, then I should be but an ill counsellor. And firstly, do not use the word shame. The ways of nature are past all explaining; if a woman be frail and easily impressed, and other circumstances concur, then in some few rare cases a thing of this sort does happen. If there be shame, it is not upon you but upon nature—to whom one would not lightly impute shame. Yet it is true that common and uninformed people might think that this shame was yours. And herein lies the great trouble—the shame would rest also on her memory."

"Then," said Sir Edric, in a low unfaltering voice, "this night for the sake of Eve I will break my word, and lose my own soul eternally."

About an hour afterwards Sir Edric and Dr. Dennison left

the house together. The doctor carried a stable lantern in his hand. Sir Edric bore in his arms something wrapped in a blanket. They went through the long garden, out into the orchard that skirts the north side of the park, and then across a field to a small dark plantation known as Hal's Planting. In the very heart of Hal's Planting there are some curious caves; access to the innermost chamber of them is exceedingly difficult and dangerous, and only possible to a climber of exceptional skill and courage. As they returned from these caves, Sir Edric no longer carried his burden. The dawn was breaking and the birds began to sing.

"Could not they be quiet just for this morning?" said Sir Edric wearily.

There were but few people who were asked to attend the funeral of Lady Vanquerest and of the baby which, it was said, had only survived her by a few hours. There were but three people who knew that only one body—the body of Lady Vanquerest—was really interred on that occasion. These three were Sir Edric Vanquerest, Dr. Dennison, and a nurse whom it had been found expedient to take into their confidence.

During the next six years Sir Edric lived, almost in solitude, a life of great sanctity, devoting much of his time to the education of the younger Edric, the child that he had by his first wife. In the course of this time some strange stories began to be told and believed in the neighbourhood with reference to Hal's Planting, and the place was generally avoided.

When Sir Edric lay on his death-bed the windows of the chamber were open, and suddenly through them came a low cry. The doctor in attendance hardly regarded it, supposing that it came from one of the owls in the trees outside. But Sir Edric, at the sound of it, rose right up in bed before anyone could stay him, and flinging up his arms cried, "Wolves! wolves! wolves!" Then he fell forward on his face, dead.

And four generations passed away.

CHAPTER II.

Towards the latter end of the nineteenth century, John Marsh, who was the oldest man in the village of Mansteth, could be prevailed upon to state what he recollected. His two sons supported him in his old age; he never felt the pinch of poverty, and he always had money in his pocket; but it was a settled principle with him that he would not pay for the pint of beer which he drank occasionally in the parlour of "The Stag." Sometimes Farmer Wynthwaite paid for the beer; sometimes it was Mr. Spicer from the post-office; sometimes the landlord of "The Stag" himself would finance the old man's evening dissipation. In return, John Marsh was prevailed upon to state what he recollected; this he would do with great heartiness and strict impartiality, recalling the intemperance of a former Wynthwaite, and the dishonesty of some ancestral Spicer, while he drank the beer of their direct descendants. He would tell you, with two tough old fingers crooked round the handle of the pewter that you had provided, how your grandfather was a poor thing, "fit for nowt but to brak steeans by ta rord-side." He was so disrespectful that it was believed that he spoke truth. He was particularly disrespectful when he spoke of that most devilish family, the Vanquerests; and he never tired of recounting the stories that from generation to generation had grown up about them. It would be objected, sometimes, that the present Sir Edric, the last surviving member of the race, was a pleasant-spoken young man, with none of the family wildness and hot temper. It was for no sin of his that Hal's Planting was haunted—a thing which everyone in Mansteth, and many beyond it, most devoutly believed. John Marsh would hear no apology for him, nor for any of his ancestors; he recounted the prophecy that an old mad woman had made of the family before her strange death, and hoped, fervently, that he might live to see it fulfilled.

The third baronet, as has already been told, had lived the

latter part of his life, after his second wife's death, in peace
and quietness. Of him John Marsh remembered nothing, of
course, and could only recall the few fragments of information that had been handed down to him. He had been told that
this Sir Edric, who had travelled a good deal, at one time kept
wolves, intending to train them to serve as dogs; these wolves
were not kept under proper restraint, and became a kind of
terror to the neighbourhood. Lady Vanquerest, his second
wife, had asked him frequently to destroy these beasts; but Sir
Edric, although it was said that he loved his second wife even
more than he hated the first, was obstinate when any of his
whims were crossed, and put her off with promises. Then one
day Lady Vanquerest herself was attacked by the wolves; she
was not bitten, but she was badly frightened. That filled Sir
Edric with remorse, and, when it was too late, he went out into
the yard where the wolves were kept and shot them all. A few
months afterwards Lady Vanquerest died in childbirth. It was
a queer thing, John Marsh noted, that it was just at this time
that Hal's Planting began to get such a bad name. The fourth
baronet was, John Marsh considered, the worst of the race; it
was to him that the old mad woman had made her prophecy,
an incident that Marsh himself had witnessed in his childhood
and still vividly remembered. The baronet, in his old age, had
been cast up by his vices on the shores of melancholy; heavy-
eyed, grey-haired, bent, he seemed to pass through life as in
a dream. Every day he would go out on horseback, always at
a walking pace, as though he were following the funeral of
his past self. One night he was riding up the village street as
this old woman came down it. Her name was Ann Ruthers;
she had a kind of reputation in the village, and although all
said that she was mad, many of her utterances were remembered, and she was treated with respect. It was growing dark,
and the village street was almost empty; but just at the lower
end was the usual group of men by the door of "The Stag,"
dimly illuminated by the light that came through the quaint
windows of the old inn. They glanced at Sir Edric as he rode

slowly past them, taking no notice of their respectful salutes. At the upper end of the street there were two persons. One was Ann Ruthers, a tall, gaunt old woman, her head wrapped in a shawl; the other was John Marsh. He was then a boy of eight, and he was feeling somewhat frightened. He had been on an expedition to a distant and fœtid pond, and in the black mud and clay about its borders he had discovered live newts; he had three of them in his pocket, and this was to some extent a joy to him, but his joy was damped by his knowledge that he was coming home much too late, and would probably be chastised in consequence. He was unable to walk fast or to run, because Ann Ruthers was immediately in front of him, and he dared not pass her, especially at night. She walked on until she met Sir Edric, and then, standing still, she called him by name. He pulled in his horse and raised his heavy eyes to look at her. Then in loud, clear tones she spoke to him, and John Marsh heard and remembered every word that she said; it was her prophecy of the end of the Vanquerests. Sir Edric never answered a word. When she had finished, he rode on, while she remained standing there, her eyes fixed on the stars above her. John Marsh dared not pass the madwoman; he turned round and walked back, keeping close to Sir Edric's horse. Quite suddenly, without a word of warning, as if in a moment of ungovernable irritation, Sir Edric wheeled his horse round and struck the boy across the face with his switch.

On the following morning John Marsh—or rather, his parents—received a handsome solatium in coin of the realm; but sixty-five years afterwards he had not forgiven that blow, and still spoke of the Vanquerests as a most devilish family, still hoped and prayed that he might see the prophecy fulfilled. He would relate, too, the death of Ann Ruthers, which occurred either later on the night of her prophecy or early on the following day. She would often roam about the country all night, and on this particular night she left the main road to wander over the Vanquerest lands, where trespassers, especially at night, were not welcomed. But no one saw her, and it seemed that she had made her way to a part where no one was likely to see her; for none of the keepers would have entered Hal's Planting by night. Her body was found there at noon on the following day, lying under the tall bracken, dead, but without any mark of violence upon it. It was considered that she had died in a fit. This naturally added to the ill-repute of Hal's Planting. The woman's death caused considerable sensation in the village. Sir Edric sent a messenger to the married sister with whom she had lived, saying that he wished to pay all the funeral expenses. This offer, as John Marsh recalled with satisfaction, was refused.

Of the last two baronets he had but little to tell. The fifth baronet was credited with the family temper, but he conducted himself in a perfectly conventional way, and did not seem in the least to belong to romance. He was a good man of business, and devoted himself to making up, as far as he could, for the very extravagant expenditure of his predecessors. His son, the present Sir Edric, was a fine young fellow and popular in the village. Even John Marsh could find nothing to say against him; other people in the village were interested in him. It was said that he had chosen a wife in London—a Miss Guerdon—and would shortly be back to see that Mansteth Hall was put in proper order for her before his marriage at the close of the season. Modernity kills ghostly romance. It was difficult to associate this modern and handsome Sir Edric, bright and spirited, a good sportsman and a good fellow, with the doom that had been foretold for the Vanquerest family. He himself knew the tradition and laughed at it. He wore clothes made by a London tailor, looked healthy, smiled cheerfully, and—in a vain attempt to shame his own head-keeper—had himself spent a night alone in Hal's Planting. This last was used by Mr. Spicer in argument, who would ask John Marsh what he made of it. John Marsh replied, contemptuously, that it was "nowt." It was not so that the Vanquerest family was to end; but when the thing, whatever it was, that lived in Hal's Planting, left it and came up to the house, to Mansteth Hall itself, then one would see the end of the Vanquerests. So Ann Ruthers had prophesied. Sometimes Mr. Spicer would ask the pertinent question, how did John Marsh know that there really was anything in Hal's Planting? This he asked, less because he disbelieved, than because he wished to draw forth an account of John's personal experiences. These were given in great detail, but they did not amount to very much. One night John Marsh had been taken by business—Sir Edric's keepers would have called the business by hard names—into the neighbourhood of Hal's Planting. He had there been suddenly startled by a cry, and had run away as though he were running for his life. That was all he could tell about the cry—it was the kind of cry to make a man lose his head and run. And then it always happened that John Marsh was urged, by his companions, to enter Hal's Planting himself, and discover what was there. John pursed his thin lips together, and hinted that that also might be done, one of these days. Whereupon Mr. Spicer looked across his pipe to Farmer Wynthwaite, and smiled significantly.

Shortly before Sir Edric's return from London, the attention of Mansteth was once more directed to Hal's Planting, but not by any supernatural occurrence. Quite suddenly, on a calm day, two trees there fell with a crash; there were caves in the centre of the plantation, and it seemed as if the roof of some big chamber in these caves had given way. They talked it over one night in the parlour of "The Stag." There was water in these caves, Farmer Wynthwaite knew it; and he expected a further subsidence. If the whole thing collapsed, what then?

"Aye," said John Marsh. He rose from his chair, and pointed in the direction of the Hall with his thumb. "What then?" He walked across to the fire, looked at it meditatively for a moment, and then spat in it.

"A trewly wun'ful owd mon," said Farmer Wynthwaite as he watched him.

CHAPTER III.

In the smoking-room at Mansteth Hall sat Sir Edric with his friend and intended brother-in-law, Dr. Andrew Guerdon. Both men were on the verge of middle-age; there was hardly a year's difference between them. Yet Guerdon looked much the older man; that was, perhaps, because he wore a short, black beard, while Sir Edric was clean shaven. Guerdon was thought to be an enviable man. His father had made a fortune in the firm of Guerdon, Guerdon and Bird; the old style was still retained at the bank, although there was no longer a Guerdon in the firm. Andrew Guerdon had a handsome allowance from his father, and had also inherited money through his mother. He had taken the degree of doctor of medicine; he did not practice, but he was still interested in science, especially in out-of-the-way science. He was unmarried, gifted with perpetually good health, interested in life, popular. His friendship with Sir Edric dated from their college days. It had for some years been almost certain that Sir Edric would marry his friend's sister, Ray Guerdon, although the actual betrothal had only been announced that season.

On a bureau in one corner of the room were spread a couple of plans and various slips of paper. Sir Edric was wrinkling his brows over them, dropping cigar-ash over them, and finally getting angry over them. He pushed back his chair irritably, and turned towards Guerdon.

"Look here, old man!" he said. "I desire to curse the original architect of this house—to curse him in his down-sitting and his uprising."

"Seeing that the original architect has gone to where beyond these voices there is peace, he won't be offended. Neither shall I. But why worry yourself? You've been rooted to that blessed bureau all day, and now, after dinner, when every self-respecting man chucks business, you return to it again—even as a sow returns to her wallowing in the mire."

"Now, my good Andrew, do be reasonable. How on earth can I bring Ray to such a place as this? And it's built with such ingrained malice and vexatiousness that one can't live in it as it is, and can't alter it without having the whole shanty tumble down about one's ears. Look at this plan now. That thing's what they're pleased to call a morning room. If the window had been *here,* there would have been an uninterrupted view of open country. So what does this forsaken fool of an architect do? He sticks it *there,* where you see it on the plan, looking straight on to a blank wall with a stable yard on the other side of it. But that's a trifle. Look here again——"

"I won't look any more. This place is all right. It was good enough for your father and mother and several generations before them, until you arose to improve the world; it was good enough for you until you started to get married. It's a picturesque place, and if you begin to alter it you'll spoil it." Guerdon looked round the room critically. "Upon my word," he said, "I don't know of any house where I like the smoking-room as well as I like this; it's not too big, and yet it's fairly lofty; it's got those comfortable-looking oak-panelled walls. That's the right kind of fire-place, too, and these corner cupboards are handy."

"Of course this won't *remain* the smoking-room. It has the morning sun and Ray likes that; so I shall make it into her boudoir; it *is* a nice room, as you say."

"That's it, Ted, my boy," said Guerdon bitterly. "Take a room which is designed by nature and art to be a smoking-room and turn it into a boudoir. Turn it into the very deuce of a boudoir with the morning sun laid on for ever and ever. Waste the twelfth of August by getting married on it. Spend the winter in foreign parts, and write letters that you can breakfast out of doors, just as if you'd created the mildness of the climate yourself. Come back in the spring, and spend the London season in the country, in order to avoid seeing anybody who wants to see you. That's the way to do it; that's the way to get yourself generally loved and admired!"

"That's chiefly imagination," said Sir Edric. "I'm blest if I can see why I should not make this house fit for Ray to live in."

"It's a queer thing: Ray was a good girl, and you weren't a bad sort yourself. You prepare to go into partnership, and you both straightway turn into despicable lunatics. I'll have a word or two with Ray. But I'm serious about this house; don't go tinkering it; it's got a character of its own, and you'd better leave it. Turn half Tottenham Court Road and the culture thereof—heaven help it!—into your town house if you like, but leave this alone."

"Haven't got a town house—yet. Anyway I'm not going to be unsuitable. I'm not going to feel myself at the mercy of a big firm. I shall supervise the whole thing myself. I shall drive over to Challonsea to-morrow afternoon, and see if I can't find some intelligent and fairly conscientious workmen."

"That's all right, you supervise them, and I'll supervise you. You'll be much too new if I don't look after you. You've got an old legend, I believe, that the family's coming to a bad end, you must be consistent with it; as you are bad, be beautiful. By the way, what do you yourself think of the legend?"

"It's nothing," said Sir Edric, speaking, however, rather seriously. "They say that Hal's Planting is haunted by something that will not die. Certainly an old woman, who for some godless reason of her own made her way there by night, was found there dead on the following morning; but her death could be, and was, accounted for by natural causes. Certainly, too, I haven't a man in my employ who'll go there by night now."

"Why not?"

"How should I know? I fancy that a few of the villagers sit boozing at 'The Stag' in the evening, and like to scare themselves by swopping lies about Hal's Planting. I've done my best to stop it. I once, as you know, took a rug, a revolver, and a flask of whisky, and spent the night there myself. But even that didn't convince them."

"Yes, you told me. By the way, did you hear or see anything?"

Sir Edric hesitated before he answered. Finally he said, "Look here, old man, I wouldn't tell this to anyone but yourself. I did think that I heard something. About the middle of the night I was awakened by a cry; I can only say that it was the kind of cry that frightened me. I sat up, and at that moment I heard some great, heavy thing go swishing through the bracken behind me at a great rate. Then all was still, I looked about, but I could find nothing. At last I argued, as I would argue now, that a man who is just awake is only half-awake, and that his powers of observation, by hearing or any other sense, are not to be trusted. I even persuaded myself to go to sleep again, and there was no more disturbance. However, there's a real danger there now. In the heart of the plantation there are some caves, and a subterranean spring; lately there has been some slight subsidence there, and the same sort of thing will happen again—in all probability. I wired to-day to an expert to come and look at the place; he has replied that he will come on Monday. The legend says that when the thing that lives in Hal's Planting comes up to the Hall, the Vanquerests will be ended. If I cut down the trees, and then break up the place with a charge of dynamite, I shouldn't wonder if I spoiled that legend."

Guerdon smiled. "I'm inclined to agree with you all through. It's absurd to trust the immediate impressions of a man just awakened; what you heard was, probably, a stray cow."

"No cow," said Sir Edric, impartially. "There's a low wall all round the place—not much of a wall, but too much for a cow."

"Well, something else—some equally obvious explanation. In dealing with such questions, never forget that you're in the nineteenth century. By the way, your man's coming on Monday. That reminds me—to-day's Friday, and as an indisputable consequence to-morrow's Saturday. Therefore, if you want to find your intelligent workmen, it will be of no use to go in the afternoon."

"True," said Sir Edric, "I'll go in the morning." He walked to a tray on a side table and poured a little whisky into a tumbler. "They don't seem to have brought any seltzer water," he remarked in a grumbling voice. He rang the bell impatiently.

"Now why don't you use those corner cupboards for that kind of thing? If you kept a supply there, it would be handy in case of accidents."

"They're full up already." He opened one of them and showed that it was filled with old account-books and yellow documents, tied up in bundles. The servant entered. "Oh, I say, there isn't any seltzer. Bring it, please." He turned again to Guerdon. "You might do me a favour, when I'm away tomorrow, if there's nothing else that you want to do. I wish you'd look through all these papers for me. They're all old. Possibly some of them ought to go to my solicitor, and I know that a lot of them ought to be destroyed. Some few may be of family interest. It's not the kind of thing that I could ask a stranger or a servant to do for me, and I've so much on hand just now before my marriage——"

"But, of course, my dear fellow, I'll do it with pleasure."

"I'm ashamed to give you all this bother. However, you said that you were coming here to help me, and I take you at your word. By the way, I think you'd better not say anything to Ray about the Hal's Planting story."

"I may be some of the things that you take me for, but really I am not a common ass. Of course, I shouldn't tell her."

"I'll tell her myself, and I'd sooner do it when I've got the whole thing cleared up. Well, I'm really obliged to you."

"I needn't remind you that I hope to receive as much again. I believe in compensation. Nature always gives it and always requires it. One finds it everywhere—in philology and onwards."

"I could mention omissions."

"They are few, and make a belief in a hereafter to supply them logical."

"Lunatics, for instance?"

"Their delusions are often their compensation. They argue correctly from false premises. A lunatic believing himself to be a millionaire has as much delight as money can give."

"How about deformities, or monstrosities?"

"The principle is there—although I don't pretend that the compensation is always adequate. A man who is deprived of one sense generally has another developed with unusual acuteness. As for monstrosities of at all a human type, one sees none; the things exhibited in fairs are, without exception, frauds. They occur very rarely, and one does not know enough about them. A really good text-book on the subject would be interesting. Still, such stories as I have heard would bear out my theory—stories of their superhuman strength and cunning, and of the extraordinary prolongation of life that has been noted, or is said to have been noted, in them. But it is hardly fair to test my principle by exceptional cases. Besides, anyone can prove anything except that anything's worth proving."

"That's a cheerful thing to say. I wouldn't like to swear that I could prove how the Hal's Planting legend started, but I fancy, do you know, that I could make a very good shot at it."

"Well?"

"My great-grandfather kept wolves—I can't say why. Do you remember the portrait of him—not the one when he was a boy, the other? It hangs on the staircase. There's now a group of wolves in one corner of the picture. I was looking carefully at the picture one day and thought that I detected some over-painting in that corner; indeed, it was done so roughly that a child would have noticed it, if the picture had been hung in a better light. I had the over-painting removed by a good man, and underneath there was that group of wolves depicted. Well, one of these wolves must have escaped, got into Hal's Planting, and scared an old woman or two; that would start a story, and human mendacity would do the rest."

"Yes," said Guerdon meditatively. "That doesn't sound improbable. But why did your great-grandfather have the wolves painted out?"

CHAPTER IV.

Saturday morning was fine, but very hot and sultry. After breakfast, when Sir Edric had driven off to Challonsea, Andrew Guerdon settled himself in a comfortable chair in the smoking-room; the contents of the corner cupboard were piled up on a table by his side. He lit his pipe and began to go through the papers and put them in order. He had been at work about a quarter of an hour when the butler entered, rather abruptly, looking pale and disturbed.

"In Sir Edric's absence, sir, it was thought that I had better come to you for advice. There's been an awful thing happened."

"Well?"

"They've found a corpse in Hal's Planting—about half-an-hour ago. It's the body of an old man, John Marsh, who used to live in the village. He seems to have died in some kind of a fit. They were bringing it here, but I had it taken down to the village where his cottage is. Then I sent to the police and to a doctor."

There was a moment or two's silence before Guerdon answered.

"This is a terrible thing. I don't know of anything else that you could do. Stop—if the police wish to see the spot where the body was found, I think that Sir Edric would like them to have every facility."

"Quite so, sir."

"And no one else must be allowed there."

"No, sir. Thank you." The butler withdrew.

Guerdon arose from his chair and began to pace up and down the room. "What an impressive thing a coincidence is!" he thought to himself. "Last night the whole of the Hal's Planting story seemed to me not worth consideration. But this second death there—it can be only coincidence. What else could it be?"

The question would not leave him. What else could it be? Had that dead man seen something there and died in sheer terror of it? Had Sir Edric really heard something when he spent that night there alone? He returned to his work, but he found that he got on with it but slowly. Every now and then his mind wandered back to the subject of Hal's Planting. His doubts annoyed him. It was unscientific and unmodern of him to feel any perplexity, because a natural and rational explanation was possible; he was annoyed with himself for being perplexed.

After luncheon he strolled round the grounds and smoked a cigar. He noticed that a thick bank of dark, slate-coloured clouds was gathering in the west. The air was very still. In a remote corner of the garden a big heap of weeds was burning; the smoke went up perfectly straight. On the top of the heap light flames danced; they were like the ghosts of flames in the strange light. A few big drops of rain fell; the small shower did not last for five seconds. Guerdon glanced at his watch. Sir Edric would be back in an hour, and he wanted to finish his work with the papers before Sir Edric's return, so he went back into the house once more.

He picked up the first document that came to hand. As he did so, another, smaller, and written on parchment, which had been folded in with it, dropped out. He began to read the parchment; it was written in faded ink, and the parchment itself was yellow and, in places, stained. It was the confession of the third baronet—he could tell that by the date upon it. It told the story of that night when he and Dr. Dennison went together, carrying a burden through the long garden, out into the orchard that skirts the north side of the park, and then across a field to a small, dark plantation. It told how he made a vow to God and did not keep it. These were the last words of the confession:—

"Already upon me has the punishment fallen, and the devil's wolves do seem to hunt me in my sleep nightly. But I know that there is worse to come. The thing that I took to

Hal's Planting is dead. Yet will it come back again to the Hall, and then will the Vanquerests be at an end. This writing I have committed to chance, neither showing it nor hiding it, and leaving it to chance if any man shall read it."

Underneath there was a line written in darker ink, and in quite a different handwriting. It was dated fifteen years later, and the initials R. D. were appended to it.

"It is not dead. I do not think that it will ever die."

When Andrew Guerdon had finished reading this document, he looked slowly round the room. The subject had got on his nerves, and he was almost expecting to see something. Then he did his best to pull himself together. The first question he put to himself was this: has Ted ever seen this? Obviously he had not. If he had, he could not have taken the tradition of Hal's Planting so lightly, nor have spoken of it so freely. Besides, he would either have mentioned the document to Guerdon, or he would have kept it carefully concealed. He would not have allowed him to come across it casually in that way. "Ted must never see it," thought Guerdon to himself; he then remembered the pile of weeds he had seen burning in the garden. He put the parchment in his pocket, and hurried out. There was no one about. He spread the parchment on the top of the pile, and waited until it was entirely consumed. Then he went back to the smoking-room; he felt easier now.

"Yes," thought Guerdon, "if Ted had first of all heard of the finding of that body, and then had read that document, I believe that he would have gone mad. Things that come near us affect us deeply." Guerdon himself was much moved. He clung steadily to reason; he felt himself able to give a natural explanation all through, and yet he was nervous. The net of coincidence had closed in around him; the mention in Sir Edric's confession of the prophecy which had subsequently become traditional in the village alarmed him. And what did that last line mean? He supposed that R. D. must be the initials of Dr. Dennison. What did he mean by saying that the thing was not dead? Did he mean that it had not really been killed, that it had been gifted with some preternatural strength and vitality and had survived, though Sir Edric did not know it? He recalled what he had said about the prolongation of the lives of such things. If it still survived, why had it never been seen? Had it joined to the wild hardiness of the beast a cunning that was human—or more than human? How could it have lived? There was water in the caves, he reflected, and food could have been secured—a wild beast's food. Or did Dr. Dennison mean that though the thing itself was dead, its wraith survived and haunted the place? He wondered how the doctor had found Sir Edric's confession, and why he had written that line at the end of it. As he sat thinking, a low rumble of thunder in the distance startled him. He felt a touch of panic—a sudden impulse to leave Mansteth at once and, if possible, to take Ted with him. Ray could never live there. He went over the whole thing in his mind again and again, at one time calm and argumentative about it, and at another shaken by blind horror.

Sir Edric, on his return from Challonsea a few minutes afterwards, came straight to the smoking-room where Guerdon was. He looked tired and depressed. He began to speak at once:—

"You needn't tell me about it—about John Marsh. I heard about it in the village."

"Did you? It's a painful occurrence, although, of course—"

"Stop. Don't go into it. Anything can be explained—I know that."

"I went through those papers and account-books while you were away. Most of them may just as well be destroyed; but there are a few—I put them aside there—which might be kept. There was nothing of any interest."

"Thanks, I'm much obliged to you."

"Oh, and look here; I've got an idea. I've been examining the plans of the house, and I'm coming round to your opinion. There are some alterations which should be made, and yet I'm afraid that they'd make the place look patched and renovated.

It wouldn't be a bad thing to know what Ray thought about it."

"That's impossible. The workmen come on Monday, and we can't consult her before then. Besides, I have a general notion what she would like."

"We could catch the night express to town at Challonsea, and——"

Sir Edric rose from his seat angrily and hit the table. "Good God! don't sit there hunting up excuses to cover my cowardice, and making it easy for me to bolt. What do you suppose the villagers would say, and what would my own servants say, if I ran away to-night? I am a coward—I know it. I'm horribly afraid. But I'm not going to act like a coward if I can help it."

"Now, my dear chap, don't excite yourself. If you are going to care at all—to care as much as the conventional damn—for what people say, you'll have no peace in life. And I don't believe you're afraid. What are you afraid of?"

Sir Edric paced once or twice up and down the room, and then sat down again before replying. "Look here, Andrew, I'll make a clean breast of it. I've always laughed at the tradition; I forced myself, as it seemed at least, to disprove it by spending a night in Hal's Planting; I took the pains even to make a theory which would account for its origin. All the time I had a sneaking, stifled belief in it. With the help of my reason I crushed that; but now my reason has thrown up the job, and I'm afraid. I'm afraid of the Undying Thing that is in Hal's Planting. I heard it that night. John Marsh saw it last night—they took me to see the body, and the face was awful; and I believe that one day it will come from Hal's Planting——"

"Yes," interrupted Guerdon, "I know. And at present I believe as much. Last night we laughed at the whole thing, and we shall live to laugh at it again, and be ashamed of ourselves for a couple of superstitious old women. I fancy that beliefs are affected by weather—there's thunder in the air."

"No," said Sir Edric, "my belief has come to stay."

"And what are you going to do?"

"I'm going to test it. On Monday I can begin to get to work, and then I'll blow up Hal's Planting with dynamite. After that we shan't need to believe—we shall *know*. And now let's dismiss the subject. Come down into the billiard room and have a game. Until Monday, I won't think of the thing again."

Long before dinner, Sir Edric's depression seemed to have completely vanished. At dinner he was boisterous and amused. Afterwards he told stories and was interesting.

★ ★ ★

It was late at night; the terrific storm that was raging outside had awoke Guerdon from sleep. Hopeless of getting to sleep again, he had arisen and dressed, and now sat in the window-seat watching the storm. He had never seen anything like it before; and every now and then the sky seemed to be torn across as if by hands of white fire. Suddenly he heard a tap at his door, and looked round. Sir Edric had already entered; he also had dressed. He spoke in a curious, subdued voice.

"I thought you wouldn't be able to sleep through this. Do you remember that I shut and fastened the dining-room window?"

"Yes, I remember it."

"Well, come in here."

Sir Edric led the way to his room, which was immediately over the dining-room. By leaning out of window they could see that the dining-room window was open wide.

"Burglar," said Guerdon meditatively.

"No," Sir Edric answered, still speaking in a hushed voice. "It is the Undying Thing—it has come for me."

He snatched up the candle, and made towards the staircase; Guerdon caught up the loaded revolver which always lay on the table beside Sir Edric's bed, and followed him. Both men ran down the staircase as though there were not another moment to lose. Sir Edric rushed at the dining-room door, opened it a little, and looked in. Then he turned to Guerdon, who was just behind him.

"Go back to your room," he said authoritatively.

"I won't,' said Guerdon. "Why? What is it?"

Suddenly the corners of Sir Edric's mouth shot outward into the hideous grin of terror.

"It's there! It's there!" he gasped.

"Then I come in with you."

"Go back!"

With a sudden movement, Sir Edric thrust Guerdon away from the door, and then, quick as light, darted in, and locked the door behind him.

Guerdon bent down and listened. He heard Sir Edric say in a firm voice, "Who are you? What are you?" Then followed a heavy, snorting breathing, a low, vibrating growl, an awful cry, a scuffle.

Then Guerdon flung himself at the door. He kicked at the lock, but it would not give way. At last he fired his revolver at it. Then he managed to force his way into the room. It was perfectly empty. Overhead he could hear footsteps; the noise had awakened the servants; they were standing tremulous on the upper landing.

Through the open window access to the garden was easy. Guerdon did not wait to get help; and in all probability none of the servants could have been persuaded to come with him. He climbed out alone and—as if by some blind impulse—started to run as hard as he could in the direction of Hal's Planting. He knew that Sir Edric would be found there.

But when he got within a hundred yards of the plantation, he stopped. There had been a great flash of lightning, and he saw that it had struck one of the trees. Flames darted about the plantation, as the dry bracken caught. Suddenly in the light of another flash he saw the whole of the trees fling their heads upwards; then came a deafening crash, and the ground slipped under him, and he was flung forward on his face. The plantation had collapsed, fallen through into the caves beneath it. Guerdon slowly regained his feet; he was surprised to find that he was unhurt. He walked on a few steps, and then fell again; this time he had fainted away.

How Will Distinguished People Spend Christmas?

The London "Evening News" reports as follows:—
[…]
"How do I propose to spend Christmas?" asks Mr. Harry Nicholls.

And then he supplies the answer:

"With my family," he replies. "There are four of us, and we're going to have such fun!

"We are going to have Sir Roger de Coverley, and a snapdragon, and a Christmas tree, and crackers, and 'Puss in the Corner,' and 'Hunt the Slipper,' and I am going to dress up as Old Father Christmas and give toys away; and we're going to have a servant's ball (when she's done washing up); and then we are going to tell ghost stories and be frightened to go to bed—at least, the other three will.

"I've bought a bottle of wassail, so I shall be all right."

Stockton Herald, South Durham and Cleveland Advertiser (Dec. 26, 1908): 5, col. 5.

Magister Monensis

The Siren

An Adventure in Manxland

The pen name "Magister Monensis" accompanied letters and news contributed to the Isle of Man Times *for over twenty years. His actual name was given in connection with it only once:* THOMAS GRINDLEY (1831-1919), *described as "school-master, Ballagarey House, Marown."*[1] *The Isle of Man is only about 1/6 the size of Long Island, thus his December 31, 1898 reading audience would have been intimately familiar with the roads and cliffs described in such painstaking detail. His emphasis on so much realism must have caused readers to wonder whether the story was a true one. The two hours of travel by horse trap northeast on the southern coast of the Isle of Man from Douglas through Onchan to Old Laxey was about double what it might have been in fair weather. Old Laxey to Ramsey by foot would take about three hours in good weather.*

PART I.

O NE WILD, STORMY NIGHT towards the close of the year 186–, the 25th of December it was, as I had good cause to remember, I was travelling along the north road from Douglas to Ramsey, in the Isle of Man. This road, as you know, keeps near to the sea throughout its entire course, in some places passing over the summits of the cliffs, which in this part of

---

1 "Local," *Isle of Man Times and General Advertiser* (June 16, 1877): 5, col. 4.

the Manx coast are from 300 to 500 feet high, and in others crossing the face of frightful precipices by means of galleries cut in the living rock. It is a singularly attractive road to travel over in the bright summer time, the views all along it, both of land and sea, being magnificent; and it is, naturally, an especial favourite with the thousands of tourists who make Douglas their headquarters during the visiting season; but in winter it is anything but a pleasant or even a safe road to be on in a dark, stormy night, such as that of which I am now speaking. At that time I was a young fellow of 28, just entering upon life, and I must say that at that time life was very pleasant to me, the past having had few real cares, and the future looking very bright and promising. But my story, gentlemen, is not a love tale, and so I will not trouble you with any account of my previous life, beyond saying that I had been learning farming with Mr. K., a highly successful farmer in the neighbourhood of Ramsey, and that I had, the preceding November, taken a small, but pleasantly situated estate a few miles south of that town, taking home to it as my wife the only daughter of Mr. K., whose affections I had been fortunate enough to win while residing in her father's house. A few weeks after our marriage, urgent family business obliged me to leave home and cross over to England—in short, I may as well say that a few days before Christmas I received a telegram from my mother saying that my father had met with a serious accident, and asking me to go at once to her help. I was very unwilling, as you may be sure, to leave home just then, but duty called me away, and hastily packing a few necessaries into my travelling bag, I bade my wife good-bye, and, accompanied by Robbie, our "serving man," to bring the trap home again, I drove off to catch the early boat from Douglas.

I found my father much better than I had expected from the character of my mother's telegram, but, notwithstanding this, and my very natural wish to get back again, I was unable to leave the old people for a day or two. When I ventured to express my wish to return home at once, the old gentleman said plaintively that I might never spend another Christmas with them, and that it would be altogether too bad of me to run away like that, leaving him laid up by the heels; and so, as I said, it was the 26th of December before I found myself able to get away. From a rather curious feeling, which, perhaps, some of you, gentlemen, may understand, I did not telegraph home to tell my wife of my return. I wanted to drop in upon her unexpectedly, and thus give my home-coming the additional charm of suddenness; and so, when I reached Douglas, after a long and tedious voyage, owing to the thick fog bank we had been steaming through for a greater part of the way, I found no one waiting for me on the pier. This, however, did not trouble me much, as I had not expected anybody; and, giving my bag to a porter, I followed him to the Royal—my usual hotel in those days when in Douglas, where I was welcomed with all his customary warmth by the genial host, my old friend, Mr. L., and shown to my room. After a hasty dinner, to which, however, the appetite given me by my long sea voyage enabled me to do full justice, I left instructions for a horse and trap to be got ready in a couple of hours, and went into the town to attend to some business matters and to make a few purchases for my wife. Thus, before I was ready to start, the short winter's day had passed away, and the darkness of a December night had closed in. This, with the road I have described before me, was not pleasant; but, to make matters still more unpleasant, the weather had changed considerably for the worse. The early part of the day had been almost perfectly calm, with a thick, damp fog resting heavily upon land and sea; but, as the night closed in, the wind, as often happens with us in the Isle of Man at this time of the year, had rapidly risen, and veering round to the north-west, now blew in heavy, fitful gusts, bringing with it blinding drifts of rain and sleet. Altogether the prospect before me, as I got into my trap at the door of the hotel, was anything but a cheerful one; and, but for an overpowering longing to get home, I would have yielded to my friend L.'s persuasions, and accepted his hospitality for the night. But I was strong and hardy, and accustomed to be out in all weathers; and, moreover, I was thoroughly acquainted with the road before me; so steadily resisting his invitation, I settled myself in the seat and started off at a trot over the rough, uneven pavement of the quaint old market-place of Douglas. For some distance my road lay through the narrow, winding streets of the old town, which were sheltered by their narrowness and the great height of their buildings as well as by the high grounds behind up which the new town was then beginning to creep; but presently, leaving the town with its lights, and its comparative warmth behind me, I passed out into the storm and the darkness beyond. After leaving the town, the north road follows the line of the shore for more than a mile, being separated from it in fact only by a low wall; while, to the left, it is sheltered towards the north and west by a succession of precipitous, wooded cliffs of great height which, while adding greatly to the beauty of the bay of Douglas, mark its former coastline. Thus, I was still only partially exposed to the violence of the storm, though my progress was rendered much more difficult and disagreeable than it had been while passing through the town. The fog had now become so thick that it was impossible to distinguish any object a few yards distant, and the light from the lamps carried by my trap scarcely reached the horse's head, or the wall which ran along the side of the road. Overhead the moon, now near the full, was obscured by heavy clouds, and its light, unable to penetrate the mist, lit it up with a strange, spectral twilight, the effect of which was heightened by the occasional appearance of the broad disc of the moon itself through a momentary opening of the drifting clouds, filling the misty air with a brief flood of pale, weird light. At intervals I passed groups of houses whose unshuttered windows threw a dim radiance around, casting broad reflections across the muddy road and over the white-crested breakers as they rolled in heavily over the sands and broken rocks of the beach. About two miles from the town the road suddenly leaves the shore, and climb-

ing by a steep ascent to the summit of the cliffs, passes behind
the great headland of Bank's Howe, which forms the northern
horn of Douglas bay into the heart of a wild and exposed tract
of country. To the left, the land rises in long, rolling swells,
broken by deep, winding glens, into the mountains of the
interior; while, to the right, it slopes gradually to the coast,
ending abruptly in a series of tremendous precipices from 300
to 500 feet in height. This district, which extends along the
entire eastern coast between Douglas and Ramsey, and is
broken about its centre by the lovely glen of Laxey, inhabited
by a numerous mining population, employed in the prosperous lead mines of the district, elsewhere it is sparsely occupied
by a hardy race of mountaineers, following agricultural
employments, and retaining more than is usual even among
Celtic races of the character and habits of their forefathers.
Their little whitewashed cottages, with their old-fashioned
thatched roofs, and the more comfortable farmsteads of the
small landed proprietors, sheltered on the weather side by
thick groves of trees, are scattered thinly over the bare uplands,
or lie hidden in the deep glens which intersect them, glistening
in the warm summer sunlight or sending out through their
curtainless windows twinkling starlike rays of light into the
black darkness of the wintry night. To the wandering tourist,
in the genial summer months, and to the enthusiastic gatherer
of decaying folk-lore, the district, with its wonderful variety
of scenery, and its primitive population with their old-world
habits and ideas, is a rich store-house of interest and information; but I now found it anything but pleasant or attractive.
Passing through the suburban village of Onchan, pictur-
esquely situated in a depression behind the great headland of
Bank's Howe, I entered upon this exposed district, and at once
began to realise the difficulties and miseries of the journey
before me. The storm, now at its height, struck me full in the
face, the frozen rain stinging like needles and penetrating my
clothing to the skin in spite of all my wraps, chilling me to the
very bone; and so fierce were the squalls as they swept shriek-

ing and howling down the mountain sides, and so overpowering the sleety drifts they brought with them that my horse, though a strongly-built, sturdy animal, accustomed to Manx roads in all weathers, was unable to face them, and I was obliged at times to pull up under the shelter of the tall earthen bank which fenced the road from the country beyond, and wait until a lull came. The cold, too, in this exposed part was intense, and the country side, thickly covered with the unmelted sleet, glimmered ghostly white in the diffused light of the obscured moon. The road itself, running for some distance past the village between high, bush-covered banks, lay in deep darkness which the feeble light of the lamps in front of my trap failed to penetrate beyond a few feet; and, as my sturdy nag slowly and haltingly plodded along carefully picking its way in the darkness, I sat crouched up in my wet wraps, shivering at their ice-cold touch. Altogether, my position was a very miserable one, and the prospect before me of a ten-mile drive, under such circumstances, was anything but cheering. But I did not lose heart; and, forcing my way through the storm, I endeavoured to draw off my attention from the discomforts of the situation by picturing to myself the light shining through my own window, and behind its closely drawn curtains the bright, cosy room and the young wife sitting by its glowing hearth.

I am not, however, going to weary you with any further account of my dreary, comfortless journey, for I am anxious to get to the strange event which so unexpectedly terminated it, and which, I know, you are impatient to come to. So I will merely say that, after some two hours' hard fighting with the storm, I reached the village of Old Laxey, thoroughly worn out and drenched to the skin; and worse still, under the circumstances, with my horse dead beaten with the efforts it had made, and unable to go any further. The latter was a very serious matter to me. The night was fast wearing on, and I had still five or six miles of a difficult and exposed road before me; and, as I found, there was not another horse procurable in the

village. But, having come so far, I was not going to give in;
but, tired as I was, I determined to walk the rest of the way.
So, leaving the exhausted animal in charge of the landlord
of the village inn, and borrowing a lantern, I continued my
journey on foot up the steep road leading from the glen to the
hilly country to the north. One circumstance, however, was
now in my favour, and I felt much encouraged by it. A change
for the better had taken place in the character of the weather.
The gale had, fortunately, turned out to be as short-lived as it
had been fierce; and before I had left the high grounds above
Laxey bay to descend into the village it had begun to subside;
and now, as I left the shelter of the deep glen, and began to
climb the northern hills, I was glad to find that the wind had
almost died out, and that the rain had ceased. The mist, however, so far from dispersing, seemed to have become denser,
and hung so heavily upon every object that, in spite of the
feeble moonlight, it was impossible to distinguish anything
a yard or two in advance. This was very awkward for me as
it prevented my taking full advantage of the cessation of the
gale, and rendered my journey still both toilsome and dangerous. But I encouraged myself with the knowledge that I was
now approaching home, and that soon the light in the window
of my own dwelling would shine before me; and I plodded
steadily on. The road, if such it could be called, up which I was
now slowly and laboriously climbing, was one of those old
horse-tracks which still remain in use in a few out-of-the-way
parts of the country, though they are too narrow and too steep
for wheeled vehicles. A good modern road branched off to the
left, and ascended the hill at a much lower pitch; but, as it was
a longer road, and I was now on foot, I struck up the more
difficult because shorter road. The darkness in this narrow
lane, bordered as it was by high earthen banks overgrown
with gorse and thorn bushes mixed with ferns and tall grass,
was so great that my lantern only cast a feeble glimmer over a
space a yard or two across, in the midst of which I cautiously
moved, endeavouring to pick my way up the steep, stony

road. My progress was, of course, both slow and laborious. One moment I would step upon a loose stone which, turning under my foot, would send me staggering among the dripping bushes by the side of the road; the next moment I would step with a sudden splash into a stream of water which ran down the middle of the undrained road, but still I kept on, and at length reached the top of the road where it joins the broader highway; and, wearied with my fatiguing climb, I sat down to rest on a large granite boulder which stood on a grassy space where the two roads met.

As I thus sat, my attention was suddenly arrested by a faint sound, something between a sob and a moan, coming apparently out of the darkness beyond the road. Startled by the sound, I lifted my head and gazed round inquiringly. Nothing appeared, however, and I was beginning to think that I must have been mistaken, when again the same strange sound came, this time more plainly and distinctly, right out of the darkness in front of where I was sitting—a low, wailing cry like the moaning of a woman in deep distress. As the fearful wail sounded in my horror-struck ears I instinctively rose from my seat, and going to the side of the road, with some difficulty climbed to the top of the gorsey bank which formed the boundary between the road and the unenclosed country between it and the cliffs. Lifting my lantern high above my head, I peered anxiously into the misty darkness and listened intently. As far as its feeble rays extended, nothing was visible but a wilderness of neglected grass-land dotted with clumps of gorse and withered ferns dripping with heavy rain-drops, and the thick, steaming mist hanging like a pall upon every object. The storm had now blown itself out, and not a sound could be heard; even the ordinary sounds of the night were deadened by the all-pervading fog, and everything was silent as the grave.

I stood thus upon the top of the bank as it seemed to me for a long time without a sound disturbing the stillness of the scene; but, at length I began to feel the silence oppressive, and, saying to myself that the sounds which I had heard, if real, were only the cries of some wild creature disturbed in its lair, and distorted by the fog or by my own excited fancy, I turned to descend the bank and resume my journey, when a third time the same terrible sound rose up on the damp night air— unmistakably the sound of a woman's voice, so wailing, and full of the direst grief that I stood for a moment awe-struck. But as the frightful cry issued out of the darkness, filling the echoing air with its quivering agony, I felt my heart give a wild leap of sympathetic feeling, and, saying to myself, it is some poor woman who has wandered out of her way and is calling for help, I turned, and without a moment's hesitation descended the bank into the waste beyond and began eagerly to explore the ground and the bushes around in search of the lost creature who had uttered such bitter cries. Step by step I carefully examined every ferny hollow and dripping bush in the direction from which the sounds had seemed to come; but, though I went some distance into the waste, I found nothing, nor did I again hear the cry which had so alarmed me. Everything was quiet, and no living thing showed itself but a few sleepy birds disturbed in their nests, and a startled hare which ran across my path out of a clump of ferns. At length, utterly confounded by the strangeness of the occurrence, and the mystery which surrounded it, unable to convince myself that the sounds I had heard were not the cries of some poor creature in terrible distress, and yet unable, in spite of the most careful search, to discover any traces of the person who had uttered them, I paused in my search, out of sheer helplessness, and again stood still to listen. But I could hear no sound in any direction; and, at last, I determined to give up so vain a quest and turn back towards the highroad.

Having come to this resolution, I was turning away to retrace my steps when once more the same sound thrilled on my startled ear—again the cry of a woman in bitter distress, but fainter and lower than before, as if she was exhausted by long-continued suffering. The sound instantly stayed my departing steps; and, as I stood with the woeful cry ringing in my ears, a strange feeling, half of vague terror, at some dimly-felt presence, from which my whole nature shrank in alarm, and half of instinctive sympathy with the suffering which that cry revealed, took possession of me, and for the moment completely unmanned me. My limbs shook as with palsy, my hair stiffened with horror, and a cold shiver ran down my spine; but forcibly shaking off the "cowardly" feeling, as I indignantly called it, I once more turned back and strode rapidly and unhesitatingly through the wet bushes and tangled grass for thirty or forty yards to the place from whence the sounds seemed to come. Then I lifted my lantern and again looked searchingly round for the creature I had expected to find. But, as before, nothing was to be seen! Not a sound broke the stillness of the damp, night-air; nothing was visible but the rain-laden bushes which encumbered the wilderness around! Utterly confounded, and thinking that I had perhaps been deceived as to the distance of the sounds by the effects of the fog, I went a few steps further, carefully examining every bush and hollow, but nothing rewarded my search; and at last, bewildered and perplexed by the strangeness of the thing, I once more stopped to think what I should do.

As I did so, other thoughts and fears began to assail me. I began to realise the danger of my own position on such a night in the midst of such a dangerous wilderness—a circumstance which, in my excitement, had hitherto not troubled me. The district into which I had been thus lured was an extensive tract of waste land lying chiefly between the highroad and the sea. In a few places, where the land was of exceptional value, some slight attempts had been made to turn it to profit; but, gen-erally, it had been left uncultivated and uncared for, and was, as I have said, a mere tract of waste land covered with tangled grass and huge bushes of gorse and heather. Toward the sea it terminated in a series of tremendous precipices, from three hundred to four hundred feet high, which, from the frequency of fatal accidents occurring among them, had obtained an ominous reputation throughout the surrounding country and caused the neighbourhood to be carefully avoided after sunset. At intervals its surface is crossed by deep ravines, whose precipitous banks are almost as dangerous in the darkness as the terrible cliffs themselves. Down these ravines small streams from the neighbouring uplands and undrained marshes find their way to the sea; their waters, especially when swollen by the winter rains, forming beautiful cascades as they leap from crag to crag to the rocks below. As this barren district lay at no great distance from my own home, I was, of course, well acquainted with its peculiar beauties, having frequently wandered over it in search of game, and scaled its cliffs for the eggs and the young of the sea birds which haunted them in myriads, and in the daylight I could easily have found my way across it in any direction. But to attempt to traverse it in the darkness of the night, and especially of such a night as this, was an undertaking so surrounded with danger that my heart failed me at the thought of it. A single incautious step might send me headlong over the cliffs or into one of the numerous ravines, to be found, as so many others had been, a mangled and lifeless corpse.

As I thus realised the dangers which beset me, the numerous stories which I had heard on the countryside of men missing from their homes, and their bodies being occasionally found dashed to pieces on the rocks at the foot of the cliffs, came back to my memory with terrible significance; and, somehow, I could not help connecting them with my own case. There was something so strange and weird in the sounds which had led me deeper and deeper into the wilderness. They were so irresistible in their woeful appeal that no heart, not stone, could hesitate to follow them; apparently so near that a few steps would bring me to the spot, I had followed them for a considerable distance, and yet, though I had carefully searched every likely place of concealment, I had found nothing; heard only at intervals, and that too when I seemed to be on the point of abandoning the search, as if some invisible presence was watching me, and was thus luring me on to my destruction. As these thoughts and fears flashed across my mind, a deadly terror took possession of me, and I bitterly repented my rashness in thus venturing so far and so heedlessly into this dangerous district. The improbability, too, of any woman being in such a place at such a time now strongly forced itself upon me, still further weakening my first belief that the sounds which had so led me astray were the cries of a woman in distress; and as I reached this point in my cogitations, I heartily wished myself safe out of the trap I had run into.

Some time had passed while I had been occupied in this way, and nothing further had occurred to attract my attention. A perfect stillness reigned around, and nothing could be seen beyond the narrow patch of light in which I stood but the heavy steaming mist feebly permeated by the diffused rays of the clouded moon. Before turning away, however, I determined to make one last effort, and, raising my voice to its highest pitch, I called out—"Is anyone here?" I repeated this cry several times, but with no effect; and then, convinced of my error, I turned and began to retrace my steps to the highroad to continue my journey.

Thoroughly alive now to the perils of my position, I moved forward slowly and cautiously, my lantern held out at arm's length before me, and anxiously scrutinising every step I took. In this way I had taken about twenty steps, when suddenly I started back in terror—right in front the ground sank sheer away, and there yawned a dark and terrible abyss before me, whose bottom and further edge were alike invisible. Another step and I should have fallen headlong into it! Shuddering with irrepressible horror, I sank down upon the ground, and covering my face with my trembling hands endeavoured to regain my composure. After a time I had sufficiently recovered to renew my attempt to get back to the road, though my nerves had received a severe shock from the frightful danger I had so narrowly escaped. But first, lying down on the grass, I crawled to the edge of the gulf, and, leaning forward, peered eagerly into its misty depths. Nothing but an abrupt rocky descent studded with a few stunted bushes met my straining eyes; but borne upward on the cold, damp air there came from below the faint sound of water dashing against broken rocks. I was either on the top of the cliffs or on the verge of one of the ravines which cross this desolate district—which, I knew not. Drawing cautiously back from the edge of the precipice, I fervently thanked God for my providential deliverance; and then, carefully retracing my steps, I tried anew to find a way of escape. Step by step, keenly scanning every inch of the ground before me, I made my way, as I thought, from the cliffs, but I had not gone many yards when again a wide chasm barred my progress, and turned me back. Still hopeful, however, I turned into a new direction, and struggled on for a few yards, but only to find myself once more confronted by an open gulf, and at last the truth forced itself upon me that I was lost—lost in this frightful wilderness! As I slowly realised this terrible fact, my resolution entirely forsook me, and, in an agony of despair, I flung myself down upon the wet grass, and burying my face in my hands, tried desperately to steady my disordered nerves and calm my excited feelings. After a time the first shock of the discovery passed away, and I gradually grew calmer, and able once more to consider my position with some degree of coherency. I was lost in this wild district, surrounded by dangers of the most frightful kind from which the darkness of the night prevented my escape. Far away from any dwelling, I could hope for no help, for there was no one to hear my cries for help. Within a stone's-throw were the awful precipices from which I had tried in vain to escape, and down which a single incautious step would cast me headlong. My sole dependence was upon my lantern, for with its aid I might even yet find my way out of the terrible labyrinth, while without its help I dared not move a step in any direction. As I thus reviewed my situation my chances of escape seemed desperate indeed; but with the sense of my danger there came also the remembrance of One who had said "Call upon me in the day of trouble, and

I will deliver thee," and, bowing my head, I uttered a brief but fervent prayer for help and deliverance in this extremity. Somewhat calmed and reassured I sat quietly for a little while pondering on my next move and thinking with regretful feelings of the home and the dear one in it whom I might never again see; but at length I was forced to renewed action by a chilly numbness creeping over me, arising probably from my damp clothes and the re-action from the terrible excitement I had passed through. Rising from the ground therefore I tried once more to find my way to the road. Slowly, and with lifted light, I moved away in a new direction, anxiously searching the ground every step I took. I had proceeded a few steps in safety, and was beginning to hope that I had at last found the right direction, and was leaving the frightful precipices behind me, when suddenly the awful cry which I had so often heard before that dreadful night rose quivering on the misty night air apparently not more than a yard or two before me. Startled by the suddenness of the sound and its seeming nearness I instinctively stopped and stood staring vacantly into the darkness from whence it seemed to come. As I thus stood, scarcely conscious of what I was doing, the cry came again, louder and shriller, the long-drawn breath at last giving place to a burst of bitter weeping. For a moment longer I stood horror-stricken, and then, excited beyond control, and forgetting everything else, I sprang eagerly forward, determined to solve the mystery of the night. One step fell on the solid ground, the next fell on empty space, and, with a wild cry, I fell headlong down the abyss! At that moment there flashed towards me out of the misty darkness a woman's face, white and beautiful, but horribly distorted by a grin of devilish triumph, and, as it glared into my starting eyeballs, there issued from its parted lips a shrill burst of fiendish laughter. One moment the evil eyes of the frightful appearance glared into mine while its mocking laughter rang through my brain, the next there came a violent shock, and I saw and felt no more.

PART II.

When consciousness returned, the faint, grey light of a winter day was beginning to dawn in the eastern sky. The fog had disappeared and the morning air was calm and cold. For some time after this I must have lain in a half-conscious condition; and I believe that I thought I was at home, for I seem to have a remembrance of talking to my wife about some family matters which were then troubling us. But gradually my senses became clearer, and memory began again to do its work; and at last, with a sudden revelation, the events of the past night flashed before me, down to their latest incident. Again I seemed to be wandering through the trackless wild, lured onward by the treacherous cries of the terrible creature that infested it; and, again, I was falling headlong down the precipice, with the triumphant eyes of the horrible appearance burning into my very soul, and its shrill, mocking laughter ringing through my burning brain—and, too weak to bear the renewed strain, my senses again forsook me.

When I once more revived, the sun was slowly rising in a crimson glow behind the Cumbrian Mountains, tipping with its rosy light their snow-laden peaks, and glancing upon the wavelets of the intervening sea, which heaved and flashed in its bright beams. For a few moments I remained perfectly still and passive, gazing quietly across the sea at the beautiful sun-rising, which, somehow, seemed to exert a soothing influence over me. But gradually memory again resumed its sway; and, with an irrepressible shudder, I buried my face in my hands to shut out the frightful visions it conjured up. After a time this feeling of abhorrent terror passed away, and a feeling of surprise at being alive—which, strange to say, I had not felt before, took its place; and I lifted my head to learn how it was that I was not lying a broken and disfigured corpse on the rocks at the foot of the cliff. A single glance showed me how my life had been saved. I was lying, I found, upon a narrow ledge of rock, about sixteen or eighteen inches broad; which, crossing the face of the precipice, gradually sloped upward to the top of the cliff, which appeared to be about thirty feet above the place where I was lying. These ledges are frequently found among the slaty rocks which form the greater part of the Manx coast-line, and are the result of the gradual waste of the rock, whose superficial layers, becoming loosened by the action of the frost upon the water lodged in their crevices, break off at the joints, and thus form these ledges which cross the face of the cliffs, at all heights and at all angles. In course of time, a thin layer of soil accumulates upon them, and the seeds of grass, ferns, sea-pinks, and other cliff-loving plants, and even of various bushes and trees, carried by the wind, or by the birds which build their nests in these cliffs, become lodged in their cracks and crevices, and germinating, cover them, in favourable spots, with a luxurious growth of vegetation. In some cases large bushes and trees, with their roots buried deep in the rock for support, and their trunks curiously gnarled and twisted by their efforts to reach the sunshine, may be found growing on the face of the steepest of these precipices.

It was, as I have said, upon one of these ledges that I found myself lying. When falling, I had fortunately—or rather, let me reverentially say, providentially—fallen upon one of these ledges at a point where a large thorn bush grew out of the face of the cliff, and had become wedged between the bush itself and the rock out of which it grew, by the force of my fall. To this circumstance I owed my safety. Had I fallen upon any other part of the ledge, which was little more than a foot broad, it would only have broken my descent for a moment. My senseless body would have rebounded off it again and been dashed to pieces on the rocks below. As it was, though the violence of my fall must have severely tested the hold of the bush upon the rock, it had withstood the shock, and held me safely through the night. As I slowly realised these facts, the extraordinary character of my preservation became clearer and clearer to me. I could not, from my position behind the bush, see downward to the foot of the cliff, but I could hear the murmurous sound of the waves as they surged against the rocks hundreds of feet below; and as I listened to the sound rising and falling in rhythmic succession, and thought of the merciful providence which had so wonderfully preserved me from such a frightful death, I breathed a fervent thanksgiving to Him who had so strangely watched over me, and asked His help in my efforts to free myself from the dangers which still surrounded me.

Meantime, while I had thus been considering my situation, the day had been steadily advancing, and the sun was now rising high in the heavens, and pouring its unclouded rays upon the rock about me, refreshing with its grateful warmth my chilled and exhausted body, and awakening within me new desires and hopes of escape. As I have said, I was lying wedged in between the smooth face of the cliff and a large thorn bush, and that the ledge upon which this bush was growing sloped gradually upward, apparently to the top of the cliff. To traverse this narrow, shelving track, though dangerous at all times, since a single slip of the foot would send the unfortunate climber headlong down the precipice, was still practicable; and I had, myself, in fact, often thus scaled these very cliffs in my expeditions after sea birds' eggs. Thus, I did not, by any means, consider my situation as hopeless. It was surrounded on all sides with danger, and the slightest error might result in certain destruction; but I had been so wonderfully preserved that I felt encouraged to believe that I should ultimately escape with my life.

The first thing to do, however, was to free myself from the cramped and painful position between the cliff and the bush, and, if possible, to take off my heavy boots so that I might be able to climb the shelving path with greater ease and security. I was lying on a thick growth of grass, mixed with tufts of springy sea-pinks, partly upon my right side and partly upon my back, with my right leg doubled in under me. My arms were quite free, but the rest of my body, and especially the lower

part of it, was tightly held between the rock and the stump of
the bush. I now cautiously set to work to release myself from
this painful position, and at length so far succeeded as to draw
my body closer to the rock and turn on my side. But, in so
doing, the attempt to move my right leg from its cramped position caused me such exquisite pain that I almost fainted again,
and I was obliged to give up the attempt. Agonised by the
efforts I had made, I lay back against the rocky wall with a deep
groan. In a few minutes, however, I had sufficiently recovered
to remember that, when leaving Douglas the night before, I
had placed a small travelling flask of brandy in an inner pocket
of my coat, and having with some difficulty got at it, I drank
a few drops of the potent spirit, and again lay back to recover
myself, and to consider my situation from its new point of
view. My case, it now appeared, was far more desperate than I
had thought. Not only was I seriously bruised by my frightful
fall from the cliff, but my leg was either badly broken, or so
greatly injured that the slightest movement caused me intolerable pain. Thus, my hope of deliverance, by making my way up
the rocky ledge to the top of the cliff, was now futile, and must
be given up. What was to be done now? From the side of the
land there seemed to be no hope of escape, for the place where
I lay so helpless was far removed from any inhabited spot, and
no one might come that way for days, or even weeks, and in the
meantime I should perish of cold and hunger. All I could do
was to wait as patiently as possible, and endeavour to attract the
notice of any passing vessel. Coasting vessels frequently sailed
by, close in with the land; and small boats out fishing, were
cruising about every fine day. Thus I hoped that I should be
able to make myself seen before my powers of endurance failed
me. This seemed all that was left for me to do; and, nerving
myself to the effort, I painfully moved myself into a position
from which I could see downward to the foot of the rocks, and
where my head and the upper part of my body would be visible
from below. Then, overcome by the exertion, and dizzy with
the pain it caused, I leaned back once more and waited.

The sun was now fast approaching the meridian, and a light breeze had sprung up from the north-east, from which the bush in front only partially sheltered me. My position now became increasingly trying. In addition to the pain which I suffered from a number of severe bruises, which I had received when falling, and especially from my injured leg, which now throbbed and burned with a gnawing agony which at times seemed almost unbearable, the pangs of hunger now began to make themselves felt. These, however, I was able to satisfy for the time with some sandwiches which I had, fortunately, placed in my pocket before starting; and thus occupied, I leaned back in as easy a position as I could assume, and waited with what patience I could for help.

I think many hours must have thus passed away. I know that they seemed ages to me. My condition became increasingly painful and trying. The sun beat upon my uncovered head, and I grew parched with thirst and fevered with pain; but as the hours wore slowly on, the sun passed round behind the high cliffs, leaving me in a cool shade infinitely grateful to my anguished body and my fevered brain. Far out at sea were the sunlit sails of several passing ships, and close in with the Cumberland coast was the dark trail of a steamer making its way southward; but they were all too far off to see me. The screaming sea-gulls flew in wide circles above my head, or perching upon the craggy rocks sat and watched me; and when, half-terrified at their persistence, I waved my arms and shouted at them, they would lazily flap their great wings, and with shrill cries soar away, only, however, to return and settle again on some point near me, to renew their expectant watch. Thus the hours slowly passed, and at length the sunlight began to disappear from the sea, and the darkness of the coming night to settle down like a shadow over the eastern sky.

And now a fresh horror began to take possession of me. While the bright sun shone, and the light of day lit up land and sea, the terrors of the past night had affected me much as a frightful dream weighs upon us in our waking hours; but, with the approach of night, an awful dread of the darkness settled down upon me; a dread lest the evil creature, whose wiles had lured me on to my destruction, should come again, and complete its narrowly-missed purpose. I cannot make you understand what I suffered from this new terror; how it gradually grew upon me as the winter twilight closed in, how my mind, weakened with a long-borne pain and hunger, became fevered with the haunting dread. All other hopes and fears seemed to be swallowed up in this overpowering horror; and so wild and excited did I, at last, become, that I believe, if I had had to spend another night upon that lone, spirit-haunted rock, I should really have gone mad with the terror, and flung myself over the precipice in my madness. But I was mercifully spared that last depth of suffering. He who had once and again so wonderfully preserved me before, again interposed for my deliverance.

I was lying back against the rock behind me, partly sheltered by the bush from the wind which blew coldly across the sea; my eyes were closed in the vain effort to shut out the dread of the fast-approaching darkness, and I think my mind must have been wandering a little, for I seem to remember talking to some one—my wife, I suppose, about home matters—when suddenly I was startled out of my brooding terror, by the sound of voices below me. Roused and excited by the sounds so long and so anxiously waited for, yet more than half fearing that they existed only in my own half-crazed brain, I opened my eyes, and, sitting up, eagerly listened. Again the sound of voices rose up from the sea—the sound of men talking and laughing, mingled with the noise of oars in the water; and never were any sounds more welcome to a human being than were those to me. They meant safety and deliverance to me— deliverance from the anguish I was suffering; deliverance from the horrible death which had stared me in the face.

"Thank God!" I cried, out of the fulness of my heart. Clinging to the bush I leaned over the edge of the rock, and looked eagerly down to the foot of the precipice; and, oh, joy!

there, at the very foot of the cliff—what a fearful depth downward it seemed!—a small fishing boat containing two men was
slowly making its way in the direction of Laxey. Now, indeed,
had come that opportunity of escape, for which I had been so
long waiting, and the hope of which I had almost given up in
despair. Almost forgetting the danger of my position in my
excitement, I put my hands to my mouth, and exerting all my
remaining strength, I called out, "Boat ahoy! boat ahoy!" The
men had heard my call, for they instantly stopped rowing,
and looked around to see who hailed them. Seeing no other
boat within hailing distance they next looked up at the cliffs;
but in the gathering dusk they failed to see me—as well they
might, for I was nearly 300 feet above them. Seeing no one,
they evidently thought they had mistaken the cry of a sea-bird
for the hail of a man, and took to their oars again. Fearing
lest they should get beyond the reach of my voice before they
discovered me, I hailed them again with the full strength of
my lungs; and, as they looked upwards towards the place from
which the call seemed to come, I leaned still further over the
verge of my ledge, and waving my handkerchief to attract
their attention, I again called out with all my might. This time
they plainly saw me, and one of them shouted in reply, "Ahoy
there! what is the matter?"

"I have fallen over the cliff, and have been lying here all day,
badly hurt. For God's sake get some help, and take me home!"

"Aye, aye! We'll not be long. Keep your heart up, and
we'll soon have you out of that!" came back in reply, as the
men pulled rapidly away, leaving me in a state of excitement
impossible to describe. I watched the boat with straining eyes
until it disappeared round the bluff shoulder of Laxey Head;
and not until the last glimmer of its white trail had died out
in the grey swell of the sea did I draw back from the verge of
the cliff. Then, utterly exhausted with my exertions, and the
excitement I had gone through, I sank down against the rock
to wait for this coming help.

How long that help seemed to be in coming! What could

be hindering the men to make them so long? Long before they could have left the village I was listening for the sound of their approaching voices, full of nervous expectation, and blaming them in my heart for loitering on the way. In this condition I could do nothing but count the moments and listen. The slightest sound—the falling of a loosened stone down the precipice, the cry of a bird settling itself for the night, the sighing of the wind among the bushes and crevices of the cliff—caused me to start in wild excitement and cry out for help. But, as the minutes passed on, this fever-fit gradually exhausted itself, leaving me weaker and more helpless than before; and, at length, in a half-fainting condition, I lay still, feebly interested in watching the changes of the approaching night. Far away, the eastern sky was already growing dark, and a deep purple haze had settled upon the mountains, through which their white snow-capped summits shone with a ghostly glare. Rising slowly from behind them the broad disk of the moon was beginning to show itself, while nearer, the cold, grey sea heaved and rolled in the dying light, and surged with a mournful, monotonous sound, against the rock-bound coast. Occasionally the silence of the scene was disturbed by the homeward flight of a belated sea-bird, which, after circling for a moment in the darkening air, would sink to its nest with a shrill scream. Gradually even these sounds ceased, and a heavy stillness settled upon the scene, which, as the time passed wearily on, became more and more oppressive. As the sun sank lower and still lower behind, the shadows of the cliffs grew steadily deeper and broader; while, in the opposite sky, the moon rose higher, pouring upon the heaving sea and rugged coast a broadening trail of silvery light. My greatest terror had been of the darkness, and as I lay watching the moonlight grow over land and sea, I felt strangely soothed. My horror of the night seemed to have fled before the mild radiance of the glorious moon; and, at last, I lay quiet in spirit and in full possession of my mental powers, waiting patiently the coming of my deliverers.

At last, after what seemed an age of expectant waiting, I heard the voices of several men on the top of the cliffs, close to where I was lying, and almost immediately a voice called out loudly, "Where are you? where are you?"

Forgetting my weakness and my disabled condition in the excitement of the moment, I started up, and called back as loudly as I could—"I'm here! on a ledge of rock here!" And as I shouted I looked eagerly upward in the direction of the voices. Directed by my shouts, the voices came nearer, and at last I saw the head and shoulders of a man leaning over the edge of the precipice, and by the aid of a lantern looking downward. As soon as I saw the welcome appearance, I shouted again, "I'm here! here!" and the better to attract his notice I excitedly waved my handkerchief.

"I see him!" at last I heard the man say to his companions above, "he is down there, lying on a rock beside a bush!" and then the head disappeared, and I heard a murmur of voices on the cliff above. In a few minutes the man's head again appeared over the top of the cliff, and when he saw that I was watching him, he called out: "Are you much hurt? Can you stand?"

"I cannot move," I replied; "my leg is broken, and I am badly hurt in other ways. For God's sake get me out of this!"

"Aye, aye," came back in reply, and again the head disappeared. Once more there was a murmur of voices above, followed by a brief silence; and then before I had time to conjecture what it meant, the form of a man appeared, stepping cautiously over the top of the cliff on to the rocky ledge which shelved down to where I was lying helpless. A lantern was fastened to his belt in such a way as to throw a glare of light upon the narrow uneven path which sloped down across the face of the cliff; and as he carefully descended it, I saw he had also a stout rope securely fastened round his body, under his arms, the other end of which was held by several other men upon the top of the cliff, whose heads I could see projected over the edge of the precipice anxiously watching their comrade's progress. I also noticed that the man who was thus adventurously coming to my help held the end of a second rope in his hand, the other end of which was also firmly secured on the top of the cliff. Step by step, slowly and cautiously the man made his way down the rugged and uneven ledge, keenly measuring each step before it was taken, and with the skill of an old cragsman, clinging with his body closely to the face of the rock. And well might he thus carefully watch his footsteps! Dangerous in the broad light of day, the path was doubly dangerous now, amid the lights and shadows of the uncertain moonlight; and in thus venturing upon this errand of mercy he was literally taking his life in his hand. Yet he faltered not. In the hope of saving the life of a stranger he was descending the face of a perpendicular precipice three hundred feet above the sea along a shallow uneven ledge of rock barely a foot wide! Deeds of valour done on the field of battle amid the heat and excitement of the conflict are rewarded with the applause and the honours of a grateful country; but what are such to heroic acts like this, done under the cloud of night, without thought of praise or reward as an act of Christian help from one man to another? Scarcely daring to breathe I watched his progress as he came slowly towards me. Once his foot slipped on a loose block lying on the path; and as he stepped backward, I uttered a cry of horror, and buried my face in my hands to shut out the sight of my would-be deliverer's destruction, for I thought he was gone. But, when he lost his footing, he instinctively crouched more closely to the cliff, and thus saved himself from falling—the stone upon which his foot had slipped falling down the precipice with a thunderous clang. After a moment's pause to recover himself, he moved onward again; and, at last, reached the place where I was lying, in safety. Panting with excitement, and unable to articulate a syllable from the very excess of my emotions, I grasped his offered hand as he reached me, and then my strength gave way and I fainted again.

When I recovered consciousness I was lying upon the top of the cliff, surrounded by a number of men, one of whom was bathing my head and face with cold water. Looking feebly around, and slowly realising that I was at last saved from the frightful death which had so long threatened me, a thrill of gratitude passed through my whole being; then all my strength seemed to fail me, and murmuring "Thank God!" my eyes again closed, and I fell again into a half-conscious condition. After a little while, I was partially roused from this state by a slight commotion among those standing around me, and then someone, who I afterwards learned was the village doctor, who had been roused by the report of my condition, and had followed the villagers to the cliffs, came up to me, and having felt my pulse for a moment, held something to my lips, and in gentle, yet firm, tones, told me to drink it. Making an effort, I swallowed the reviving cordial. The effect was extraordinary. My weakness seemed to pass away like a dream, my dull brain became clear and active, as by magic, and the memory of all I had passed through came back to me. Hardly knowing what I did, I made an effort to rise; but the agony of the moment was too great to be borne, and with a deep groan I sank back upon the grass. Dr. ——, recognising the character of my injuries, placed his hand firmly upon my shoulder, and said—"Do not move; lie still."

"I am ——; and I live at ——," I gasped, faintly. "Please take me home!"

Dr. —— again felt my pulse; and then, after giving me a few more drops of the restorative, he gave some directions to those standing near, and I saw them bring forward a door, which, in anticipation of this use of it, they had taken off its hinges, and brought with them, together with a pillow and some blankets. Lifting me with gentle care, strange to see in such rough looking men, they placed me upon the door, and putting the pillow under my burning head, and wrapping me carefully in the blankets, they raised it to their shoulders, and moved away, Dr. —— walking beside me, and occasionally moistening my lips with the cordial, when the pain of the journey seemed too great for my strength.

My remembrances of that terrible journey are like those we

retain of some frightful dream. Thanks to the care and skill of
Dr. —— I retained my consciousness throughout; but it was
only to suffer the more. As we approached my home, I began
to get excited again, until, as we came in sight of the house,
my thoughts began once more to wander. I have a distinct
remembrance of our passing up the avenue to the house, with
the bright moonlight shining through the trees, and throwing
broad waving shadows across our path; and I remember, as we
came in front of the house, seeing my poor wife, whom the
doctor had considerately prepared for our coming by a message sent on before, meet us at the door, with a white, scared
face, and of feeling her throw her arms around me, and with a
brave effort to keep back her tears, kiss my fevered brow; and
I remember, too, that, as she bent over me, I lifted my hand to
touch her blanched cheek, and made a mighty effort to gather
my thoughts to speak to her. Then all became a blank, and I
remembered no more.

When next I remember, I was lying in my own bed, and
the sun was shining with a subdued brilliance through the
closed curtains. A strange stillness pervaded the room, and the
only sound audible was the muffled ticking of my watch, in its
pocket above my head. For a moment I lay perfectly still, looking quietly about me, and trying to remember how I got there.
Gradually the horrors of that dreadful time came back to me,
but in a strange and curious way. Somehow they seemed to
have lost all power to affect me personally. I recalled them
now as if they were so many scenes in a story I had read, as
something strange and terrible, but altogether outside myself,
as something in which I had no direct interest or concern; and
for a while—I don't know how long, but it seemed a very long
time, I lay quite still, going over again the frightful experiences
of that awful day. At last I remembered that I was at home, and
in my own bed, and then I began to wonder how I got there,
and where my wife was that I had not seen her; and so thinking
I tried to call her. The sound of my voice was a fresh surprise
to me, it was so weak and faint; but before I could think more

about it, the slight noise I made brought my wife to the bed-side, from another part of the room. When she saw that I was awake, and knew her, she burst into a flood of irrepressible tears, and with an exclamation of thankfulness stooped over the bed, and kissed me again and again.

Surprised at this outburst of feeling, I looked at her inquiringly and asked, "What is the matter, my dear?" But, again, I wondered at the sound of my voice. It was little more than a faint whisper—the merest echo of my own lusty voice. My poor wife, too! How thin and pale she looked, with great dark shadows under her once bright eyes, which were now hollow and sunken, and looked full and heavy as if with long watching.

"Hush, my darling!" she said, "You have been very ill, very ill indeed. But, thank God, you will soon be better now." And, as she spoke, she smiled upon me through her tears.

"Have I?" I began; but with a smile she laid her hand—how thin and transparent it had become!—upon my lips, and said, "Hush, dear! You are not to talk now. I will tell you all you want to know by-and-bye, when you are stronger. Take this, now, and then try to sleep." And she brought me a small basin of broth, and with tender persistence fed me with her own dainty hands. Then she smoothed my pillows, and kissing me again, left me, and I soon fell into a quiet sleep.

From this my recovery, though slow and tedious, was persistent. The shock to my nervous system, and my long exposure upon the rocks had resulted in a dangerous attack of brain fever, complicated by strong rheumatic symptoms, which had brought me to "death's door"; but through the skill of Dr. ——, and the devoted care of my wife, aided by a naturally strong constitution, I had escaped with my life. But it had been a narrow escape. For several weeks I had been hovering between life and death; and though the crisis had terminated favourably, it was many weeks before I was sufficiently recovered to leave my room. Gradually, however, I regained my strength; and though it was long years before I was the same man that I was before, I was at length again able to go about my ordinary employments.

Note.—In connection with the preceding narrative, it may be well to relate a local tradition—that of the Fairy Wren—which afterwards came under my notice; and which, I think, may help to account for the mysterious occurrences of that dreadful night. Among the unsophisticated inhabitants of the north-eastern parts of the Isle of Man, the legend is still current, and may occasionally be heard related by some ancient gossip of the district, of a wicked spirit, which, in "the days of old," haunted the wilds, through which ran the rough horse-track which then served as a road between the northern and southern districts of the country. Often the belated traveller, journeying along the dreary road, would see a maiden of wondrous beauty, sitting by the wayside, with disordered attire and bathed in tears, bewailing bitterly her wrongs, and begging pitifully for succour. Should the traveller be deceived by her tale of woe, or be allured by her seductions and venture from the plain roadway with her—woe to him! Evil was sure to follow, and frequently death in one of its most terrible forms. In various ways she would entice him deeper and deeper into the wilderness, until he got irretrievably mired in its treacherous bogs, or fell headlong over its tremendous precipices.

At other times, for her wiles were as various as her moods, or her victims, the passing stranger would see a lovely girl dancing lightly upon the grassy sward in the mellow moonlight, and singing joyously to the music of the silvery bells attached to her flying feet. If he yielded to her blandishments, and quitted the straight road to toy with her in the grassy waste, his fate was certain. None ever escaped her in such moods.

It was noticed, too, as time passed on, that it was generally the young and the brave, the very flower of the Insular chivalry who thus suffered from the wiles of this terrible creature; and so numerous were her victims that at length it began to be feared that the kingdom itself would become exhausted of its noblest defenders, if some means were not found of destroying the power of the syren, or of driving her away from her favourite haunts. To attain this much-desired end, various expedients in great repute in those days for such purposes were accordingly adopted. The matter appearing to pertain to the spiritual power, the Church very properly brought its forces into the field, and the ecclesiastics of the district, headed by the Prior of Douglas, marched in solemn procession through the infested country, and with bell, book, and candle, formally exorcised the evil spirit. In vain! It was reported, and commonly believed by the people, that when the holy prior concluded his exorcism by condemning the wicked one to confinement in the foul depths of the Red Sea, a burst of fiendish laughter rang through their midst, making the boldest tremble with fear; and certain it was that the very next day the disfigured remains of one of the bravest of the king's knights were found lying at the bottom of a precipitous declivity, in the very heart of the haunted country.

But this failure of the regular forces of the Church to cast out the destroyer only roused the ambition and zeal of the volunteer soldiers of the Holy Mother; and a revered hermit, who had lived for many years in a comfortless hole in the side of one of the neighbouring mountains, and who was, accordingly, greatly venerated throughout the country for his sanctity, next entered the field of holy conflict, and attempted to deliver the people from their destroyer; but with even less satisfactory results. The syren not only refused to be driven away, but actually tried her arts upon the holy man himself; and with such success, that he barely escaped with his life! The beautiful demon mocked at their spells, and continued unchecked her evil course.

But all things have an end; and we are told that a way was at last found to put an end to her wicked practices. About this time there came to the court of the King of Man a stranger knight, famed equally for his deeds of valour in the Holy Wars, and for his pious and austere life. Learning at the court of King Godred of the evil doings of this fallen spirit, and of the ignominious failure of every attempt to destroy her power, or expel her from the desolated country, he, in the spirit of true knight-errantry, announced his determination to ride straight to the districts haunted by this evil one, and attempt her destruction. Being a stranger and a guest, and one high in the favour of his suzerain, the King of Norway, Godred was exceedingly loath to let him venture upon so hazardous an enterprise and strove to persuade him from it; but incapable of fear, and doubly fortified against the temptations of enticing spirits by the valiant deeds he had done for the Christian faith, and by the vows of chastity and abstinence which he had taken, he persisted in his resolution, and taking his leave of Godred and his Queen, Phingola the Fair, he rode away, alone and unattended from the Castle of Rushen, on St. Stephen's Day, to the spirit-haunted country of Garff.

Not for long was he left unassailed. With all her wiles, and in all her guides, the wicked fairy assailed the good knight— as a distressed damsel, wronged and oppressed by tyrannical neighbours, and as a merry laughing maiden, full of wanton smiles and alluring graces, she even assumed, as we are told the greatest tempter of all once did, the appearance of goodness and virtue to deceive to his ruin and death the faithful soldier of the Cross. But all in vain! He possessed in his breast a talisman of unequalled force which rendered all her witcheries harmless, and, stripping her of every disguise, revealed her in her true character to his calm and steadfast eye. All her old power thus failing her, she, in her turn, began to be terrified at such extraordinary virtue, and attempted to escape from the invincible hero; but he now assumed the offensive, and followed hard after her. Long she fled before him, by hill and dale, by wood and marshy heath; and throughout the long pursuit his unswerving faith sustained and preserved him. At last, it seemed as if her last chance had gone, and as if she must yield to his persistence. Making a mighty effort to seize her by her long flowing locks, she eluded his grasp only by changing herself into the form of a Wren; and fluttering across a stream of running water. As she thus escaped, she gave a triumphant chirp, and disappeared from his view in a thick wood beyond the river. But though the evil spirit thus evaded the destruction which threatened her, her power for evil was broken, at least for the time, by the good knight's victory. Henceforth she was comparatively harmless, while a spell was from this time cast over her, by which she was condemned on every succeeding St. Stephen's Day, to reassume the same bird-like form, with the definitive sentence that she must in that form perish by a human hand. Hence the extraordinary pertinacity with which the pursuit and slaughter of the wren on this day has been continued from that time to our own day; and yearly, as the anniversary of the Siren's defeat comes round, bands of youth and boys go out into the country "to hunt the wren." And, having caught their victim, they carry it in triumph from door to door throughout the country side, singing an ancient and uncouth doggerel descriptive of their joy in this traditional sport.

Baroness de Bertouch

The Tryst

BARONESS BEATRICE CAROLINE ELMSLIE DE BERTOUCH (1858-1931) *authored books of poetry, some poems set to music, and a biography of Father Ignatius, O.S.B., the Monk of Llanthony. She contributed poems, short stories, and social notes to various periodicals and was patron of the London Poetry Society and of a school of journalism and secretarial training for women in London. She was the wife of Montagu, 2nd Baron Bertouch, Master of the Hunt to the King of Denmark. This poem appeared on Christmas Eve, 1898 in the* Hampshire Telegraph.

(An old Yule Legend.)

Who walks i' the Glen to-night
　By the light of the pale Yule Moon?
　　Where the snowdrops sleep
　　And the drifts are deep,
　And the owls come to woo and croon.
　　'Tis My Ladye fair,
　　With her dusky hair
Loos'd down, like a veil of Night.

Who speeds to the Glen to-night,
　Over moors and by frozen fells?
　　And spurs his good horse
　　Thro' the snow-topp'd gorse,
　And the ghost of the heather bells.

185

'Tis My Ladye's Knight,
Who in armour bright,
Rides out to the Tryst to-night.

Who creeps to the Glen to-night
By the gleam of a traitor's knife?
Thro' the tangled brake
Like some starving snake
That's athirst for a victim's life;
Just a stifled breath
And a cry of death
Who flees from the Glen to-night?

Who weeps i' the Glen to-night?
It is not the wail of the sea;
Nor the sleeting rain,
But a woman's pain;
For she kneels at the Trysting Tree,
With her proud head laid
On her lover's plaid,
Who dies i' the Glen to-night?

Who walks i' the Glen to-night,
Tho' a hundred long years have flown?
"Canst thou find no rest
In the snow's white breast,
Lovely Ghost with the starry crown,
That thou comest still
At each Yule-tide chill,
To walk i' thy Glen at night?"

Adeline Sergeant

The Mummy Hand

A Story of One Christmas Eve, as Narrated by Eustace Ormerod

The Victorians were taken by Egyptomania, with a particular boom in fiction in the 1890s of which Richard Marsh's The Beetle (1897) *and Marie Corelli's* Ziska (1897) *were a part. The interest fueled not only literature but also research, of varying scientific worth. According to one account, an hour-long December 18, 1889 lecture by British Museum Egyptologist Wallis Budge was followed by an hour-long unwrapping of a mummy.* EMILY FRANCES ADELINE SERGEANT (1851-1904), *author of nearly 100 novels, frequently wintered in Egypt. The following text is taken from the* Alcester Chronicle *of December 28, 1901.*

YES, IT IS RATHER AN ODD STORY, and I never can help thinking of it at Christmas time. But my wife says there is something uncanny about it, so I don't usually refer to it in her presence. Women are a little sensitive and nervous about these things. But I will tell you what happened if you like. And a very odd experience I had, on Christmas Eve, when I was in Upper Egypt.

I had had rather a run of ill-luck. I was engaged to Mabel, but her father was doing his best to break off the engagement, because I was such a bad match for her.

To begin with, I had scarcely any money, except what I made by illustrations for papers and magazines, and old Sir John did not take a very high view of the artistic profession.

Then my health had broken down, and the doctor said I ought to winter in a warm climate—which did not look very well for the future, did it?

Old Sir John was quite kind and paternal, but inexorable too. "My dear boy," he said to me, "I like you immensely, and Mabel likes you too, but as long as you are a pauper and an invalid, it is not much good proposing to marry her, for I think too well of you to suppose that you want to live upon my money."

It was a little hard to listen to a statement of that kind, but I had to swallow it, because I did not want to quarrel with Sir John, and I knew that Mabel would be true to me. So I said good-bye to them both, and made my way to the office of the paper for which I worked.

The editor was Wilkins, an awfully kind chap. I told him the whole story, and he said a great many pleasant things to me about my work, and told me that he would consult with the directors, and see whether there was not some permanent post that they could offer me.

He was as good as his word. The very next day I got a proposal from him that I should go out to Egypt, at the expense of the paper, and visit the scene of some recent excavations, making sketches as I went, of temples, statues, sarcophagi, or anything that struck me as interesting.

They proposed to utilize these sketches partly in the paper, for a set of articles on the buried cities of Egypt, and partly for a handbook on Egyptian antiquities, that somebody or other connected with the firm was going to bring out. Anyway, he said that they would pay me handsomely for the job, that I could take my own time over it, and so forth, and that they would not grudge any reasonable expense. They also intimated that if I acquitted myself well, I could count upon permanent employment, as one of the staff.

This was good news for me, and I closed with their offer immediately. I saw Mabel at once, and said good-bye to her, then started immediately, for the November fogs were coming on, and I had a nasty cough that I wanted to get rid of.

I knew nothing at that time of Egyptian history or hieroglyphics, and I can assure you that I had never heard the name of Mr. Flinders Petrie. So I had my work cut out for me, even on the voyage, to get up the subject.

I need not dwell upon my difficulties, nor upon the steps I took to start my expedition. I reported myself to a bigwig, and got as much information as I could about the recent discoveries. Thanks to the introductions I had brought, I lost very little time in getting to work, and by the middle of December I was comfortably established in my own dahabeeah, and had got some distance up the Nile.

I must tell you—though without wishing to boast—that I have always had rather a knack at languages. I can usually become pretty fluent in a new tongue in two or three months time, and Arabic was not entirely new to me, because, you know, my father was something of an Oriental scholar and I had learnt various Eastern languages from him. So that it was not altogether remarkable that I should soon put myself into communication with any Arabs that I came across, and more particularly with the Bedouin tribes upon the river banks.

They soon learnt to understand the interest I took in old tombs and temples. And, of course, I did my best to ingratiate myself with them, because I thought it very likely that they might know of places upon which no Englishman's eye had rested and the discovery of which might add to the value of my work and also to my reputation.

It was also lucky for me that on one or two occasions I was able to give some assistance to a boy, who turned out to be the favourite son of one of the sheiks—in point of fact I saved the young monkey from being gobbled up by a crocodile, and the sheik's gratitude was boundless, or so at least it seemed to me. I may as well add that in considering the matter afterwards I thought there had been a good deal of deliberate calculation mixed up with it.

He came to me one day, and after the usual greetings, the cup of coffee and the chibouk which were handed to him, he intimated that he had something special to say. Would I like to go with him to a city partially buried beneath the sand, which no Englishman had ever seen? I asked him a good many questions about it, and what he said distinctly raised my curiosity.

"It is the City of the Princess," said the sheik, with a face like a mask, and eyes which sedulously avoided mine.

He was a handsome old man, brown, and lithe, and slender, as Arabs generally are, but of great stature, and considerable strength. His features were regular and delicate; he wore no beard, and his arched eye-brows and fine dark eyes, lent a rather peculiar character to his face. He had very beautiful hands. I used to watch the movements of the long, slender fingers, as if I were fascinated by them—and yet I hardly knew why. I had already received hints from Cairo that old Sheik Muhammed was not altogether to be trusted, and indeed, I believed him to be the most thorough-going scoundrel and cut-throat on the banks of the Nile. But he had the supple grace of a tiger, and I shall never forget the velvety softness of his eyes. He sat cross-legged before me, on a carpet, his white robes and turban immaculately clean, his demeanour as cool and dignified as that of an emperor. But he looked more like a sage and a poet than a Bedouin sheik.

"Why do you call it the City of the Princess?" I inquired.

He bowed gravely, touching his forehead and chest. "She was the daughter of a great king," he said. "It was by her orders that the city was built. And her tomb is in the midst."

"Her tomb—does that still exist? Can you take me to see it?" I cried.

"If the Effendi has no fears," said Sheik Muhammed, "I can show him the place where the Princess used to lie."

"Does she not lie there now?" I asked. "Who then has broken open her tomb? You say no Englishman has been there before."

The sheik simply shook his head. "In this land there are many thieves," he observed, "and perhaps the body was removed to a place of greater safety. But the Effendi shall see, and judge for himself."

It is needless to say that I consented with alacrity. Such a chance was not to be despised: I should see what no other Englishman had seen, and I might make valuable and important discoveries. I waited, with impatience, until the moment came for setting out upon my expedition to the buried city.

The sand of Egypt is as the waves of the sea, it overthrows and submerges the works of man, and shows merely the smooth unbroken surface above them; where no one can discern, or even guess, at the existence of the things that have been lost. As we journeyed over the vast expanse I wondered how it was possible for my guides to know their way, or for their eye to distinguish any landmark by which our destination could be known, for, as the sheik had explained to me, we were not going to look for ruin visible to the eye of man, but for some subterranean passages and buried cities, which had not seen the light of day for hundreds of years.

We had set out at dawn, but the sun was high before we paused at what looked to me, like a flat, round stone, buried in the sand, and shaded by one or two palm trees. The ground, by its verdure, showed the presence of underground water-springs.

I looked on with deepest interest while my escorts formed their camp, and then removed the stone from its place. As I had expected, I saw that it covered the entrance to some underground building, for there were stone steps, and above them a domed roof, and a passage, into which the sun's rays penetrated only a little way.

The sheik, who was accompanied only by two of his sons, and one or two of his most trustworthy servants, looked at me with triumph in his eye. "Did I not tell you," he said, "and now, if the Effendi chooses, I will show him the burial place of the Princess. Will the Effendi follow, or——"—with an unmistakable touch of scorn in his voice—"is the Effendi afraid?"

For it must be confessed that I had hesitated, as a breath of chill, dank air came from the vault, like a foreshadowing of death. But at the sheik's question my courage returned to me, and I haughtily begged him to hold his peace and go forward.

I shall never forget the curious sensations produced in me by that expedition. One of the servants went first, holding a lantern, and then came the sheik, and then myself, while one of the sheik's sons brought up the rear. But for the light of the lamp we should not have been able to see a step before us. The steps went down for some distance, and were succeeded by a level passage. But that also went down until we seemed to be descending into the very bowels of the earth. Worse than that, the walls narrowed on each side until I almost thought that it would be impossible to proceed. The lithe figures of the Arabs hopped easily from the narrow steps, but I, a tall and broad-shouldered Englishman, had considerable difficulty in squeezing myself along the passage. Once or twice I almost came to a full stop. But it occurred to me that there was nothing to be done but to go forward. One could never turn in that narrow passage. It was a case of going further or being wedged for ever in the darkness. At last, to my unspeakable relief, the passage widened until it opened out into a large hall or chamber, supported by pillars and illuminated by dim radiance, which must have come from the outer day, although I failed to see the shafts which must have communicated with the outer world.

But what surprised me was that there seemed to be no outlet from the chamber. Looking round it I saw no door and no passage, except the one by which we had come. But the sheik smiled at my bewilderment. "Look up," he said, "on your right side, to the East. Look up!"

He took the lantern from the Arab's hand and hung it aloft, so that I could see a great opening high in the wall, and as the light streamed into it I could see that it was a vast and magnificent chamber adorned with brilliant wall paintings, with carved images of sphinxes and colossi, and with some great objects in the middle of the chamber, which I could not at first make out. "What is it?" I asked, pointing to the black central mass.

"It is the tomb," he said, briefly. "Look, I will show you."

And to my surprise he put his foot into a small crevice or cleft in the rock, and swung himself up to the opening, with the lightness and dexterity which only an Arab could have shown. Then standing aloft in the large dim chamber, his white robes making him a noticeable object, even in the semi-obscurity, he looked more like a phantasmal form, some presiding genius of the place, than mere human flesh and blood. The other Arabs clambered after him with lighted torches, which they held high above their heads, thus enabling him to see the wonders of the place.

There was an enormous sarcophagus of rose granite, supported on a great marble slab, with granite pillars; it was here no doubt that the body of the Egyptian Princess reposed—a mummied body wrapped with spices in linen clothes, which I ardently desired to unroll, in order that I might add some scrap of knowledge to the great sum-total of Egyptian archæology.

But disappointment awaited me. I tried in vain to swing myself up to the opening in the inner chamber, as the Arabs had done. I was too big and heavy for the operation. The crevices which had afforded foothold to the Arabs did not suffice for me, and even when two of the men supported me, and the others tried to pull me up by my arms, it was found that the attempt was impossible. The only way was to come there again, with ropes and other implements, so that I might for myself examine the chamber, and all that it contained.

The Arabs were evidently disappointed with the result of our visit. Evidently they had wanted me to examine the sarcophagus, but I told them I would do so in the course of a couple of days, and that in the meantime, if they would keep silence they should be handsomely rewarded.

There was certainly nothing more to be done that day, and we determined to make our way to the upper earth again.

I took some hasty notes of the place where we stood, and

of the different things I could see, not failing to remark that the great stone coffin had already been, to some extent, tampered with, for its great cover had been removed and partially broken. But the contents of the sarcophagus I was assured were still intact, and I was consoled with the thought of opening for myself the gilded mummy case, and removing the poor mummied body from its swaddling bands.

I went back to my dahabeeah in a state of wild excitement, and occupied myself for some hours in getting ready or sending messages for the implements that I thought I should require. On the second day, however, I received a shock. My movements had evidently not been unobserved. The Government had got wind of my private researches—so at least I supposed, for here was an official letter from the Director of the Museum in Cairo, stating that he was on his way to join me, as he thought that some valuable Egyptian remains were to be discovered near the village, beside which my boat was anchored.

Now I know very well that all antiquities belonged to the Egyptian Government, and may not be carried out of the country and that everyone who could be proved to be defrauding the Government in this matter was liable to punishment. Of course, I had not meant to appropriate anything that I might find, but I did want to have the honour and glory of my discoveries all to myself, and I was very much annoyed that M. Bougier should in any way anticipate me. But there was nothing to be done. He might arrive at almost any moment, and would certainly not be later than the following day.

I sat and fumed secretly while I gave all necessary orders for the entertainment of a guest. In the dusk of the evening the Sheik Muhammed sent word that he wished to come on board and speak to me. I received him with all the ceremony which he considered proper to his position, and as we sat opposite to each other drinking coffee and smoking in our respective modes—for he preferred a narghilek, while I restricted myself to the customary cigar—he entered, after some preamble, upon the subject of conversation he wished to make. "The Effendi has had a letter!"

"True," I answered, oracularly.

"The letter is from the Great One in the City, who has control over everything that is ancient in this country. He comes soon and will demand tribute."

"How the devil do you know?" I asked, rather forgetting my manners in my surprise. The glimmer of a triumphant smile passed across the handsome old face.

"Pardon, Effendi, but all the people know it. The letter was carried to Effendi by a messenger, who has seen letters of the same kind at other times. It is of the blue colour, and it has the name of the Great Man in writing upon it. If the Effendi looks at it he will see that it is so. We all know the look of that covering and the signature."

I hastily withdrew the director's epistle from my pocket, and looked at the envelope. It was a blue, official-looking document, and the director had carefully inscribed his signature outside.

Possibly he had no idea that the Arabs knew it just as well as an Englishman or Frenchman would have done.

"Well—you cannot have read it!" I exclaimed.

"No, Effendi. But we know when a letter of that kind comes, the Great One follows. He will be here to-morrow or the next day. Is it not so?"

"Yes, you are right!" I said, thinking it no use to deny what was so well-known. "And what of that?"

"It is just this, Effendi, that the coming of the Master means ruin to my house. The Effendi does not know the methods of the Great One. He will come and ask questions, and he will frighten those of my household and force them to tell things that they should not; also, he searches our houses and ourselves, and if he finds but a mummy finger, or a tarnished ornament of no value, or a little carbon stone, he sends us to the Black Prison, and deprives us of our goods. Now the Effendi knows that there are always small things that even the children pick up in the sands, and some of them may have been brought by chance into my tent, and, therefore, if the Great Lord comes and searches me and my house, behold I am a doomed man, and a price will be put upon my head."

"Not quite so bad as all that," I said. "There will be a fine, I suppose; and perhaps imprisonment. I don't know. But you will get off lightly, I think. Besides, why don't you clear out all these curiosities and make a present of them to the Government if you are afraid they will be discovered?"

The old man's eyes twinkled. I was somewhat inexperienced in oriental wiles, but it struck me that Sheik Muhammed was bent upon concealing something valuable for himself, and I hardly knew whether to aid and abet him or to side with the director, who was certainly very much in my way. I fell back upon my generalities. "We must all obey the law," I said. "The things belong to the Government, who will give you a fair price for your labour in digging. But if you keep and sell them to strangers, most assuredly, Sheik, you will be put in jail and suffer great loss beside."

The sheik said nothing. His hands had been folded in the large, white garment which he wore, but he now slid them out of the folds and exposed them to my view. On one of the long, brown fingers, I at once observed there gleamed a jewel of extraordinary size and lustre; it seemed to be a blood-red ruby set in dim gold. Without a word he quietly slipped it off his finger and held it out to me upon his flat, thin palm.

"What is it?" I exclaimed. "What a magnificent ring! Why, it's ancient! Where did you find it?"

He made no immediate answer, but motioned to me to take the ring. "It is for the Effendi. The Effendi can keep it for himself."

"Antica?" I said, using the word that every Arabian knows. "If I take it I must give it up to M. Bougier." But I took it from the sheik's hand and tried it on, conscious at the same time of a sudden flash of something like triumph from the sheik's brilliant, dark eyes. Though what he had to triumph about I could not exactly see.

"It is yours, Effendi," he said, in a low voice. "But do not show it to the Great Man from Cairo. Keep it safely, for it is worth much gold."

"That is impossible," I said, gazing at the jewel as though it fascinated me, for I could not accept such a valuable gift, and I had not enough money to purchase it.

"Keep it then for a little while. Keep it until this visit is overpassed, and then we will speak of barter."

"Oh, now I understand!" I cried, bursting into hearty laughter. "The fact is, you want me to conceal this ring from the eyes of the officials, because you know very well you have stolen it. It would be very convenient for you, I have no doubt, if I kept it concealed until the director had gone back to Cairo, and then presented it to you again."

I spoke in English, but I think the sheik understood me, although he sat grave and immovable. "Where did you find it?" I asked curiously, in Arabic.

"Where we went together. In the chamber of the dead Princess."

"You have not meddled with the sarcophagus, have you?" I cried.

"Allah forbid. I have left it for the Effendim and their servants. But the ring has virtues. Without it no one can open the door which leads to the sacred chamber. Unless the Effendi will keep it safe we cannot go to see the chamber again."

I began to understand. The ring was a bribe, most assuredly. I was to conceal it, and return it to the old sheik when the director had returned to Cairo, and as my reward, I should be shown the sarcophagus, and be allowed to explore its hidden treasures. Under these circumstances what should I do?

It flashed across my mind that if I refused to keep the ring or presented it to the Government officials I should lose the sheik's friendship, and with it probably every chance of making discoveries in that part of Egypt. With the loss of this chance went also a certain amount of my chance of winning Sir John's consent to my marriage with Mabel. I really could not afford to sacrifice the old sheik's protection for the sake of a scruple, and yet it was hardly fair or honest to defraud the Government of what was its due.

"I should like to examine the ring a little," I said. "For the present I will keep it, and return it to you later on. I should like to find out what these hieroglyphics mean," I said, and I pointed to some characters roughly inscribed on the inside of the little circlet.

Not a muscle of the sheik's face changed, although he must have thought that he had secured a tremendous triumph. He went on in a bolder tone, "There is one other thing, Effendi. One of my house has found for himself an ancient mummy, such as the English love to take away to their own country. We dare not keep it because of the search which will shortly be in our house. But if the Effendi would but buy it for himself——"

"The mummy, as well as the ring," I observed. "How much more? No, I don't want any mummies, sheik. Why don't you bury it in the ground until the director has gone, if you want to get off free?"

It was a very improper statement to make, no doubt, and the old man's eyes twinkled shrewdly.

"It is difficult to do it without many knowing," he said, "and I fear me lest we should be betrayed. But if the Effendi will allow me to bring it to his boat he can see if there is some little corner where it can be kept safe from prying eyes. It is only a small mummy, Effendi—and it is not quite complete, it is only partially unwound—and if the Effendi would but keep it a little while——"

I laughed, in spite of myself. "I have no room for it," I said, "and I should like to know what the director would say if he found me concealing a valuable mummy. No, no. Be content, sheik. I have got your ring, but really I cannot take the mummy too."

But perhaps there was something in my face that told of yielding, for at night, when the darkness had fallen, and I was sitting alone in my cabin writing up my journal, the sheik himself reappeared, with two of his sons, informing me in the humblest of tones that they had found a hiding place for the mummy, if I would but let it remain. And when I inquired the nature of this hiding place, I was quietly shown the upper bunk in my sleeping apartment, which had hitherto stood empty, and was a receptacle for all kinds of rubbish.

Certainly no one would think of hunting there for curiosities, and the men's ingenuity was so great that I at last consented to allow their precious burden to be deposited there. And early next morning M. Bougier arrived.

I entertained M. Bougier at dinner. He was a clever, amiable little Frenchman, full of anecdotes, and very inquisitive concerning my relations with the Arabs in their neighbourhood. Especially was he anxious to know whether I thought the Sheik Muhammed had made any recent discoveries. I was pleased to be able to state that I did not know. It was a rather illusive answer, I am afraid, because I implied that I did not know whether the sheik's discoveries were recent or not. Only I did not take the Director into my confidence respecting the buried city, the mummy in my bunk, or the wonderful ring. He would know about all these things, no doubt, in good time, but I was not going to betray the sheik's confidence.

We spent a very pleasant evening together, and he did not leave me until late. It must be confessed that I was rather glad to get rid of him, as my thoughts wandered incessantly to the concealed treasures in my cabin. I was restlessly anxious to know that the ring was safe, and went so far at last as to take the ring from its hiding place and conceal it in my pocket. I should have worn it if I had not been afraid of attracting M. Bougier's attention. But when he was gone I took it out and slipped it over my fourth finger, as it was too small for any of the others. There was something about it that fascinated me. I wished with all my heart that I could afford to buy it, and that it was fair for me to do so. I knew very well that I should have to advise Sheik Muhammed to report his treasures to the Director, or if not should ultimately be obliged to do so myself. But at present I very much wished to put off the evil day.

Moved by new, strange impulses for which I could scarcely account, I took the candle and let its rays fall upon the covered shelf which contained the sheik's mummy. I wondered vaguely why he attached so much importance to it. Finally, I took off the covering and made a superficial examination of the mummied figure. It had been partially unrolled, and I could make out that the mummy was that of a young woman, slight and small. But evidently, from the nature of the wrappings and the spices employed, a person of distinction. I speedily made another discovery which startled me a little. The right hand had been severed from the body, but not taken away. It lay amongst the wrappings, long, brown and ghastly, and it struck me that one of the fingers had also been mutilated. Though of this, in the dim light, I could not be sure. I resolved to ask the sheik for the full history of this mummy, and why the hand had been severed from the arm. The full significance of it did not strike me at the time. But I came to see afterwards that it was easy to conjecture why the sheik or one of his family had committed this outrage upon the dead.

I recovered the mummy, put the ring in a box, which I locked for greater security, and went to bed. I think I never had a worse night. I woke continually, and dreamt frightful dreams at intervals. The air seemed curiously thick, and there were strange rustlings, probably caused by the presence of some lizard or scorpion which had crawled into the boat.

At last I lighted a candle and read till morning. Then, feeling strangely weary and unrefreshed, got up and joined M. Bougier, who was holding a sort of bit-de-justice on the river bank.

"Ciel! It is the twenty-fourth!" he ejaculated, as he made his last note towards the close of the sitting. "It is the eve of Noel! And we so far away from all Christian festivities! You, Mr. Ormerod, will be able, I hope, to furnish a Christmas dinner. I will supply the wine, which I brought from Cairo. Is it a bargain?"

"It is, indeed," I said, with satisfaction. "I was thinking that my Christmas Day would be a somewhat dreary one, but in your company, M. Bougier, I shall no doubt spend a very agreeable time."

"Very well," said Bougier, in extremely good humour. "Then you dine with me to-night, my friend, and I dine with you to-morrow, Christmas Day. That is so, is it not?"

He gave me a very good dinner that evening on board the dahabeeah, and I came back to my own boat in good spirits, though by no means unduly excited. I mention this fact because a kind friend has now and then suggested that I had dined too freely. I can assure you that I, Eustace Ormerod, was never more sane, more clear-headed or light-hearted, than I was that Christmas Eve, when I looked at the dim, glimmering waters of the Nile, and thought of the Christmas bells that were ringing out across the cold Northern lands and of the girl that I knew was waiting for me at home.

"I wish I could send her a Christmas gift," I said to myself. "By the way that ring of the sheik's would please her immensely. I wonder if I could get Muhammed to sell it at a low price, and Bougier to wink at my keeping it. It is too small for a man; it is evidently meant for a woman's hand." So saying, I unlocked the box, took out the ring, admired it and held it up to the light, then put it as I had done before on the little finger of my left hand. But this time I did not take it off again. I looked upon it as a possible gift to Mabel, and I pleased myself with the idea of wearing it first.

I fell asleep in my berth almost immediately. But in a short time I awoke just as I had done on the previous night with the sensation of having had a horrible dream of which I could not remember the details. I said some angry words to myself on the subject of these bad nights, and then composed myself to sleep again. But this time I did not lose consciousness. I dreamt, and yet I was awake, for I knew that what I saw was not all a dream. It seemed to me that the air was full of a strange presence. That some hungry, malignant creature was going to and fro in

the room, not speaking or crying out, but full of a deliberate
enmity towards myself, and a determination to take my life.
Once or twice the thing seemed to come near me, then drew
back as if afraid. I knew, in a vague way, that it waited for me
to sleep, and I tried with a growing horror, which I cannot
express, to awake myself thoroughly, and to drive away from
me this creature of darkness to the realm to which it belonged.
But I was paralysed. I could not move hand or foot. The terror
of a sort of nightmare was upon me, and I was absolutely helpless.

The thing certainly came nearer. It hovered over me. It
almost brushed my face. Then it seemed to take shape and
form. I knew it, only my eyelids were shut—and I saw beside
me for one dazzling moment a young and beautiful girl, with
long almond eyes, full of passion and fire, red lips, and brown
shapely limbs, on which glimmered costly robes, jewels and
flowers. I felt the scent of the rich blossoms overpower my faculties. Yet mixed with it there was a strange, rank odour, like
that of corruption and death. Yet the girl's glowing face, the
lithe yet rounded figure breathed nothing but life and energy!
It would have been the most beautiful vision I ever beheld, had
the face possessed any softness or tenderness of expression, but
it was disfigured by terror and by hate. It seemed to me that
she sought for something that she could not find and that she
was determined to avenge herself on me as upon an enemy.
Her slender brown fingers closed upon my throat, and then
at that moment I knew that one of the fingers was bleeding
and broken, and that there was a strange red circlet about the
slender wrist.

I knew no more. I did not come to myself for some hours,
and I believe I narrowly escaped brain fever. It seems that at
that supreme moment of my nightmare, if so it may be called,
I uttered a strange, stifled cry, which brought Said, the most
faithful servant that I ever possessed, to my side. He said that
I seemed to be in convulsions, with my hands tearing at my
throat, and my face almost black; and there were strange

discoloured marks such as could only be made by clutching fingers upon the flesh.

He told me that M. Bougier had doctored me to the best of his ability, and that the old sheik had manifested every sign of alarm and distress, when he heard that I had been taken ill. He had also demanded back from Said the precious mummy which he had conveyed to my cabin. But Said, with an infinite reverence for things in his master's apartment, had refused to let him touch the mummy figure, which still therefore reposed upon the empty berth opposite my own.

As soon as I was able, although still feeling very weak, I crawled out of my bunk and lifted the coverings with which the mummy was hidden. "But someone has been here," I ejaculated involuntarily, "or you, Said, have rearranged the wrappings." Said swore that he had not touched the figure, and also that he had not admitted anyone into the cabin. But all the draperies and wrappings had been rearranged, and lay in straight stiff folds about the figure, almost as if the swathing was complete. The hands were entirely hidden, but my curiosity impelled me to remove some of the easily loosened bandages, and then I saw—what I had vaguely expected to see—that upon one of the slender brown fingers of the mummy's hand was the ruby ring which I myself had worn when I went to sleep on Christmas Eve.

I sent for M. Bougier and confided to him the whole story. With his help we partially unrolled the mummy, and found it in a very good state of preservation.

The face was especially perfect. It was that of a young girl, whose beauty it was easy to conjecture had been very great, and it seemed to me that it was the face of the woman who had hovered over me, with cruel clutching fingers, in my dreams.

"She was of Royal race," said M. Bougier. "The hieroglyphics tell us that, and here is a papyrus roll, which we may be able to decipher. I remember hearing some tradition of this Princess. She died of grief, because of her lover's death, and was buried with his ring upon her hand. You must have heard this story, my friend, and you dreamt that she came back from the dead to take back her ring."

"I did not dream at all," I answered, somewhat angrily. "She—it—the Thing, whatever it was, was here, and I saw it."

"Ah, well," said the little Frenchman, placidly, "there is no saying. We dream very wonderful things sometimes. It strikes me this mummy was taken from the sarcophagus that you saw in the buried city. The sheik wanted to steal a march upon us all. I should like to arrest him and hear what he has to say."

But Sheik Muhammed had fled. He had scented danger as soon as he knew that I was ill, and he and his family were never seen again. Nor could we recover a clue to the buried city, which still, therefore, remains unexplored. I entreated Bougier to let the dead Egyptian Princess keep her ring, and he, with some reluctance, consented. But I couldn't persuade him to abandon the idea of adding the mummy to the other exhibits in his museum. She lies there to this day, in a glass case, duly ticketed and labelled, but with her lover's ring still safe upon her mummy hand, and, perhaps, with this she is content.

But although I have been a happy and successful man for many years, and have married the girl I loved, and spent many a joyous Christmas in my own English home, I shall never forget the weird experiences of that gruesome Christmas eve upon the Nile. And upon my throat I still carry, and shall carry as long as I live, the marks of that murderous mummy hand.

James Skipp Borlase

The Dead Hand

A Tale of a Weird and Awful Christmastide

JAMES SKIPP BORLASE (1839-1909), *a native of South West England, worked for some years as a solicitor, but was also a prolific contributor of adventure and crime fiction to penny dreadfuls, boys' magazines, and newspapers. Many of his books drew on his time spent in Australia in the 1860s. His* Ned Kelly, the Ironclad Bushranger *was reviewed as being "as disgraceful and disgusting a production as has ever been printed."*[1] *Borlase wrote several ghost stories wherein he adapted historical legends and folklore and gave them Christmastime settings. The hand is an actual relic kept at the Catholic Church of St. Oswald and St. Edmund Arrowsmith in Ashton-in-Makerfield, Greater Manchester, and there are traditions of its being a healing "holy hand."*[2] *The opening lines of the story come from "The Hand of Glory, or, The Nurse's Story" in Richard Harris Barham's* The Ingoldsby Legends *(1837). This tale first appeared in the* Rugby Advertiser *of December 15, 1903.*

---

1 "James Skipp Borlase (1839-1902)." *Yesterday's Papers*. Sept. 19, 2010. http:// john-adcock.blogspot.com/2010/09/james-skipp-borlase-1839-1902.html (citing *Saturday Review*, Nov. 26, 1881.)
2 Owen Davies and Francesca Matteoni, "'A Virtue Beyond All Medicine': The Hanged Man's Hand, Gallows Tradition and Healing in Eighteenth- and Nineteenth-Century England," *Social History of Medicine*, vol. 28, 4 (2015): 686-705. https://www.ncbi.nlm.nih.gov/pmc/articles/PMC4623855/

CHAPTER I.

THE DEAD HAND OF BRYN HALL. A LOVE TRYST BY MOONLIGHT.

> "Open, lock,
> To the dead man's knock!
> Fly bolt, and bar, and band;
> Nor move, nor swerve,
> Joint, muscle, or nerve,
> At the spell of the dead man's hand."

IN ENGLAND, UP TO A HUNDRED AND FIFTY YEARS AGO (as in Russia at the present day), a wondrous power was supposed to dwell in a dead man's withered hand.

Housebreakers set great store by it, for not only would it, when properly used, point out to them every spot where valuables were concealed, but the lock of the stoutest chest or door would fly open at its mere touch, bars shoot back, chains drop noiselessly to the floor, and the inmates of the mansion, or cottage, as the case might be, be cast into a deep sleep so long as the burglars remained on the premises.

Indeed, an old rhyme promises even more than that, saying:—

> "Love, wealth, and power, shall he command,
> Who useth the charm of the Dead Man's Hand."

A century and a half ago one of the most famous dead hands in Great Britain was treasured, as a rare and precious relic, in the ancient mansion of Bryn Hall, near Widnes; for it was the right hand of a good and faithful Catholic priest, called, in life, Father Arrowsmith, who was hung, drawn, and quartered, in the reign of William III., for having celebrated Mass, on three divers occasions, at Warrington, in the year 1693.

As the venerable divine had been a faithful and zealous serv-ant of God during his life, so, after his death, his hand continued to perform many a good deed, (if common report is to be relied on) for many a long year, the following case having been recorded with great minuteness:—

"In the year 1736 a boy of twelve years, only son of Caryl Hawarden, of Appleton-within-Widnes, was cured of a fatal malady by the application of the dead hand of that blessed martyr for faith, Father Arrowsmith. The child had been ill for over fifteen months, totally deprived of the use of his limbs, with loss of memory, and impaired sight. In this condition, which divers physicians had declared hopeless, his parents sent to Sir Geoffrey Wynn, of Bryn Hall (as many had done before them in an equal emergency of bodily illness) for the loan of the dead hand, which, being forwarded under safe custody, packed in a box and wrapped in fair linen, Mrs. Hawarden, the boy's mother, devoutly took the hand, and after making the sign of the Cross, with the fingers thereof stroked down either side of the child's backbone, praying fervently to the Lord Jesus the while, that her son might be restored to perfect health. Thereupon the patient, who had before been perfectly helpless, sprang with great joy to his feet, and ran about the house, thanking and praising God for his great deliverance, and from that day forth his pains entirely left him, his memory was wholly restored, and his health fully re-established, as was testified to by many friends and neighbours."

But there was shortly to come a time when the dead hand of Father Arrowsmith was to be borrowed for a wicked and nefarious purpose, instead of for a good and righteous one, and it is that gruesome incident which gives me the materials for the terrible tale which I am about to tell.

★ ★ ★ ★ ★

Mary Morgan was, in the year 1739, a pretty girl of nineteen, vain, good-natured, credulous, and thoughtless, fond of having a sweetheart, and, as yet, prone to frequently change them.

She was a servant maid at Bryn Hall, where she was a great favourite, because she was never out of temper and ever ready to do anyone a kindness.

Alas, it was these very good qualities (because they were untempered by prudence and caution) that were fated to involve the entire household in great peril and even to threaten some of its members with a bloody death.

It was a clear, calm night in the Christmas week of the year just mentioned, and about seven of the clock, when Mary escaped out of doors in order to keep tryst with her last acquired lover and by far the best favoured that she had ever possessed, a young gipsy named Will Boseley, who would have served as a model for Byron's Corsair, so noble was his form and so handsome his face, though we may add that no corsair or pirate who ever lived had possessed a blacker heart than he.

But he was gentle of manner, soft of speech, and could make love in a really wonderful way, considering his station in life, for his compliments and his flattery, though, perhaps, sometimes a little rough, were never coarse or vulgar, and he kissed a pretty girl not as though he longed to eat her, as ordinary clod poles do, but rather as an ardent devotee will press his or her lips against hand or foot of the statue of some miracle-working saint or madonna.

On all these accounts, as well as by reason that Will had a neat taste in the matter of neck and cap ribbons, and during their brief acquaintance had given her many little presents of that kind, poor, foolish Mary, who knew nothing whatever of his past life, thought him "the nicest and dearest fellow in all the world," and would have been ready to lay down her very life for him, had such a sacrifice been required of her, instead of which, by her folly, she was unknowingly about to run the risk of, at the very least, jeopardising the lives of an entire family.

We need not describe that lovers' meeting at length, for such interviews are all alike, or very nearly so.

Bill Boseley, to do him bare justice, was no libertine, so that a pretty girl's honour would have been safe with him at any hour, and in the loneliest of places, for, in truth, gold was his sole goddess, and the bottle his only much-loved sweetheart, wherefore he did not even kiss the maiden girl who had given her whole heart to him, more than diplomacy required, and as soon as he had come to the conclusion that he had made sufficient love for the nonce, he began to talk of a beloved sister, who had been taken suddenly and dangerously ill in the gipsy camp, which was pitched some three miles away in the direction of Warrington, and to wish that the dead hand of Father Arrowsmith could be used to bring about her cure.

"If you would but call at the Hall and tell my master about your poor, dear sister, she would not lack a cure for want of the laying on of the holy hand, for it is ever at the service of the poorest as well as of the richest," answered Mary.

"Not when the poor happens to be of gipsy blood, Polly," rejoined Will Boseley, with a heavy sigh. "Your master hates all our race, because we believe that hares, pheasants, and such like, being wild creatures of the woods and wastes, are our lawful spoil, and treat 'em accordingly. His gamekeepers shoot our fellows down without remorse whenever they are caught trespassing, and when one of them was tried and convicted of poaching at Warrington Police-court, a month ago, your master, who sat on the bench as one of the magistrates, wished aloud that he could hang every gipsy in Lancashire, man, woman, and child."

"Oh, dear, what then can be done?" sobbed tender-hearted Mary.

"Well, much could be done if you have but the pluck to do it, my dear."

"Oh, tell me, tell me?" pleaded the girl.

"You have informed me, Polly, that you are the first to rise and the last to go to bed of all the servants at the Hall."

"Yes, that is so. I am trusted to do all the locking up at night, after the others have gone upstairs, and I am also always the first down in the morning. But what of that, Bill?"

"Why, you might save my poor sister's life by lending me the holy hand, unknown to your master. Leave the box containing it on the back kitchen window-sill, when you fasten and bolt the window on the inside, ere you go to bed, and you shall find it there at whatever hour you come downstairs in the morning."

"Oh, Bill, it will be as easy to manage as putting on my shoe, and I am sure that I can trust you, even with so sacred a relic as the holy hand."

"Trust me? Why of course you can, Polly. I would not get you into a row, through the dead hand being missed, on any account, and by your pluck you will have saved my sister's life. My goodness, how the dear girl will love and cherish you when you become her own brother's wife, and that will be before very long, my brave and darling girl."

That was the ruse by which the most daring band of robbers in all Lancashire, and, if it were expedient, murderers as well, of whom Bill Boseley was leader and captain, procured possession of the Dead Hand, whose magical power they believed would make their midnight raid upon Bryn Hall an easy and safe task.

CHAPTER II.

MARY BEHELD A SIGHT THAT MADE HER VERY BLOOD RUN COLD.

The hand of the dead priest was easily come by, for it was kept in an ebony box which always rested in a niche in the wall on the first landing of the broad old oak staircase of Bryn Hall, a staircase so wide that a dozen people might have ascended or descended it abreast.

Thus, when all the family, as well as the servants, except Mary Morgan, had gone to bed, at the then considered late hour of ten o'clock, Mary could abstract the case containing the precious relic without any chance of its being missed until Sir Geoffrey and his maiden sister, Tabitha, came down to breakfast the next morning, for there was a common place—an uncarpeted back staircase—for the use of the domestics.

So she possessed herself of the ebony box as soon as she could safely do so, and, by a quarter past ten, it stood on the outside sill of the scullery window, which she then fastened and next secured by closing and barring its shutters on the inside; whereupon Bill Boseley emerged from behind a big laurel bush that rose close by, secured the talisman, and made off with it.

He was an ignorant fellow, after all, and though he knew something about dead hands, it didn't amount to much, or he would never have supposed the hand of a man who had led a holy life could be made to work evil after its owner's death.

The only hand, indeed, that could have really aided him and his brother rogues in their nefarious design to rob Bryn Hall, without risk and peril to themselves, would have been that of a malefactor who had been hanged upon a roadside gibbet, a common enough incident at the period of which this story treats.

The great Lancashire novelist, Harrison Ainsworth, who was as deeply versed in witchcraft, spells, and all such uncanny lore, as he was in English History, in his glorious romance of "Rookwood," describes the preparation of the only sort of Dead Hand that can be of any practical use to criminals as follows:—

> "From the corpse that hangs on the gallows tree,
> A murderer's corpse it needs must be,
> Sever the right hand carefully;
> Yea, sever the hand that the deed has done
> Ere the flesh which clings to the bones be done,
> In its dried veins must blood be none.
> Those ghastly fingers, white and cold,
> Within a winding sheet enfold.
> Count the mystic count of seven,

Name the planets high in heaven.
Then in earthen vessel place them,
And with dragon wort encase them.
Bleach them in the noonday sun,
Till the marrow melt and run,
And next within their chill embrace
The dead man's awful candle place.
Of murderer's fat must that candle be.
You may scoop it neath the gallows tree,
Of wax and of Lapland Sisame.
Its wick must be formed of the hair of the dead,
By the crow that brood on the wild waste shed.
Wherever that magical light shall burn
Vainly the sleeper may toss and turn,
But his leaden eyes shall he ne'er unclose
So long as that magical taper glows.
And were he to open them, then nought would he see
For he who grasps the dead hand will invisible be
But of black cat's gall let him aye have care,
And of screech owl's venomous blood beware!"

Yes, Bill Boseley and his three fellow robbers were but
novices in the art of necromancy, and the reading of evil
spells, as they, at eleven of the clock, on that clear and frosty
Christmastide night, crouched, amidst a clump of gorse,
about half a mile away from Bryn Hall, twining five of the
thin and taper rushlights of the period about the wrist of the
grizzly hand, clumping the united grease of their centres in
the hollow palm, and, finally, twisting their upper portions
around the thumb and four fingers, so that the wicks should
o'ertop the nails by half an inch or so, and be all ready for
lighting when the proper time came.

And whilst they pursued their weird task they endeavoured
to make light of it by coarse jesting; yet, for all that, they
wished that the night's work was well over, and their dead ally,
as they deemed the desecrated hand to be, got well quit of; for,
as they manipulated it and the greasy rushlights, each man felt
his blood run cold within him, and as though live worms were

wriggling up and down his spine, whilst his hair every now and then seemed as if rising on end like the quills of a frightened hedgehog. Indeed, but for frequent recourse to a square bottle of Hollands, or "liquid moonlight," as Ben Boseley poetically called the potent spirit, it is doubtful whether they would have had sufficient nerve to have concluded their gruesome work.

And whilst they were engaged upon it, poor Mary Morgan was lying awake in bed in a state of semi-rapture, produced by the belief that, through a very venial fault of her own, if fault it really were, her brave and tender-hearted lover was, by the miraculous power of a holy martyr's hand, saving a beloved sister from agony of death, and even, more likely not, restoring her to a condition of perfect health and strength.

Vainly she tried to go to sleep, so that she might be sure to wake with the earliest dawn on the morrow, in order to take in and return the dead hand to its accustomed niche in the wall ere anyone else in the old mansion was astir.

But sleep she could not.

She heard the great clock in the hall strike eleven, and then twelve, and, as it sounded the last stroke of the midnight hour, another and unaccustomed something seemed to appeal to her sense of hearing, a something that appeared to be the cautious opening of a window, whose hinges creaked somewhat.

This rendered her wider awake than ever, for she was well aware that her master was reputed to be a miser, possessing plenty of hoarded wealth, and she knew, for a fact, that the silver plate at Bryn Hall was of great value.

Presently she heard a yet more ominous sound, though dulled by distance, of a chair or some other article of furniture being upset in one of the rooms below, and being a brave girl, she at once leapt out of bed, hurriedly donned a few articles of clothing, and then, leaving her chamber, ran downstairs in her stockinged feet, and stood listening in the hall for something that should guide her further course.

She had not to wait long ere she heard the sound of footsteps and of muttering voices in the library hard by, and creeping towards the door thereof, she peered through the keyhole and beheld a sight that made her very blood run cold, for four masked men had just broken open a great iron-banded oak chest, and were bending over it, examining its contents by the light of five glaring rushlights that o'er topped the thumb and the four side-expanded finger tips of a dead man's hand.

Poor Mary knew that hand at a glance, and the conviction struck home to her that her lover had been robbed of it on his way back to the gipsy camp, perhaps murdered besides, and that the wretches who had despoiled him of that whereby he had hoped to save his sister from death, and even restore her to a state of perfect health, were now using the holy relic for a villainous instead of for a good and righteous purpose.

"What should she do?" she hurriedly asked herself, reflecting the while that were she to alarm the house her master would be one of the first to appear upon the scene, and then her share in the abstraction of the dead hand might be discovered, and, as a consequence, she would certainly lose her place, and perhaps be imprisoned, or even hanged in addition, for in those days a person might be, and often was, hanged for stealing anything above the value of fourpence-halfpenny.

On the other hand, she was not a girl to suffer her employer to be robbed with impunity, and knew herself to be agile, muscular, and, to use a metaphor, she was somewhat partial to "as strong as a horse."

So, as none of the would-be robbers appeared to be armed, and the hall in which she stood was hung round with ancient rapiers, daggers, pistols, and other offensive weapons, she resolved to arm herself, rush in upon the housebreakers, and terrify them (as she believed it would be easy to do) into taking a rapid and ignominious flight.

So she seized hold of a dagger with one hand, and a formidable-looking horse-pistol with the other, feeling as brave as a modern Joan of Arc, and pushing open the library door with a foot, for though "shut to," it wasn't fastened, she suddenly appeared before the masked robbers, exclaiming, in hoarse tones, for her agitation was great:

"Put down that holy hand, and then clear out of the house, or some of you shall be dead men in the twinkling of an eye."

On hearing those words, and beholding their utterer, three of the robbers gave vent to howls of dismay, as they discovered that the dead hand had neither rendered them invisible, nor sent everyone in the house to sleep, but the fourth swore a fierce oath, and then softening his voice, as he pulled off his mask, said:

"Don't be a fool, Polly. You would not sell your own Bill to the mare with three legs [gallows], I know full well, and a good part of this rich spoil will be our wedding portion, my pretty lass."

"Oh, Will, dear Will," gasped poor Mary, in an almost whisper, for she was afraid to raise her voice for fear of bringing destruction upon her lover, "I will share in no stolen riches. I would far rather wed you and then beg for you from door to door. Do go away now with the other men, and henceforth lead an honest life, for I will not have anything to do with a—a—thief."

Then, to soften the effect of her last word, which had been, as it were, dragged out of her, she rushed forward, and flung herself, sobbing violently the while, into her lover's arms.

But even as she did so two shots rang shrilly forth, and that lover, with a groan of mortal anguish, slipped out of her encircling grasp to the floor, falling across the body of a second robber, who had also received his quietus, and, glancing wildly round, Mary Morgan beheld her old master, looking grim and stern, standing in the open doorway with a pistol in either hand, each still smoking at the muzzle, whilst she was also aware that the two uninjured robbers were on their knees before him praying for mercy.

CHAPTER III.

"'TWAS YOU WHO MUST HAVE GIVEN THE ROBBERS THE
DEAD HAND."

Now, Sir Geoffry Wynne was a justice of the peace as well as a
baronet, and never did he feel more inclined to exercise sum-
mary jurisdiction than on the present occasion, as he gazed in
turn on the sparkling gold and silver revealed by the upraised
lid of his treasure-chest, on the dead hand of the blessed Father
Arrowsmith, as it lay on the floor, with every thumb- and
finger-entwined rushlight now extinguished, on his unfaithful
servant, as he deemed poor Mary Morgan to be, as she bent,
weeping and wailing, over the dead body of her lover, and on
the two cowardly miscreants who still knelt at his feet, vowing
that they had been tempted into taking part in the housebreak-
ing by their defunct companions, but that they had hitherto
led perfectly innocent and blameless lives, with much more to
the same effect.

Had he had the power, as he certainly had the will, the
choleric old gentleman would certainly have bidden the three
men servants who stood at his back, each grasping a bare
sword, drag the whining cowards forth and string them up to
the nearest convenient tree branch.

As, however, he did not dare go so far as that, he ordered
them to be bound with ropes and locked up in the cellar until,
on the morrow, he would be able to commit them to Warrington gaol.

Then, as they were being dragged away, still howling for
mercy, Sir Geoffry strode across the floor to where Mary
Morgan still knelt beside her dead lover, and, gripping hold of
her arm, he dragged her to her feet, exclaiming the while, in a
voice hoarse with passion:

"Miserable and ungrateful girl to betray the master who

placed such trust in you, and whose bread you have eaten, as did your mother for twenty long years before you were born. 'Twas you who must have given the robbers the Dead Hand, in the hope that it would have enabled them to accomplish their villainy undetected, thus adding sacrilege to your treachery, so that, girl though you are, you shall swing for this night's work. Aye, by the sainted hand which you have profaned, I swear that you shall swing," and as he concluded he shook her as a terrier might shake a rat.

"Oh, master, dear, kind master," shrieked poor Mary, wildly; "I did lend the dead hand to my sweetheart, Bill Boseley, but it was that it might cure a sister who, he said, was sick, well nigh unto death, in the gipsy camp three miles away, and he swore that he would return it ere dawn of day. And—and when I heard the robbers downstairs, I tried to drive them away with a dagger and pistol that I helped myself to in the hall. See, they lie upon the floor now, to vouch for the truth of what I am saying."

"A likely tale," retorted Sir Geoffry, mockingly. "I doubt not but that you conveyed the rascals those weapons in order that they might defend themselves therewith, for they don't seem to have had any of their own, in case they were interrupted in the execution of their villainy. I know that I caught you in the arms of one of them, and I presume that he was paying you in kisses for the assistance that you had rendered him and his fellow rogues."

"Oh, master, how cruelly you misjudge me," sobbed Mary at this bitter retort, and then, womanlike, she fainted dead away.

When she recovered consciousness, she found herself in her own room, but bound fast with cords to the foot of the bedstead.

The day was just breaking, but for long hours she was left there alone, and during these hours, what with grief for the death of her handsome lover, horror at the thought that those who had hitherto so implicitly trusted her now believed her to have been the confederate of thieves, and the dreadful fear that she would be tried, condemned, and hanged for a crime of which she was altogether innocent, her mind gave way, so that when at last some male members of the household came to conduct her to Sir Geoffry Wynne's presence, in order that she might be judicially examined, in place of the merry, laughing girl of the day before, they found a raving maniac.

A dreadful warning was poor Mary's fate to all thoughtless maids who chose for a sweetheart a man with a handsome face and faultless form, but of whose character and antecedents they knew nothing.

Mary Morgan had, therefore, to be despatched to a madhouse instead of to a gaol, and a madhouse of those days was by far the most dreadful asylum of the two.

In the course of a couple of years her unmerited misfortunes ended in the grave.

Bill Boseley and the other dead robber were buried without funeral rites, on the site of the deserted gipsy camp, and there, too, a couple of months later, the twain who had been taken alive, after being duly tried and condemned to death, were hung in chains, thus affording plenty of material, after the crows had done with them, for the manufacture of Dead Hands to be used by other rogues who had any inclination for following in their steps.

Sir Geoffry Wynne lived to be a centenarian, and his sister Tabitha to the age of a hundred and three.

On the latter's decease Bryn Hall fell into other hands, long ere which time the hand of the martyred priest had become anything but an enviable possession, for though, immediately after the abortive burglary, it was reverently cleansed and laid again, wrapped in fresh linen of the finest quality, in its ebony box, which was replaced in the accustomed niche in the wall on the first landing of the old oak staircase, it would no longer lie tranquilly at rest, but often, in the dead of night, would burst open its sarcophagus, wriggle thereout, creep down the wall like a great brown spider, and thereafter run as a rat runs,

or else leap like a grasshopper, all over the house, entering bedrooms, whose doors were fastened and locked, just as easily as
though they stood wide open, thereafter sometimes, to creep
up the bedclothes, and even crawl over the faces of the sleepers.

These antics of the Dead Hand were, of course, very hard
to put up with, but they were more or less patiently borne in
consideration of all the good deeds which the aforesaid hand
had done in life, until it at last struck the owner of Bryn Hall
that the Dead Hand was no longer content to dwell in a place
where it had been put to such vile and unholy uses, and that its
constant wanderings were made in an attempt to escape therefrom, which, for want of the sense of sight, it had hitherto not
succeeded in doing.

So its owner having at length convinced himself on this
point, determined that selfishness should not stand in the way
of the hand's apparent desire for a change of lodging, and presently secured it a new home at Garwood, the seat of another
family of the Old Faith, by the name of Gerard.

Thither it was removed, in a new casket of solid silver, with
all due reverence and solemnity, and there, apparently, tranquillity and contentment were restored to it, for never more
was it known to wander.

On the extinction of the Gerard family, about 1842, and
Garwood passing into the possession of a Protestant owner,
who had little liking for so gruesome an heirloom, the silver
casket and its contents were presented by him to the Catholic
priest of Ashton-in-Makerfield, who was doubtless as glad to
receive the famous relic as the donor was glad to get quit of
it, and we believe that the Holy Hand of the martyred Father
Arrowsmith is still treasured in the Catholic church or Presby-
tery of Ashton-in-Makerfield, though we cannot vouch for it
as a fact.

But the strangest part of the story has yet to be told, for,
though the real Dead Hand was, as we have stated, removed
from Bryn Hall to Garswood, and appeared to be well contented with its change of lodgings, a spectral Dead Hand

almost immediately took possession of its old abode, and there began to play the very pranks that the actual hand had done, creeping out of an equally spectral ebony box in the dead of night, and running or hopping over the floors, and up and down the stairs, but the latter noiselessly, and not with the flop, flop, flop of its bony predecessor. This spirit hand could also, on occasion, fly like a bird, and suddenly alight on a sleeper's nose or elsewhere—(doubtless the general wish of the household tended towards the "elsewhere") but it has never been known to work any worse harm than to occasion a severe fright.

THE CHRISTMAS NUMBER HORROR.

The Christmas number, whether of periodical or newspaper, is now one of the horrors of Christmas. [...]

"Christmas is supposed to be a genial, joyful time of the year, and it would be so still if it were not for the Christmas number. All the ghastly, gruesome, and horrible stories that can be collected are gathered together and published in the Christmas numbers. The healthful, roystering, rollicking humorous stories of Washington Irving and Charles Dickens have given place to the vain pessimistic strivings of a lot of young men, each trying to outdo the other in writing something loathsome and distressing. They vainly imagine that this is a sign of strength, whereas it is just the reverse, and we predict that the thing has about come to an end. If the average Christmas number continues to be what it has been for the last few years, it will be left on the book-stall unbought by the great British public. The future of the present style of Christmas number lies with the waste-paper man."

Dundalk Herald [Louth, Ireland], Dec. 30, 1893: 3, col. 4.
[Quoting the *Detroit Free Press*]

James Skipp Borlase

The Wicked Lady Howard; or, The Coach Made of Dead Men's Bones

As with "The Dead Hand," Borlase chose a setting further back in time than most Christmas ghost story authors. Of the subject, author Arthur Hamilton Norway wrote, "As far as history tells us, she was simply a woman of great force of character, who managed her estates admirably, and was tenacious of her rights against a greedy husband." In spite of that, she has been given a reputation as a monstrous black widow in Tavistock, West Devon, South West England.[1] The story has also been told in song form, one collected by Sabine Baring-Gould, "My Ladye's Coach," in Songs of the West *(1891), and a 2013 bluegrass composition by the Carrivick Sisters, "Lady Howard." This story first appeared in the periodical* Wicklow People *on Christmas Eve, 1905.*

CHAPTER I.

"I INTEND TO KILL YOU DURING THE HAPPIEST HOUR OF YOUR LIFE!"

IT IS CHRISTMAS EVE of the year 1643, and the annual ball is in full swing in the great assembly room of the quaint old borough town of Tavistock, in Devon, a room which had once been the refectory of its noble abbey of Saint Mary the

[1] Arthur H. Norway, *Highways and Byways in Devon and Cornwall* (London: Macmillan, 1897): 162-163.

Virgin and St. Ramon, and it was a common belief of that day that on such festive occasions as the present the ghost of one or other of the for long dead Black Monks would glide, mist-like, amongst the guests, with stern visage and clasped hands, whenever one of them was destined to die a violent death within the following year.

Upon the present occasion, however, not one amongst the two hundred or so of dancers gave a thought to the ancient Benedictine Brothers, whose once holy home they were profaning with their frivolous pleasures; and yet not all of those lovely girls and handsome cavaliers were so happy as they seemed to be, for Violet Fitzroy, the acknowledged belle of the assembly, was almost monopolised by middle-aged Lord Howard, whom she had consented to marry on account of his title and his wealth, whereas, in secret, she hated him with all her heart, whilst the young cornet of dragoons whom she loved with an equal degree of passion was powerless to worship her, save at a distance, and so found nothing better to do than to gnaw his amber-hued moustachios, play with his sword hilt, and wish, over and over to himself, that he could plunge the blade of the weapon guard-deep into his successful rival's body.

How he cursed his fate in that he was a younger son and a mere cornet of dragoons, with more gold lace upon his brilliant uniform than gold coin in his purse; aye, he would willingly have sold his very soul to the foul fiend at this moment to become suddenly as rich as Lord Howard, who was owner of the great estates of Oakhampton Park and Fitzford Chase, with a rent-roll of some thirty thousand a year; for well he knew that in such case the lovely Violet would have cast off her middle-aged suitor as carelessly as though he had been a split glove, and bestowed on him, the penniless cornet, her person as well as her heart.

And Lord Howard, unhappily for his peace of mind, was quite as well aware of this as ever his rival was, and being of a highly jealous disposition he gave back Hubert Molyneux hate for hate, even though he knew that he held the game in his own hand, for he had long ago discovered that Violet Fitzroy loved rank and wealth far more than she was capable of loving a mere man, and these he could offer her whilst Molyneux could not.

Yet, for all that, it maddened him to perceive how often his promised bride cast stolen, and, as she thought, unnoticed glances, at the handsome young Royalist officer, and which glances were invariably returned with interest, though throughout the evening she dared hold no closer communion with him, as her stern old father was present, and had vetoed the lovers exchanging anything beyond a formal bow, and well did Violet Fitzroy know that disobedience on her part would subject her plump, milk-white back, and lovely dimpled shoulders, to a sound horsewhipping as soon as she reached home.

Hubert Molyneux might have danced with many a lovely girl, had he felt so inclined, for the daughters of fair Devon were as renowned for their beauty in those far off times as they are at the present day; in which case he would have owed such favour not only to his own good looks, his dashing uniform, and his gallant bearing, but also the great victory which the King's army had gained over the vastly superior forces of the Parliament a few months previously, on neighbouring Bradock Downs, and in which he and his regiment of Royal Dragoons had borne a very conspicuous share.

But Cornet Molyneux had no eyes or heart for any of these rural belles; indeed, for the entire evening, his gaze seldom wandered, for more than a minute at a time, from Violet Fitzroy and Lord Howard, who seemed to be bound up in each other.

Howard, on the other hand, cast many a glance towards the Royalist officer, each, if possible, more malevolent than those which had gone before, and at length, when, for a wonder, Violet was dancing with some one else, he crossed the floor to where the cornet of dragoons stood, and said with extreme insolence of tone:

"You seem to take an impertinent interest in Miss Fitzroy and myself."

"Psh! my venerable Lord, I have been infinitely amused at beholding a man of your age playing the ardent wooer to a young girl not yet out of her teens; but doubtless your wealth and title more than compensate for your two and a half score of years and your lack of good looks," was the scornful answer of the penniless soldier.

"I shall be happy to prove to you that a gash from a sword-blade across your face will set our personal comeliness upon a par," answered Lord Howard, hotly, and drawing off a glove he struck Molyneux sharply across the cheek therewith.

By this time the angry rivals were surrounded by a wandering crowd, most of whom expected that a tragedy would follow.

But Cornet Molyneux received the dire insult that had been offered him with an ironical peal of laughter, and so soon as he had recovered therefrom he bowed to his assailant, and said, in gay tones:

"A palpable challenge, which I accept with ecstatic joy and deep thankfulness. It is the etiquette of the duello, however, that the challenged party may wage the combat when and where he chooses, wherefore, I have the honour to inform your lordship, within the hearing of all present, that *I intend to kill you during the happiest hour of your life,* which I shall wait for with the greatest possible patience."

With that Molyneux made his rival a supercilious bow, and then pushed his way through the wondering circle that had hemmed them round.

A minute later he had left the assembly room, which saw him no more that night.

Lord Howard, though brave enough under ordinary circumstances, felt a cold shiver pass through his frame as Molyneux parted from him, for the devilish gleam in the cornet's eyes had altogether belied the conventional smile upon his lips.

"I intend to kill you during the happiest hour of your life!"

The words recurred to him again and again, for they seemed to partake more of a prophecy than a threat.

"The fellow doubtless intends to slay me on my very wedding day," next presented itself to his mind with the force of a conviction, so 'tis little wonder that all feeling of happiness and even comfort abandoned him for the rest of the evening.

Indeed, he was by no means sorry when the ball had ended, whereupon he accepted Sir Ralph Fitzroy's invitation to accompany his daughter and himself home to their fine old family seat in the suburbs of the town.

As for the lovely Violet, she was as gay and light-hearted as ever, for she had been in the supper room when the contretemps between her two lovers had taken place, and had since heard not even so much as the vaguest rumour thereof, which was certainly somewhat strange.

The night was not destined to pass, however, without terror striking even *her*, for, as the trio were crossing the Abbey Green, where thirteen malefactors dangled from the long crossbeam of a single gallows, as a result of the Winter Assizes having been recently held in Tavistock, because Exeter, the county town, was being ravaged by the plague, the ghostly figure of a "Black Monk" barred their way.

It seemed to have arisen out of the very ground, and as the wind blew back the cowl which covered its head, the moonlight revealed, not a face, but a fleshless and grinning skull.

Then one bony hand was placed on Violet's right shoulder, and the other on Lord Howard's left shoulder, whilst a hollow voice ejaculated mournfully, "Repent, repent, or both within a year! Repent, repent, or both within a year!" and the next instant the ghostly monk had vanished as suddenly and as mysteriously as he had appeared.

Sir Ralph Fitzroy saw naught of the unearthly visitant; but Violet and Lord Howard not only beheld the monk but also fully understood his grim warning.

Alas! well would it have been for both of them had they not so soon forgotten or disregarded it.

CHAPTER II.

The Christmas of 1643 has passed away, New Year's Eve has arrived, and with it a clear, frosty, moonlight night.

Under the shadow of Betsy Grimshaw's Tower, so called because of the murder of a young woman of that name therein, whose ghost, on the night of "All Souls," is still believed to haunt that now detached remnant of the ancient Abbey, Cornet Hubert Molyneux is anxiously keeping tryst for the fair Violet Fitzroy, and as the clock of St. Eustachius' Church strikes the hour of nine, the blue-eyed, golden-haired girl, warmly clad in furs, hastens towards and joins him.

A silent embrace, and she demands of him eagerly:

"Why did you insist upon my meeting you here to-night, Hubert, for you must know that, as the betrothed wife of Lord Howard, it was most unfitting that I should come."

"D— Lord Howard," was Molyneux's angry retort. "You have come here to hear me vow that you shall never be his wife, inasmuch as I intend to kill him on his very wedding eve. I gave him the promise that I would do so in the presence of a crowd of witnesses at the Assembly Ball, and as a man of honour I cannot break my word."

"And do you feel sure that you *can* kill him, Hubert?"

"Well, as I am the best swordsman in the King's Dragoons, I regard it as a dead certainty, my dear girl."

"And then you would fain marry me, I presume, and sup-port me on your munificent pay of five shillings a day; for let me assure you that my father, were I to commit so rash an act, would turn me penniless from his doors."

"Love will enable me to carve you a fortune with my sword, Violet."

"What, in the service of a bankrupt King, to bolster up

whose fast-sinking cause your father has ruined himself, like many another gallant cavalier? Your words are words of folly, Hubert."

"It seems to me that in your heart you are bent on marrying Lord Howard, in which case you could never have truly loved *me*."

"On the contrary, I love you with every whit as deep and true an affection as you can possibly feel for me. Added to that I will become your wife if you will accept me as Lady Howard instead of as Violet Fitzroy."

"What on earth do you mean? You speak in riddles."

"Riddles very easy to guess, I should think. Well, I will give you a clue to their answer. Kill Lord Howard *after* he has married me instead of before, and then you will wed a wealthy widow instead of a penniless maid."

"My vengeance will scarcely bear waiting so long. Besides, I vowed, and that in public, that I would kill him during the happiest hour of his life."

"And don't you think that with so lovely a girl-wife as I shall be, every succeeding hour of his lordship's wedded life will be happier than the preceding one? Taking which for granted, after he and I are once wedded you cannot help but kill him during the happiest hour of his life, be it when and where it will," rejoined Violet Fitzroy, smilingly.

"I will slay him the day after he has wedded you instead of the day before," exclaimed Molyneux with a fierce oath.

"No, that would look too much as though we had planned his death between us, added to which I would like to flaunt it for a few months as 'My Lady Howard.' During those months I will so cozen the old fool that he shall execute a will in my favour, leaving me all that he possesses. Will it not make your revenge the sweeter the knowledge that you have won from him his broad estates in addition to his wife?"

"Ay, perhaps it will. Yes, most assuredly it will," laughed the dragoon cornet, continuing: "And for how long do you want to pose as 'My Lady Howard?'"

"Oh, I shall be sick of the role within the New Year that is on the point of opening. I make no doubt."

"You want well nigh twelve months to indulge your folly in. My God, Violet, have you forgotten, as until this moment, in the charm of your presence, I have done, that the Black Monk has marked you as well as Lord Howard for the tomb within the year that you so lightly speak of?"

"Oh, for that matter, ghosts may err as well as living men, so I snap my fingers at the Black Monk's warning, or at all events at that portion of it which refers to myself. The old must die, and 'tis very fitting that they should, but I am young and lovely, and so can afford to laugh at death. Well, Hubert, our arrangements are settled, and I must be gone, lest my father should discover my absence from home at so late an hour."

Her lover agreed with her that to part at once would, under the circumstances, be the wisest plan; so, after a rapturous embrace, they separated, and Violet sped homewards.

★ ★ ★ ★ ★

Within a few weeks, dating from her last interview with her lover, Violet Fitzroy became Lady Howard, and was installed as mistress at Oakhampton Park, an almost princely residence which is now fast falling to decay and ruin.

In a very short while she ruled her middle-aged husband with a rod of iron, notwithstanding that the iron was concealed by roses.

Her slightest will became his law.

She presently made him take her to London, where she shone for awhile as the very queen of loveliness at the Royal Court.

But ere long her fitful nature pined for yet another change, for she thought how pleasant it would be to return to Devonshire, and there dazzle all her former friends with her newly-acquired London airs and graces, and with the grand dresses and costly jewels that had there been purchased for her adornment.

She even cajoled Lord Howard to present her with a wonderfully painted and gilded coach, with six beautiful milk-
white steeds to draw it, and in this sumptuous vehicle, with
winged cupids and other allegorical figures carved thereon,
they made the return journey, their coachman and two footmen being magnificent-looking specimens of their kind, and
adorned with well-nigh as great an amount of gold lace as was
the rich velvet hammercloth, on each side of which the arms
of Lord Howard gleamed, parted, per pale, with those of his
wife.

But their reception, on their homecoming, was not such
as they had anticipated, for, in order to pay for the extravagances of Lady Howard, his lordship's bailiff had oppressed
the tenantry to such a degree that the hitherto prosperous
had become impoverished, and those who had been merely
poor were actually famine-stricken, wherefore, in lieu of the
expected cheers, hoots and hisses arose on all sides.

But the lovely Violet Howard only laughed at these hostile
demonstrations, and presently proceeded to inaugurate a series
of costly fêtes, in order to afford herself the opportunity of
displaying her flashing diamonds and her grand court dresses,
whilst all the while she was in secret correspondence with her
lover, Hubert Molyneux, whose regiment was quartered at
Exeter.

And at last the time arrived when she even grew tired, to use
her own words, of flaunting it as my Lady Howard, and then
she pined more eagerly with each passing week to give herself
wholly to the only man on earth whom she really loved.

Meanwhile winter had again come round, a second Christmas was nigh at hand, and there was to be a repetition of the
annual county ball at the Tavistock Assembly Room.

"Lord Howard and I will attend that social function on
Christmas Eve," she wrote to Molyneux, "and shall start for
home at the stroke of midnight. I will make the commencement of the drive the happiest hour of his lordship's life, for
never previously shall I have looked so lovely or behaved so

graciously to him. It will be for you to render that happiest hour of his life, his last hour on earth, and at the same time to make me your own for ever."

And when the night of that annual ball arrived Lady Howard was once more the acknowledged belle of the room, and many a gay cavalier envied her husband the possession of so young and so lovely a wife. Her eyes were as sparklingly bright as her diamonds, and her laughter far sweeter than the music of the orchestra. She danced every dance, and was in the highest of spirits throughout the long evening.

Then when, at last, the midnight hour struck, and the old church bells began to ring forth their joyous Christmas peal, her husband handed her into her gorgeous coach (the like of which had never before been seen in those parts), and a minute later, with its cocked-hatted coachman on the box, and the two stately footmen standing erect behind its body, the six milk-white steeds broke into a trot and the pretentious equipage rolled away in the direction of Oakhampton Park and—*destruction*.

CHAPTER III.

A DUEL TO THE DEATH.—A FELON SHOT.—THE COACH OF DEAD MEN'S BONES.

The road from Tavistock to Oakhampton is a wild, rugged, and lonely one, skirting, as it does, the dreary lower reaches of Dartmoor.

But Lord Howard recked naught of this, for the carriage was as brilliantly lighted within as it was without, and his beautiful girl-wife lay in his arms, with her plump and snow-white neck and shoulders all bare, and her soft, round breasts rising and falling with the violence of the emotions under which she laboured.

"Violet," his lordship exclaimed at length, as he strained her to his embrace, "never before have I seen you look so lovely. This—this is, indeed, the happiest hour of my life."

Scarcely had he uttered the words when a harsh voice called upon the coachman to pull up, three horsemen loomed out of the surrounding gloom, and, a second later, one of these dismounted, approached the carriage, lugged open the nearest door thereof, and then doffing his plumed hat and making its inmates a polite bow, he exclaimed airily:

"My lord, you and I have a little account to settle which is just twelve months overdue, so if you will kindly alight, my sword shall give you acquittance in full for the debt so long owing. My name, as you will doubtless remember, is Hubert Molyneux."

"Mr. Molyneux," answered his lordship stiffly—aye, as stiffly as his beautiful wife now sat upright in the carriage by his side, with a baleful light in her violet eyes, "strange as is the time and place that you have chosen for our duello, I acknowledge that you are acting within your rights, and, therefore, I shall be most happy to oblige you."

So saying, he stepped forth from the carriage to the ground, and whilst two of Cornet Molyneux's troopers overawed the coachman and footmen with levelled pistols, Howard and Molyneux sought a patch of level turf whereon to wage their duel to the death, and, having found it, courteously saluted each other, then drew their rapiers, and waited impatiently for a cloud to pass from off the face of the moon so that they might have its full light to fight by.

As soon as ever the orb of night shed its silvery radiance over the scene, their blades rasped and ground together till sparks of fire flashed from the tempered steel, whilst lovely Lady Howard watched the fierce combat through the open window of her gorgeous coach, with contracted brows and evil eyes, sending up an impious prayer to heaven the while that her husband might fall death-stricken, and her lover presently approach her unhurt.

But Lord Howard was a better master of fence than the

cornet of Dragoons had suspected. He fought with great coolness and skill, and more than a quarter of an hour elapsed before it was at all certain how the combat would end.

Oh, what an agonizing quarter of an hour that was to the beautiful, but wicked woman, who watched the deadly strife. She had, weeks ago, coaxed her husband into the making of a will which would bequeath to her all that he possessed, and now she positively yearned to share those vast estates and that magnificent rent roll with the man who had always owned her affections.

"The beast will not let himself be killed," she hissed, at length, between her tightly clenched teeth: and the next instant she could scarcely repress a shriek of anguish as the moonlight shone full upon the white enamelled lace embroidered belt that traversed her lover's breast and she observed that it was encrimsoned with his blood.

At the sight, a wild rage, which amounted almost to madness, possessed itself of the beautiful fiend, and oblivious of the fact that such an act, if successful, would constitute her a murderess, and, more likely than not, ensure her a felon's doom, she plucked a horse pistol from out the receptacle which all carriages in those lawless times were furnished with for that special use, and, steadying the long steel barrel on the window ledge, took steady aim at Lord Howard's back, which at the moment was broadly presented to her, and then pressed the trigger.

Shrilly the shot rang out, a shriek of mortal agony followed, and Lord Howard, dropping his sword, fell prone to earth.

At the sight, the murderess gave vent to a truly diabolical laugh of triumph, which was, however, suddenly changed to a cry of intense mental agony, when she beheld Hubert Molyneux reel and fall prostrate in turn, gasping with his last breath:

"Violet, I'm sped!"

Fain would the self-made widow have leapt from the carriage and rushed to her lover's side, but by now that carriage was in rapid motion, for the six milk-white steeds, terrified by the pistol shot, after a brief struggle with their driver, had overmastered him, and were tearing along homewards at a headlong gallop.

The two mounted dragoons made no attempt to follow, for they had their officer to attend to, so the coach rushed on in its wild flight, rocking and reeling like a Dutch galliot in a choppy sea, owing to the roughness of the road, and every instant threatening to capsize altogether, whilst its lovely occupant had enough to occupy her mind in contemplating her own imminent peril, for well she knew that a mile or so further on, a narrow stone bridge had to be crossed that spanned a chasm at least a hundred feet in depth, with jagged rocks and a rushing torrent at the bottom.

The coachmen and footmen knew this equally well, and one by one leapt to the ground, whilst Lady Howard endeavoured to open first one and then the other of the carriage doors, in order to follow their example, but her trembling hands failed to accomplish her desire.

Her end quickly came—that is to say, her end as a mortal woman—for, as a pallid ghost, she will haunt these wild regions for evermore.

The maddened horses swept around an abrupt curve in the road, the bridge lay directly in front of them, the dip between it and them was too steep to allow them to turn evenly upon it, whilst the cumbersome coach pressed hard upon them, forcing them up against the bridge parapet. The rough unmorticed stones gave way before their involuntary on-rush, and with a crash like that of thunder, a mass of those stones, the six milk-white steeds and the gorgeous coach with shrieking occupant, crashed down that horrible chasm to be dashed to pieces at its bottom.

* * * * *

And, a few seconds later, another coach—but, oh, how

dissimilar an one—came rushing up out of the gorge of death, and, by supernatural agency, gained the mountain road.

It was a coach in shape exactly like Lady Howard's, but it was black, and made of dead men's bones (the bones, it was afterwards reported, of those wretched tenants of Lord Howard, whom, to minister to his wife's extravagances, he had rack-rented and oppressed until they and theirs had died from famine). Imps of Hell were carven thereon, in place of chubby Cupids, there was a pall for a hammer-cloth, a dead babe on either side for doorsteps, and a grinning skull at each corner of the coach top where gay plumes had previously waved. Behind the awful vehicle stood two fleshless skeletons in place of footmen, the driver was a horned and tailed fiend, and the six coal-black steeds that he drove had eyes of fire, and snorted flame from their nostrils as they tore madly along.

And within that death coach sat the pallid wraith of the beautiful Lady Howard, clad now in a winding sheet, which was no whit whiter than her horror- and terror-stricken face.

On tore the coach, its wheels passing over the bodies of the dead duellists, and scaring away, with shrieks of terror, the two dragoons, who had only just mounted their horses to ride back to the Exeter barracks.

Lady Howard could hear the cracking and scrunching of her husband's and her lover's bones as the heavy wheels passed over them.

Next she became aware that the coach had quitted the road, and was tearing along the open moor, over the so-called Soul Path, across which the souls of all those who die in those parts flit, on their way to eternity, pursued by the spectre huntsman and his hell hounds, vulgarly called, throughout Devonshire, "the devil and his dandy dogs."

No sooner did this knowledge reach the poor ghost than:

> She heard the black hunter, and dread shook her mind,
>   Ne'er before had she felt such a fear,
> She heard the black hunter's dread voice in the wind,

She heard his cursed hell hounds run yelping behind,
  And his steed thundered loud on her ear.

And now he appeared, through the gloom of the night,
  His plume seemed a cloud in the skies,
His form the dark mists of the hills to the sight,
And as from a furnace leaps forth the red light,
  So glared the fierce gleam of his eyes.

He blew from his bugle so dreadful a blast,
  His hounds howling hideous the while,
That all nature trembled and shook as aghast,
As when some great castle's high battlements brast,
  And fall in one tottering pile.

Yes, the demon hunter and the hounds of hell were undoubtedly in full cry after the soul of the wicked Lady Howard, even whilst the church bells of many a distant town and village were ringing out their merry Christmas peal.

The huge, open-mouthed black dogs, breathing smoke and flame, were continually leaping up at the windows of the death coach, as the ghost of the once lovely Violet Fitzroy shrieked and shivered within it, and so on, mile after mile, over the desolate moor, the hunt continued, until, at last, a great gulf suddenly yawned in the ground directly in front of the mingled flight and chase, and down into that apparently bottomless abyss plunged the six black horses, dragging the coach and its ghostly occupant with them.

A hollow roar, as of thunder, accompanied its descent, with an upward flash of a thousand lambent flames, and then the earth closed again over the awful tragedy that it had buried in its deepest recesses, and the Black Hunter and his hounds, with a wild "View hallo!" and a chorus of fiendish howls and yelps swept onwards along the dreary "soul path," doubtless in quest of other victims not yet "run to earth."

But the ghost of the wicked Lady Howard, in the coach made of dead men's bones, on stormy and tempestuous winter nights, is said to still revisit the "glimpses of the moon," and not only to confine itself to the desolate regions of Dartmoor, but, with its demoniac driver and its skeleton footmen, to rush at headlong speed from Oakhampton Park Gates on to, and even through, the streets of Tavistock, the pallid ghost of Lady Howard its sole occupant; and, as it passes the Assembly Room of the latter town, the still beautiful wraith gazes piteously thereat, and wrings its hands, doubtless remembering the two Christmas balls at each of which it was once the acknowledged belle.

True, the ghostly equipage has not been seen of late years, but the author of this tale remembers, when he was a boy, and dwelling in Tavistock, that on the eve of All Souls' Day, and that of Christmas, neither he nor his companions were brave enough to look forth from door or window as the dread midnight hour drew nigh, lest they should behold, clattering along the cobble-stone paved street without, on its way to Oakhampton Park, the coach made of dead men's bones, with its six black horses, its demon driver, its skeleton footmen, and the beautiful wraith of the long dead and gone Lady Howard looking out through one of its windows, and, as an unfailing consequence of the gruesome sight, die a violent death within the passing year.

Huan Mee

Ghost of the Living

Huan Mee was the jocular pseudonym for brothers Charles
Herbert Mansfield (1864-1930) *and* Walter Edwin
Mansfield (1870-1916). *Together they authored several
books and short stories and even dabbled in song and theatre.
Their ghost stories "The Tragedy in the Train" and "Phantom Death" have been anthologized in recent years, but this
Christmas ghost story is reprinted for the first time since running
in several British newspapers in 1905. Unusually, in October
the* Hastings and St. Leonards Observer *began teasing the
story's appearance with a contest. In early December, they would
print a "skeleton story" with just the story's title, character
names, locality, and general plot. First and second prizes of 15
and 5 shillings would go to readers who could, using only those
elements, compose a story of their own that would turn out "most
like the original."*[1]

C HRISTMASTIDE, THE TIME OF MERRIMENT and good
cheer, always seems to associate itself with the supernatural. Perhaps it is for vivid contrast, but no Christmas party
seems complete unless chairs have been drawn to the fire and
some ghost story has silenced the merriment for a time.

The house party at Colonel Rupert's has been a glorious
night of Christmas jollity. Christmas dinner at six, and at nine
dancing and games commenced, which ran the evening and
part of the morning through at lightning speed.

---

[1] "Skeleton Story," *Hastings and St. Leonards Observer* (Oct. 7, 1905): 4, col. 9.

It was a really genuine Christmas country-house party of the best old-fashioned sort. One of the kind where the servants join heartily in the merriment and all class distinctions are pushed upon one side. Sir Rupert headed one quadrille with his housekeeper, and I was one of the side couples with a lady's maid, who, I must confess, danced delightfully.

In the early hours of the morning, when the dancing was over and the womenfolk had retired, we men found ourselves in the billiard-room just for a final nightcap and a yarn before bed.

Then the conversation turned to ghosts.

"Any of you youngsters believe in ghosts?" said the Colonel suddenly.

"I believe in spirits," one of our party murmured, as he mixed himself a whisky and soda.

"It's all very well for you to try and be funny," the Colonel continued, with a good-tempered laugh; "but you know ghosts are serious things. I've got one now that is costing me about a hundred a year."

"Do you pay him weekly?" asked the humorist.

"I don't pay him at all," the Colonel answered, with another laugh; "but there's a splendid little house on the border of the estate by the forest, and I can't get anybody to take it. Directly a tenant comes to look over it he hears the talk in the village that it's haunted, and either he is frightened himself, or his womenfolk are, so it never goes off.

"It's very hard luck indeed," the Colonel continued, selecting a cigar with as doleful a face as if the hundred a year really mattered a pin to him.

"You should follow the ideas of the fairy tales," said the humorist, "and offer your daughter's hand to the man who would sleep there for one night and lay the ghost."

Now Webster Charrington was engaged to the pretty daughter of the Colonel, so, of course, as we laughed, we all glanced towards him.

He smiled quietly at the thought of winning his sweetheart

in such a manner, and then his face grew serious.

"I would not sleep in that house for a million paid in advance," he said, and then, as if to make it stronger still, "I would not stay a night there alone, not even to please Ethel."

"But, my dear boy," the Colonel exclaimed, gazing in astonishment at his future son-in-law, "you don't mean to say that you, a sensible man, believe in ghosts."

"I've had the fortune to meet a ghost of a living man," he answered. "That was bad enough. I never want to see a ghost of the dead."

"A ghost of a living man," the Colonel ejaculated. "Oh, ridiculous!"

"Perhaps you'd like to hear it all," Webster Charrington replied, with a glance that took in the circle, and there was a murmur of assent from everyone.

"I've often wanted to tell it to someone," he continued meditatively; "but have never cared to. I may as well to-night, just for the sake of company.

"For the sake of company?" I exclaimed. "It's a strange idea, Web."

"Yes, it is strange," he answered, in his quiet way; "but, do you know, for years past I have wanted to tell the yarn, as I say, just for company's sake. I can't bear to put up with it myself any longer. As I start to talk of it now I feel as though my head had been shaven, and an icy wind was blowing on it. My whole skin is prickling with the remembrance."

Instinctively we drew our chairs nearer the blazing fire, and one or two took a drink from the glass beside them. Webster Charrington thought, fully filled his pipe, and then turned to us again.

"I think I'd like to tell you," he said. "Some of you perhaps have got more brains than I have, and you might be able to explain it for me. I can't. It happened years ago, and I've never found a solution. I wish I could, but there isn't one."

He slowly lighted his pipe, thoughtfully blew a cloud ceilingwards, and commenced the story.

"It's about ten years back now. I hadn't got anywhere near finding a living. I starved best part of the week, and went hungry the rest. I had great ambitions, and kept them in a very small room in a dingy square near King's Cross.

"I had the first floor front, and another man—an artist like myself, but a cleverer man—had the first floor back. He was introduced to me by his cough one day—poor fellow—and at a glance I saw all there was to see. We became friends, he and I, and I saw the rough sketches which he had made of a picture which was to bring him fame when he was able to afford the money for canvas and paint. I couldn't help him to that extent. I used to wish I could. I could only help him not to starve, and, genius that he was, I think he used to love me, just like a dog might."

Webster Charrington's pipe had gone out, and he slowly lighted it.

"It was at Gower-street it happened," he continued, after a while. "I met a friend up West. A real friend who saw that I hadn't been overfeeding of late.

"He took me out to dinner, and as he was going to Portland-road we took the underground from Paddington, where we had dined. He left me at his station, and I had the carriage to myself. First-class, too, a luxury I had never before enjoyed in my life.

"I tell you I was perfectly happy, perfectly contented, and perfectly sober. It's as well to tell you fellows that, for you make a joke of everything. I've been an abstainer all my life."

Several of us nodded. No one felt inclined to make a joke of anything, for we realised we were on the eve of a tragedy. Again Charrington drew thoughtfully at his pipe.

"I told you I lived at King's Cross," he said, "and my friend left me at Portland-road. The next station is Gower-street, and as the train started moving out of the station I heard the sound of a man running by the side of the carriage; I heard the pat-pat of his feet as he jumped upon the footboard. I saw the handle move as if the door had been opened; after a second I saw it twitch again, as though the door had been closed, but no one had entered the carriage—no one that I could see.

"I did not realise anything then. I did not understand. It seemed to me that someone had tried to enter the carriage and had fallen beneath.

"I expected the train to be stopped, and I sprang to my feet in alarm, but the train swung clear of the station into the tunnel, and then I realised something—I know not what? but from every pore of my skin there broke an icy, clammy sweat.

"In that empty corner there was a sound of breathing that came high above the roar of the train in the tunnel. Above the roar, too, came a tap as though something had been dropped upon the floor.

"'You fool!' I yelled to myself. 'You're going mad. You're like a boy. Do something.'

"In a spasm of bravado I rose to my trembling legs and flung myself into the empty seat.

"I'm not going to try to describe the result of that folly, or to picture the horror of that contact. It's something I want to forget if I ever can. I know I rolled from the seat on to the floor, and crouched there for what seemed an eternity—it could only have been a minute or so; you know the whole journey is short—in such terror as no living man but myself has ever felt. The blurr of the lights at King's Cross as we ran into the station brought me to half-consciousness and sanity, and I staggered out of that awful carriage out into the open-air, and had the first and only drop of brandy in my life.

"I scarcely know how I got home that night, for the terror seemed still to hang upon me wherever I walked. It was with a feeling of relief that I saw my fellow-lodger's door was open and he was there at work on his sketches.

"It was company at least, and I was frightened to be alone.

"'Well, old chap,' I exclaimed, as I stood in the doorway. 'How do you feel?'

"He did not trouble even to turn his head—a most strange

thing, for, as I have told you, he was devoted to me for the few small human kindnesses I had done for him.

"He just answered, with his back turned towards me—

"'Oh, badly; it's always bad, and always will be. It's worse than usual to-night. I've just been fooling about over the rough sketches which I shall never get a chance of reproducing in my picture, and I dropped asleep and dreamed. What do you think in all conscience I dreamed, Webster? Dreamed I was well. Isn't it laughable? Isn't it funny?'

"He laughed a discordant mocking laugh, and I hastily crossed the bare little room and laid my hand on his shoulder.

"At once he was upon his feet, and stretched his hands impulsively towards me.

"'Webster, old man,' he said, 'what a cad I am; what a despicable ingrate to worry you—you, my dearest friend, with my childishness.'

"I sat on the edge of the table and lighted my pipe. I had forgotten my own troubles at the vividness of his.

"'Jack, old man,' I said; 'don't you go and get the blue devils. I've got some good news for us both. I met an old friend to-night—a real friend, who took me out to dinner, and looked at some of the sketches I always carry with me in the hope of finding someone to admire them. He told me I was a clever chap, and he'd soon see that I had an opening on one of the weekly papers at a good screw. Now, Jack, I'll get him to interest his generous self in you, and we'll share a glorious studio somewhere round Regent's Park. How does the idea strike you?'

"'Splendidly,' he replied, and he spoke with enthusiasm—I believe so that he should not seem to discourage me."

Charrington again paused, and again lit his pipe, which had got such a knack of going out during this story, and one or two of us needed the matches too, for we had become too absorbed in this tragedy to keep our pipes going.

"You'll be pleased to hear," he continued presently, "that I had got rid of all my superstitious fancies by the morning. The broad light of day seemed to put a great deal of commonsense into me. I came to the conclusion that I had dropped asleep, dreamed it all in a few seconds, and been awakened by rolling from the seat of the carriage. I called it a nightmare caused by indigestion brought on by a heavy meal in a stomach that was used to being thin. A good solid, rational interpretation, was it not?"

We nodded, but with reserve, for there seemed to be a touch of deep cynicism in Webster Charrington's tones.

"I called upon my friend again that day," he continued, "to gain his interest in my fellow-lodger as well as myself; and he, like the good chap that he was, promised that he would call and see his work, and if it was as good as I said it was—and he counted me no mean judge—he would interest artistic patrons in him and, maybe, he said in his jovial tones, 'Make my friend's fortune.'

"I trod the air when I left him that night. Surely luck was on the turn now, and all was bright. The thought of my terror of the previous night came back to me, and I laughed a jeering laugh at my own folly, and then determined to do a silly thing. I would prove what an imaginative dyspeptic I was, I said, by covering the whole journey again, and then the joke should be one I would tell at my own expense, and raise shrieks of laughter for the rest of my life at the incident."

We could all see by the expression on Webster Charrington's face that the height of his story was near, and to some of us, I think, came that cold, prickly feeling that he had felt himself.

"I went to Paddington again," he quietly continued, "and wasted my money on a first-class ticket to King's Cross; the train went through to Portland-road, and there I glanced at the time. It was coincidence indeed: I was in the very same train as on the previous night. I whistled an air from the latest opera to keep my spirits up, and we ran into Gower-street.

"Then as the train started moving, my whistle died as if it had been frozen. The same pat-pat of feet came on the platform as the train started to move from the station, and again came the click as of a hand unfastening the door.

"Then I turned my face from the door, but a second after gave a laugh and a sigh of relief, for I saw reflected in the window by my side at the far end of the carriage the figure of a man who had entered the compartment.

"I admit I had crouched into a corner of the carriage when I heard what I thought were the ghostly steps upon the platform; but now my courage came back to me, and I laughed as I thought how easily I had been frightened—just because a man had rushed for the door as the train was moving.

"He was enveloped in a heavy travelling cloak, a cap was pulled down over his forehead, and a thick scarf enveloped the lower portion of his face.

"Above the roar of the train came his breathing—that strange, gasping breathing which brought to my mind the dream of the night before.

"Then suddenly something dropped on to the floor of the carriage, and it lay before blood-stained, but still glinting in the light of the lamp above us.

"It was a white-handled razor—one I fancied I had seen somewhere before, and with a cry I jumped to my feet and sprang to the figure seated in the corner. In my mad fright I expected my hand to pass through the form that my sight told me was there, but my frenzied brain told me was not. My out-stretched hand touched a solid body, and as it was pushed back under the vigour of my grasp the cap slipped off and I saw the eyes of my fellow-lodger looking into mine.

"'I didn't expect to see you in a first-class carriage, Web-ster,' he said, chokily. 'I did not know anyone was here, I thought the carriage was empty. I'm sorry, old fellow. I didn't want to worry you. It's just fate, that's what it is.'

"He fell forward into my hands so suddenly that I dropped upon my knees just as I had done the night before.

"'But, Jack,' I cried; 'Jack, old fellow, what have you done? Why have you done it all? We were going so well—'

" 'Going well!' he gasped, and the tears ran down his cheeks. 'I got tired of life, and I've ended it. You know I dreamed I was well last night.'

"The blurr of the lights of King's Cross came again, as the night before, with a flash upon my numbed senses, and I thrust open the door and called for assistance. He was dead, poor old Jack, and he died in my arms. I believe he would have chosen that, but in his grand unselfishness he tried to die like a dog.

"That is my story," Charrington continued slowly. "I must leave it to wiser heads than mine to explain it all.

"He had written in a letter to me, which I found at home, that success had come to me, and he was not going to be a dead weight upon me. He could never be strong enough to do any good, he said, and my friend might get tired of running two artists, one half dead. So he said good-bye. He had slept the night before, he said once again, and dreamed he was quite well. He wished me luck in his simple style, and then went out, not knowing it was written that we were to meet again.

"There's the whole story," Webster Charrington exclaimed, rising to his feet. "I don't know whether any of you fellows are wise enough to explain whether I imagined it all the night before it happened, or whether, while he slept and dreamed, he was in his spirit, the ghost of a living man, anticipating what was to be, and so came to me in that carriage. I have never been able to puzzle it out myself, but I'm glad I've told you the story. As I say, it's company to share a thing like that with someone else. Good-night, boys. Good-night Colonel."

Harry Grattan

A Christmas Ghost Story

Thomas Edison (1847-1931) first invented the phonograph in 1877, but each playback would significantly degrade the recording. It would be some time before it was a marketable product, and still longer before durable recordings were possible. The reading of the following story by Englishman HARRY GRATTAN *(1867-1951), recorded in November 1905, added a new dimension to the oral transmission of ghost stories—making this perhaps the most widely-told Christmas ghost story for a time—and, since 1951, has permitted people to hear the voice of a dead man telling it. At the time of writing, Grattan's recording was available for listening on YouTube.*

PEOPLE NOWADAYS DON'T BELIEVE IN GHOST STORIES, but the following things actually happened to me, and that is why my hair is white, and though not a nervous man I can never forget that awful night four years ago. Then, as now, the old church clock was chiming out the midnight hour. I was sitting in the library, reading a book in which I was much interested, when the thing appeared. It was a horrible night. The wind howled as though all the lost souls in Purgatory were screaming through the world the tale of all their blood-clotted crimes and the agony of their remorse. The dim candles flickered and fluttered, casting ghoulish, gruesome shadows in the corners of the room that fancy turned to evil spirits, then suddenly went out. Darkness, relieved only by the fitful flare of the slowly dying fire. Then, gradually I heard slowly drawing nearer, nearer the clank, clank, clank as of someone dragging a heavy chain along the passage. Nearer, nearer it came and as I listened I felt, or rather I knew, that the door opened, and an icy cold swept into the room bringing with it a chill not of this earth, but the chill of death. It came nearer, then stopped, and then a moan. A moan so fraught with agony that my blood curdled in my veins. Then something touched my shoulder. At that, beads of sweat broke out on my head, my tongue clinged to the roof of my mouth. I was unable to cry out. Oh, the agony of that moment, sitting there waiting for what would happen next. Silence! Deep silence. Suddenly, the moon breaking through the storm, black clouds cast a sheet of light across the room. A shriek! A frightful, blood-curdling shriek rang through the house. I turned in my chair and saw— "What's that!"

I found myself on the floor. I had fallen out of my chair, and as I woke up! . . . I'd trodden on the cat.

CHRISTMAS GHOST STORIES.

Does anybody desire to know a good ghost story for Christmastime? One of the brightest which has been related to me recently is that of the two men in the train. They were sitting opposite each other, and the train was tearing along at an enormous rate of speed. "Beastly train, isn't it?" observed the first man. "Yes," the second replied. "I have always thought so. I was killed in this train three years ago." Some of us are glad to know that the ghost in which we had delighted is not going to die yet, despite the predictions of people who have invented something with which they fondly hope to supersede it. The ghost will walk, but let us hope it will be this year rather more cheerful than the variety which developed out of the devil-worship of the Reformation.

G. K. CHESTERTON.
Daily Citizen [London] (Dec. 24, 1912): 4, col. 6.

Arthur Walter Berry

Woden, the Wild Huntsman

ARTHUR WALTER BERRY (1870-1934), *a native of Tam-worth, Staffordshire, West Midlands had a number of poems published in newspapers and journals between 1906 and 1917. Among the many names of the poem's subject, Woden (also known as Wotan or Odin) was Jólfaðr: the Yule Father, an influence on Father Christmas and Santa Claus.[1] The Wild Hunt is one of the deep roots of holiday horror, with versions recorded across Scandinavia, Northern Europe, and the British Isles, led by different figures in different places. Berry's poetic witness to the hunt is a fearless one, as traditionally people would thrown themselves to the ground to avoid being taken up into the sky. The poem is from the* Tamworth Herald *of December 23, 1911.*

'Tis Christmas eve, the falling snow
Wraps tree and spire like sheeted ghosts;
This night the bitter north winds blow
A doleful dirge across our coasts.

While wandering down the dismal lane,
A sight appeals my startled eyes;
For I behold a spectral train
Of huntsmen uttering frenzied cries.

1 See, *e.g.*, "Don't Take Odin Out of Yule," *Norwegian American Weekly* (Dec. 19, 2014), available at https://www.norwegianamerican.com/dont-take-odin-out-of-yule/

Awe-struck I gaze upon the pack
Of murderers and suicides;
Who sit astride each bony hack,
Commencing their nocturnal rides.

They race unto the four cross-roads,
Woden falls lightly from his horse;
And points unto the doom'd abodes
Of many a soul-forsaken corse.

Anon dismount the ghostly train,
Bemoaning their clay counterpart;
While sounds of strife and clanking chain
With ghoulish yell doth rend my heart.

The huntsmen mount again their steeds,
These spectral forms on bony backs,
In torment for their life's misdeeds,
Pursue thro' snow their midnight tracks.

The restless phantoms disappear,
The chanting of their raucous wail
Re-echoes in the dying year,
Then dies upon the winter's gale.

With heavy heart do I return,
And muse where spectral huntsmen go;
While cottage-fires now dimly burn
Mid ghostly trees enwrapp'd in snow.

F. G. Grundemann

Squire Humperdinck and the Devil

A Christmas Story for Children

As best as can be determined, the author was FREDERICK GLASIER GRUNDEMANN FOSTER. *Foster served on the Earby Urban District Council and the Education Committee of the West Riding County Council. He was active in the Socialist and Labour parties; his wife Elizabeth L. "Lizzie" Glasier was active in the Socialist Sunday School movement and edited* The Young Socialist. *"Squire Humperdinck and the Devil" appeared in the December 23, 1913* Manchester Daily Citizen, *an official organ of the Labour Party. The story has some elements and a spirit reminiscent of the Cornish Christmas play* Duffy and the Devil, *a later version of which, by Harve Zemach, was the 1973 winner of the Caldecott Medal for illustration.*

IN A VILLAGE VERY FAR FROM HERE, that neither you nor I have ever seen, lived an old squire. He was a very rich and very cross old fellow, who never by any chance spoke pleasantly to anyone, least of all to those who worked for him and made him wealthy. He owned all the surrounding fields and houses and barns and living things; indeed, everything that was ownable in the village of Humperdunken was his, including his work folk. Among the latter was a lad named Cheukari, or Chuck, as he was more often called.

By day the boy would feed the animals belonging to his master, and toss hay into the big, lumbering hay-carts. He was supposed to make himself generally useful; what he actually did, however, was to get into everybody's way and plague the life out of the poor farm hands so that they could scarcely attend to their duties.

Chuck was a very genius of misadventure. He was born to mischief and prank playing. Should he carry a message he would most certainly forget what it was about, and have to come back to find out what it was he had gone for; when he went again he would remember the message but forget for whom it was intended; and the third time he would find the person and deliver the message wrongly. Squire Humperdinck reaped little profit from his employment of young Chuck.

Years before Humperdinck had been poor like other people. One evening it happened that he strolled towards some woods that were near his farm. The day's work was over, and he was feeling glad within him at the thought of his thriving little crop, and the hard work his hands had done that day. The birds were singing in the woods, and this added to his content. Suddenly a queer-looking red figure confronted him. It was laughing, and it leaned against a tree stump looking with wicked eyes full at the young farmer. The smile of it was most unpleasant.

"Who are you?" asked Humperdinck. But he seemed to know already, for he trembled horribly.

"I'm the Devil," answered the other, still smiling. He appeared to be in a frivolous mood.

"What do you want with me?" inquired the farmer nervously.

"Don't be afraid, friend Humperdinck," said the other; "I merely wish to make you a business offer. I find that this village is capable of development; now I want a representative. I can't keep pace with things alone, you know, and I'm no great believer in work myself. Be my agent, and I'll promise you excellent and liberal returns."

"What shall I have to do?"

"Just what I tell you, and no more; as my accredited representative you would simply follow out my instructions, and grow rich and prosperous."

"And—and, afterwards?" inquired the farmer, who was of a very superstitious nature.

"When you die?" laughed the other. "Ha! Ha! Leave that to me, Humperdinck. I'll make you my doorkeeper in Paradise as likely as not."

In the end the farmer's scruples were overcome. At the thought of the rich reward his fears vanished. He promised to do all the Evil One desired, and in the course of time the Devil's words came true. Humperdinck grew rich and prosperous.

In was nearing Christmastime in Humperdunken. The spirit of Christmas was stealing into all honest souls, filling them with the warm, lovely feelings of friendship and brotherhood. One morning the observant Chuck, who never missed seeing anything it was not intended that he should see, perceived a strange-looking crow perched upon the wicked squire's window-sill. He watched it creep through the slightly open window into the squire's bedroom, and presently voices reached him from within.

"Tell your master," said the squire's voice, "that I have raised the rents, as he ordered."

"Master! master!" repeated Chuck, who was listening intently, "who can he mean, I wonder?"

"And that I now make them work an hour longer each day," went on the voice of Humperdinck.

"That's us!" gasped Chuck, in amazement. "The beast!"

"And that I've taken away the bushel of corn usually allowed them for Christmas baking."

The boy waited no longer. "I'll just catch you, my beauty," he said, referring to the crow.

Young Chuck swarmed up the ivy that grew thick about the squire's window; presently the black messenger reappeared. In a trice he was gripped by a deft hand, and thrust under Chuck's coat.

"Don't kill me," whined the crow.

"Why shouldn't I?" asked Chuck.

"I'm only a crow."

"I've heard that excuse before," answered the boy; "what's the good of you anyway?"

"Look here, boy, I'll tell you all about it if you'll spare me."

"Right," agreed Chuck. "First, then, who is your master?"

"The Devil."

"Where does he live?"

"In the woods."

"How long has he lived there?"

"Years and years."

"How far is it?"

"Twenty miles, crow-measurement." And finally, the crow told him the whole story.

"So Squire Humperdinck is the Devil's servant; and you are their messenger, eh? You nasty black thing!"

"I ran away once," whispered the creature.

"Ugh! I ought to kill you," remarked Chuck; "but I cannot."

Now it happened that young Chuck possessed a crow of his own. All crows are alike in appearance; in nature, of course, some are nobler than others. Chuck had found his crow one winter's day lying upon the ground half-frozen with cold, and almost starved. The tender-hearted boy had shared his breakfast with the bird, and laid it gently inside his rough shirt, so that his warm body might restore it. Since that day the two had lived together in friendship.

"I want you to do me a service," said the boy to his black comrade.

Chuck's crow had been waiting for this for years, never doubting that some day his opportunity would come.

"Anything in the world for you, Chuck," he answered.

"In yonder woods," said the boy, "stands an old house, and in that house the Devil lives. Go to him and say, 'Squire Humperdinck has put the rents up as he ordered, and lowered the wages, and taken away the bushel of corn from his workpeople, and what is your Majesty's pleasure for Christmas?' Bring the answer to me."

Next day the crow came back.

"Old woman Künd is to be turned out," he reported, "she and her children. The Devil is quite upset about it. He keeps raving and shouting loudly, 'No rent, no house-room!' He nearly struck me because I said she was old."

"Go to Humperdinck," said Chuck, "and say, 'Your master tells you to prepare a present for Widow Künd at once. He is to fill a hamper with tea, sugar, currants, bread, cake, raspberry jam, and toffee sticks, and the Squire's boy is to deliver it.'"

Next morning the faithful crow crept through the Squire's window. Humperdinck had been sleeping unsoundly, and tossing restlessly in his bed. Perhaps he had been dreaming of paradise. The crow's voice woke him abruptly.

"The Devil's compliments," began the bird, who observed his ill-humour.

"Confound the Devil," said the farmer crossly.

"Yes, sir," agreed the crow, thinking it better to keep on the right side of him. Then he delivered his message.

"Fill a hamper with what?" gasped the amazed Humperdinck.

"Good things, sir," said the crow. "I'll mention them all again, if you like. I remember every one."

"The Devil has gone raving mad!" cried Humperdinck; "I know he has!"

"He was when I left him, anyway," said the Crow.

Humperdinck dared not disobey the command. He dismissed the Crow, who made his way as quickly as possible to Chuck.

"Now go to the house in the woods," said the boy, "and tell the Devil that old widow Künd is out of doors in the cold."

Next morning was Christmas Day in Humperdunken. Cheeks were ruddy and smiles were plentiful as flowers in the spring. Good-fellowship filled the little village with laughter and hearty greetings.

The Crow again returned. This time he appeared to have had adventures. His feathers were ruffled, and he was all a'tremble with fear. "The Devil's in an awful rage," he began. "Last evening he happened to go to a town house of his, to stay the night, and the bells outside began to ring like anything."

"Bells always get on the Devil's nerves," explained the captive crow.

"Then some children came beneath his window," continued the other, "and commenced to sing something about 'Herald Angels.' The Devil rushed out in a temper, and the 'Herald Angels' scattered in all directions. I think they thought he was the real Devil," remarked the Crow.

"Well, so he is," said the boy.

The Crow went on, "The Devil says that no one in Humperdunken is to sing carols, or make merry; the bells must not ring; there's to be no Christmas trees; and everyone must be in bed by eight. I'm to stay and watch."

"And supposing no one does it?" asked the boy.

"The Squire Humperdinck will have to go away with the Devil."

"Go to the Squire," said the boy, "and tell him the Devil orders the big barn to be made ready at once. He is to entertain the village folks. Say that he is commanded to roast an ox, and boil a hundred plum puddings. After the supper there must be music and dancing. Say that on Christmas morning all the churches must ring their bells as hard as they can, because it's Christmas. And tell the Squire that the boy Chuck is to take the big wagon into town and load it with oranges and crackers and distribute them among the village folk, with the compliments of Squire Humperdinck and the season's compliments."

Here the boy and two crows had to stop and laugh. They were all quite good friends by this time. "And tell Humperdinck," said Chuck, "that on New Year's morning all the villagers are to have their houses given them as a New Year's gift."

"And never pay rent any more?" asked Chuck's Crow.

"Never more," said the boy—"now that we've caught the Devil. And tell the farmer," he added, "that his master will explain everything later on." Again the three conspirators were convulsive with joy. The Crow flew away on his mission.

Never before was so gay a feeling abroad in Humperdunken. Everybody was smiling, and nobody knew why. Everybody was happy, and everybody's heart was just bursting with good will for everybody else. It was gracious to be alive, and to feel the sweet touch of the keen morning wind and to see the honest faces all aglow.

Then the bells started to ring out; they crashed and clanged and jangled and argued. Now at any time, bells pealing one against the other are bad enough, but this time they were worse. It was as though the bells understood and were doing it on purpose. From all quarters the noise arose, and the violent peals reached the Devil in his home in the woods.

The Crow had spoken truly. If there was one thing Old Nick hated more than another it was bells—church bells. He could tolerate—from interested motives—the slow, regular toll that sometimes woke the solemn echoes of the evening, but this violent, joyous jangling nearly drove him frantic.

He leapt up as the sound reached him. With a single bound he was out of the house, and racing in the direction of Humperdunken. He did not even stop to close the door. He was in such a hurry.

Squire Humperdinck saw the bounding figure coming straight towards him. Peeping from behind the window blind, he observed that something had put the Devil seriously out of countenance. He guessed it must be himself. There was rage in every bound. The Squire flew to the window and fastened it. He barricaded the door with chairs and tables. He set a heavy chest against it to make it doubly secure—but it was of no use. The Devil came through as though nothing were in the way. Humperdinck crouched beneath the bed; his craven heart filled with fear, and his limbs were trembling as they had trembled long ago in the woods when he had sold himself to the Evil One—for money.

A long red arm reached under the bed, there was a stifled

cry from the Squire, followed by a wicked chuckle of Satanic mirth, and Squire Humperdinck's soul left the merry village of Humperdunken. Where it went the Devil alone knows.

GHOSTS FOR CHRISTMAS.

Brisk Demand for Haunted Houses for the Festive Season.

Haunted houses are in great demand just now.

"Spending Christmas in an old house which has the reputation of being haunted is the beau ideal of many Americans and a few Englishmen," said a prominent West End real estate agent to the Daily Mirror yesterday.

"In response to the demand we keep on hand a list of ancient houses which are claimed to be visited with apparitions.

"There is a haunted house near Guildford which I can especially recommend to ghost-loving Americans. Its reputation is sinister in the extreme.

"Some time ago a family moved into the house, and on the second day the servants left in a body. They flatly refused to come back; the house, they said, was haunted by a fearful spectre.

"Some Americans are particular in their tastes regarding ghosts. They like one that is an original kind, particularly one that has any historical association.

"I believe that if you could convince one of these Americans that a certain house was haunted by the shade of Queen Elizabeth, he would pay any price you demanded for it.

"English people, on the whole, however, dislike ghosts, and English ladies have a horror of them.

"As it is, there are several haunted houses in England which can be supplied to clients at reasonable terms."

Daily Mirror (Dec. 5, 1907): 5, col. 4.

CPSIA information can be obtained
at www.ICGtesting.com
Printed in the USA
LVHW081641121121
703175LV00014B/211/J

9 781954 321540